PRAISE FOR WELCOME TO YOUR BODY

Welcome to Your Body has its finger on the clotted pulse of society, baring the rotting viscera of patriarchy, capitalism, and healthcare for all to see.

—Eric Raglin, author of *Extinction Hymns*

In *Welcome to Your Body*, authors wield their pens as scalpels, delving beneath the skin of nightmares to return with a gory, suppurating harvest. Indeed, by the end of these seventeen stories of abnormal anatomy, you may find yourself questioning your own flesh, distrusting your own limbs, and doubting your own senses. I can guarantee, however, that your fingers will definitely betray you—but only into turning more pages.

—TJ Price, author of *The Disappearance of Tom Nero*

Welcome to Your Body is the next evolutionary step for anthologies. Every story feels like its own extraordinary species crawling out from the primordial ooze of horror, blossoming into something far more terrifying than what we've ever read before.

—Clay McLeod Chapman, author of *What Kind of Mother* and *Ghost Eaters*

In *Welcome to Your Body: Lessons in Evisceration*, Ryan Marie Ketterer has collected a fantastic variety of body-related horrors ranging from cyberpunk and historical fiction to dark fantasy, from the subdued and lyrical to pulpy and fun. Here we're reminded of all the ways the body can fail us, all its potential for discomfort, dread, and disgust. If you've ever been frightened of your own body, you need this book!

—Christi Nogle, author of the Bram Stoker Award® winning first novel *Beulah*

Welcome to Your Body makes it viscerally clear: no part of you is safe. From head to toe, disease to delusion, every inch of the human body is vulnerable and volatile, and these authors show that in a myriad of inventive ways. If you love body horror, this is the book for you.

—J.A.W. McCarthy, Bram Stoker Award and Shirley Jackson Award finalist, author of *Sleep Alone*

Welcome to Your Body is a sensory bouquet of slippery delights, a marrow-deep exploration of the self, and a misophoniac's nightmare. These fantastic stories slide between cartilage, tooth, and bone, and get right under your skin. An unforgettable collection.

—Marissa van Uden, Acquiring Editor Apex Books

Welcome to Your Body is a strong anthology of mostly new-to-me writers, expertly curated for maximum impact. Body horror that hits on all the most evocative tenets of the subgenre, each story was also imbued with the heart and empathy so vital to effective horror. Entertaining yet riddled with unexpected and sometimes painful truths, I stopped often just to process a poignant line or idea that struck my heart.

—Laurel Hightower, author of *Crossroads* and *Below*

A chaotic ride through both the failures and perhaps what some would call triumphs of the human form. Within these pages, there's a little something for every lover of body horror.

—Kristi DeMeester, Author of *Such a Pretty Smile*

WELCOME TO YOUR BODY

Edited by Ryan Marie Ketterer

Published in the United States by Salt Heart Press.
www.saltheartpress.com

Front & back cover image by Daniel Andersson
Book design by M. Halstead.
Formatting by M. Halstead.
Interior illustrations by P.L. McMillan.

First printing edition 2024.

For all the writing groups out there.
Keep doing what you’re doing.

CONTENTS

Welcome to Your Body: Lessons in Evisceration

A Foreword

Paula D. Ashe

Of all the terrible decisions I have made, having a body is—by far—one of the worst (only second perhaps to having consciousness, which is another lamentation for a different day). I never 'decided' to have a body as I never 'decided' to be born. I was born into/with/having a body and as such have continued living and my body continues with me. The ambiguity of 'my' relationship to my 'body' is so fraught I didn't even previously know what article to use to describe it. Throughout our lives we are in possession of a body that constantly changes, is constantly threatened, and is constantly sinister. Having a body means that sometimes you don't really know what's going on in/on/with it. Anything could be ticking away in there, illness and injury are always imminent.

Like death, it's only a matter of time.

There are of course some benefits to embodiment. Bodies can experience both starvation and satiation (of all kinds), pain and pleasure, a full spectrum of sensations. Bodies drive cars and write novels and steer wheelchairs and cook dinner. Hell, some bodies make other bodies which is absolutely nuts if you think about it. You cannot live without a body (we think) and the better your body conforms to the ergonomics of spatial power, often the better quality of life you have. Although, in all honesty, no matter how 'good' your body may be, it eventually decomposes and decays the same as everyone else's.

Which is really why we're here, in this genre, and with this book.

Horror as it stands, almost always involves the body (I know there are some notable exceptions, don't @ me). So much so that there is one subgenre dedicated wholly to its exploration, the aptly named, body horror. Clive Barker made the connection quite clear when he wrote, "every body is a book of blood, whenever we're opened we're re(a)d". Body horror then, is all about the contradictory experiences offered by embodiment and its attendant abjection.

Welcome to Your Body takes that conceit and runs with it at hypersonic speeds, shredding the body from head to toe in the process. Each story is a lesson in evisceration, sure, but you'll also find lessons in liquefaction, lessons in amputation, lessons in laceration…there's a lot to learn.

This collection assembled by Ryan Marie Ketterer showcases how the functions and expectations of the body can go wrong in so many horrific yet compelling ways. As a result, there's something here for every…body.

The Head:

A woman battles the strange side effects of a rare cancer, another woman battles her fraught self image and a manipulative partner through a series of increasingly unhinged haircuts, a family's generational traumas come to light at a gruesome and ritualistic reunion, and a translator discovers that cybernetic technology always comes with a high price; an audio engineer finds revenge is a dish best served quietly, a young woman discovers a supernatural figure desires her teeth, and a bridesmaid's desperation to impress her friends leads to a gruesome decision with a diamond-tipped drill.

The Limbs:

A runner experiences a strange skin condition that remains invisible to everyone else, a middle-aged widow's isolation and depression manifest in painful visions and striking revelations, a lonely bar hopper meets an alluring woman with an intoxicating secret, and a grieving mother finds solace in a gruesome keepsake.

The Middle:

A man who can see into the spirits of those around him discovers a love that leads to devastation, a newly arrived doctor and his wife run afoul of rampaging uteri hellbent on comeuppance, and a woman struggling after childbirth finds her body transforming while she fights against her own mother's overbearing behavior.

The Rest:

A nineteenth century medical student has a ghastly encounter in the city's crypts, a scorned lover finds transformation a balm to temporarily soothe their jilted soul, and finally, a disgusting plague provides the means for a struggling art student to challenge her condescending opposition.

Welcome to Your Body won't make you feel any better about the fact that you have a body, but it will make you grateful these authors have no control over it.

Paula D. Ashe
4-17-24

Section I

THE HEAD

THE HOLLOW MARCH OF DECAY

ALEX WOLFGANG

"Seeeeeeping in…"

The tinny, distant voice cut out as quickly as it came, Rachel's fingers tingling at the sound. They ran cold and sluggish across the strings of her instrument. She told herself it must have been the amp, where she'd picked up countless snippets of radio broadcasts over the years. She sat across from her rig and waited to see if the voice would return. There was only silence. The entire room felt muffled and stuffy, isolated from reality, but she shook off the feeling and cranked the amp's volume, ready for the crunchy tone that always sharpened her brain the way morning coffee never could.

She plucked one of her bass strings, but the sound was barely audible, like she was hearing it from a neighbor's house. The fierce vibrations from her amp suggested the problem laid not in her external equipment, but that didn't stop her from fiddling with the dials anyway, desperate for an easy answer. It didn't come. She put her instrument down and headed for the stereo, where she put on the thickest, sludgiest album she could think of. It far more resembled the tinny, static sounds of black metal from a distance. She paused the music and cleared her throat, but even that sound seemed to emerge from deep underground.

It was early. She was congested. She and Henry had gone to a show last night, and she'd forgotten her ear plugs. All excuses, all woefully inadequate to explain the problem. It wasn't until Henry entered the room, mouthed words that she knew she should hear in the deep, gravelly voice he always had after waking, that she began to panic.

"Something's wrong," she said. "Nothing sounds right."

Her voice was a light muffled hum, and she was unsure if she'd said the right words at all. The sensation was nauseating, panic-inducing. She could tell by Henry's expression that he shared these feelings.

All thoughts of the strange voice in the amp deserted her.

The rest of that day was a blur. Henry must have called off work for both of them, not that she could have gone in anyway. They sat in the ER for two hours, Henry typing out messages on his phone to keep her distracted. She forced smiles and empty replies. Patients sat around her coughing and fiddling with phones and magazines, the dull roar softened into a distant, hushed static. She tried and failed to distract herself. When Henry tapped her shoulder to indicate they'd called her name, she nearly cried from relief.

The relief was short-lived. The doctor couldn't help her there, but according to Henry's messages, they referred her to a specialist, one who mercifully had an afternoon appointment available. It came and went. An MRI. The doctor looked confused and offered little guidance, saying the results would be ready in a week. She hadn't expected an immediate answer, but this conclusion did little to offset the anxiety that had dug into her so deeply it had left her nauseous.

With no further steps to take that day, the blur came to an abrupt, agonizing halt. They went home. She sat on her couch and stared at the wall for so long that time seemed to dilate. Henry put his arm around her, but she could feel the tension in his muscles better than she ever could with her senses entirely intact. He spoke to someone on the phone, and though she couldn't make out the words, she could feel the agony oozing out of them.

For the first time in what felt like years, Rachel was unsure what to do with herself. No music to hear, no conversation to be had. She flipped the TV on with subtitles, but her brain wouldn't allow her to be distracted. She pictured it sitting in her skull, chastising her ears for their failure.

Though the sun still seeped in from her windows, she longed for the hour of sleep to come, when maybe she could get some respite. Until then, she pretended to care about what was happening on screen, more for Henry's sake than her own. Possibilities circled her thoughts in a manic whirl. She knew very little about medicine, but one very ugly word kept worming its way into her mind: cancer. Each time it did, another image of her brain manifested in her mind's eye, that of it being eaten alive by rogue cells, malicious little monsters with a taste for her flesh, crying out to the rest of her body for help that wouldn't come. A masochistic part of her wondered how her brain might taste.

When ten o'clock rolled around, Henry's eyes already drooping as he rested his head on her shoulder, she was desperate for consciousness to fade away. Maybe this was all a bad dream, and she'd wake up to the sound of something beautiful and melodic and clear.

Sleep didn't come easily. When she was in bed, submersed in silence, she could almost pretend for a moment her ears were normal. Inevitably, she would remember, and she could almost feel the cancerous cells digging into her brain matter, altering her perceptions, rotting her from the inside out. She had to stop saying the C word. There was no reason to believe it was real until her doctor confirmed it. Surely there was another explanation, but that didn't stop her from assuming the worst.

After an hour she heard whispers. Sure they were her imagination, a cruel trick played by her ailing brain, she ignored them and tried to return to sleep. But they wouldn't stop. Vague and distorted, they sounded like they came from somewhere far below her.

Within an hour she was on the verge of losing her mind. Henry slept undisturbed, so she crawled out of bed and, feeling justifiably insane, put her ear to the ground.

She heard a familiar voice like an old door opening on a rusty hinge. "Seeeeeeeping in."

Another like slow-dripping ice. “It’s sleeping. Take its place. Become it.”

Though they exchanged words, she couldn’t be sure they were addressing each other.

“Feels gooooood. Alive.”

“Eat and move. More more more.”

“So much. So hungry.”

Rachel lifted her head from the floor. The voices lingered in her ears and chest, their rust and ice creeping through her veins. Had they been speaking since that morning? It wasn’t until that moment she considered the fact she could understand them. The first spoken words she’d comprehended all day. She wondered if she was losing her mind, if this was a minor insanity personified. Standing in her dark room, she could no longer make out the words, so she lay back on the ground and put her ear to the hardwood again.

“Can’t stop. A drug.”

Shuddering, she lifted her head, and the voices once again became muddled whispers. They sounded as if they emerged from the floorboards, from somewhere deep below the ground. But of course, this couldn’t be possible. Maybe it was the blood rushing to her head as she put it to the floor, her brain transforming the sound into something comprehensible in a desperate attempt to believe she could hear. She lay back down on her bed, her body just as prone as it had been on the floor. But the whispers were no more audible than they had been while she was standing.

She was dreaming. That had to be it. A nightmare, justifiable under the circumstances. She tried to meditate, to clear her mind, but sleep remained elusive. The whispers never ceased. They became more frantic, sadistic in tone. She was grateful not to understand any more.

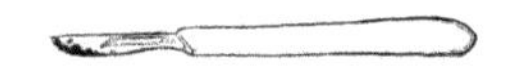

In the morning she said nothing to Henry of the whispers. She decided they were a bad dream and nothing more, manifestations of her anxieties. They sat together over coffee and toast. Rachel stared at the woodgrain on the table and did nothing while Henry scribbled a message for an agonizingly long time.

He slid a paper across the table into her field of view. The message was annoyingly short.

I have to work late today. You gonna be okay?

She looked up and nodded, doing her best to make her expression look genuine. In truth she dreaded his departure. With her bravest face on, she kissed him goodbye and opened a book she hoped he believed she would read.

She didn't make it past the first page. Her internal monologue wouldn't allow her to focus on anything. Instead it swirled and stormed and pelted her with useless stones of pessimistic hail. *You'll never hear again. Your brain is broken. Your career is over. You're going to die.*

Meditation helped a little, but the moment she stopped counting her breaths, the hailstorm resumed. She tried television. Tried video games. Tried smoking weed. None of it opened the bars of the prison cell her brain felt trapped in. Eventually she made her way out to the garden, where she'd been neglecting the small enclave of vegetables she and Henry had been trying and failing to grow. Weeds had sprouted around them, and she took a little pleasure in clearing them out and watering what remained. The lawn didn't need to be mowed all that badly, but she did so anyway, edging and weedeating afterward until everything was as neat as it had been the day they'd moved in. If nothing else, the work kept her active, and the sun felt pleasant on her skin.

Afterward she had little desire to go back inside, so she dragged a lawn chair out of the garage and lay on it, letting the light warm her and wrap her in a cocoon. Without the sound of the motors to block them out, the whispers returned.

"Seeping in…growing big and strong…"

She hummed to herself and counted her breaths until the voices drowned out. Hours passed. The sun receded, and eventually Henry tapped her on the shoulder, grinning at the sight of her productivity. It must have looked like the healthiest way to cope with her condition. Maybe it was, but deep down, she knew it couldn't last.

The following week brought nothing resembling respite. There was truly nothing to do with her time alone. Her hobbies were now moot. Couldn't play music. Couldn't run without risking being hit by a car. Couldn't even watch a movie without the subtitles reminding her of how important sound was to the experience. Now that the lawn looked perfect, there was no more she could do to improve it. But she couldn't tell Henry any of this. What good would it do? He was stressed out enough already. The silence between them grew chasmous.

Going to work felt out of the question. There was no way for her to function, but she couldn't bear to call her partners and tell them she may never record another song again. Henry must have done it for her, because the texts came sweeping in.

We love you Rachel. Get well soon.

Feel better. We miss the hell out of you.

We're all pulling for you.

All vague niceties, but what else could she expect? What do you say to an audio engineer who suddenly can't hear, who may never hear again? Can't wait to get you back in the studio? She could hardly blame them.

In a last-ditch attempt to cope with the eternal hours, she took to exercising all day, every day in the hopes that she could exhaust herself into sleep before the voices returned each night. Yoga mat laid out on her floor, she'd follow the instructors online as they took her through endless cycles of yoga and cardio workouts, forcing herself to read their subtitles. Mercifully, the technique worked. Each night, the whispers barely wormed their way into her ears before she was unconscious.

A week after her doctor's visit that first day, the phone call finally arrived. Henry reached out and squeezed her hand before typing out a message: *Your results came in.*

An hour later the doctor slid a piece of paper across her desk. She already knew what it would say.

Your tests have come back positive for acoustic neuroma. It's a type of cancer that affects the part of the brain that processes sound. Your case is a little unusual in how quickly the symptoms came on. Usually it starts in one ear and sometimes spreads. It's also usually accompanied by dizziness and numbness. Have you experienced anything else strange lately?

She shook her ahead. Beside her, Henry tensed up. He grimaced when they met eyes, trying to keep his composure. He asked the doctor something she couldn't understand. The doctor again wrote something down, and this time, the wait was agonizing. Her insides clenched up, desperate for him to tell her he could cure her. Eventually he slid his paper across the desk.

We're going to keep a close eye on it for now. It's serious, but most of the time this type of cancer ends up benign. If you start to get headaches, dizziness, anything, call me immediately.

"Will I get my hearing back?" she asked, unsure how the words came across.

He wrote something again.

At this stage, we can't say one way or another. It's certainly possible.

'Possible' was far from an encouraging word.

If nothing else, her diagnosis gave her a way to occupy her time. For the next several days, she dug deep into research about acoustic neuroma, but learning more didn't do any good. It was supposed to be slow, gradual. Most cases didn't lead to hearing loss, and when they did, it usually wasn't so sudden. But sometimes cancer didn't behave the way it was supposed to. Her research turned up another disturbing fact: how much more common cancer had become in recent years. Some scientists seemed to believe this was the fault of modern diets and exposures to toxicity, but many agreed on something more fundamental. People were simply living longer. The longer you live, the more likely cancer becomes. It isn't an if but a when.

After Henry had left one morning, she went to the window and looked outside. A beautiful day in May. Another day in the house sounded exhausting, unbearable. Maybe she couldn't run in the streets like she used to, but there was a park nearby with a loop, and even though it was small, it was better than nothing. Without a better idea, she put on her workout clothes and headed that way.

She reached the park and did the short loop thirty times, until she was panting, drenched in sweat, and feeling ever-so-slightly better. Then she sat in the grass and stared up at a tree, trying not to think about how much easier music and podcasts usually made her runs.

"More, bigger, deeper, further."

Once again the whispers came from beneath her, not from her floorboards but from the grass and dirt itself. More fascinated than terrified, she kept listening. For the first time, she didn't want to drown them out.

"Good, good. Done here. Not much left."

Compelled by something beyond her understanding, Rachel shoved her hands into the dirt. It had rained the night before, so the soil was soft and malleable. She dug and dug until her fingers were pruned and covered with mud. A foot down, the soil changed. While it started as a rich, dark brown, packed with insects and water and organic compounds, it became a sickly gray, thin and dry. It rubbed her skin raw before dissolving like ash in her fingers. She withdrew her hands and cried out, but there was nobody nearby.

This wasn't soil. Maybe it had been once, but something had turned into another substance entirely, a foreign one that felt deeply out of place. Nothing would grow from here, nothing could live in it.

"Shhhhh. Something here."

Rachel froze and listened, but the whispers ceased. She sat and listened to silence for what felt like an hour.

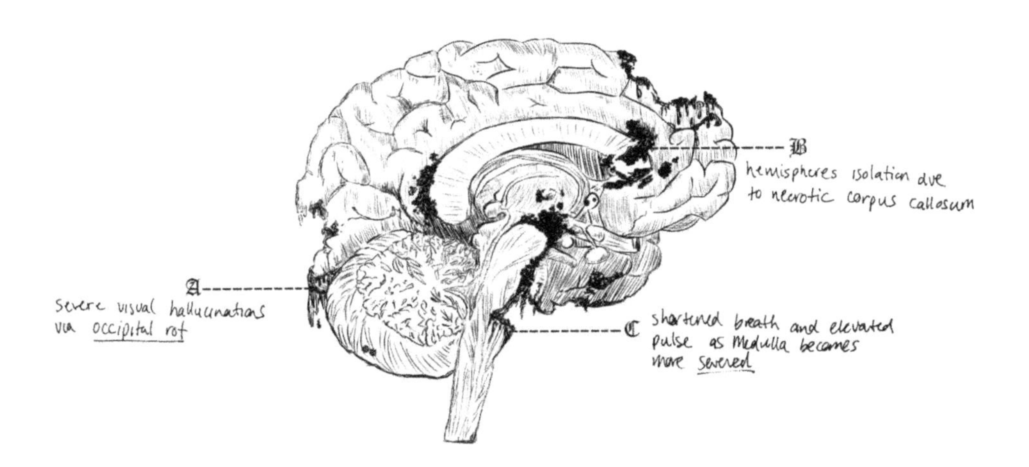

On her way home, she passed by her neighbor's house, a young blonde woman she barely knew named Rita. The woman lay sprawled across a lawn chair, sunbathing in a red bikini while her little Pomeranian shook with terror at everything in sight. Rachel had seen her neighbor do this a thousand times on beautiful days.

Rita waved as Rachel passed, mouthed something, then quickly covered her mouth as if embarrassed. It occurred to Rachel quickly that Henry might have spoken to Rita about her condition. Her husband became a chatterbox when he was nervous, and her inability to hear him was likely enough to drive him insane.

She wished Rita would've left it at that, but the woman waved her over and began typing frantically on her phone. Rachel waited with a patient indifference. She had nowhere else to be anyway. Finally Rita handed her a phone with a message scrawled across the front.

So sorry to hear about your condition. I had cancer once. I bet you can beat it, too.

Rachel had expected to be annoyed, but she found herself touched by the heartfelt simplicity. Tears welled up. Rita took her phone back and typed something else.

I'm sorry! I didn't mean to make you cry!

Rachel shook her head. Rita took the phone and typed something else.

I don't know if this is helpful, but when I got my diagnosis, I took a lot of comfort in spirituality. I have some books if you want to borrow them. I started seeing my body as one manifestation of Earth. We're all made of the same things...atoms and molecules that get recycled. Your body isn't any different than mine or Scruffy's or the grass or the bugs. It helped me a lot to think of it that way, instead of thinking something was wrong with only me.

Rachel stared at Scruffy while the dog cocked his head. She tried to imagine him as a part of herself. Maybe pieces of them had been the same tree or trilobite or triceratops millions of years ago. Rita was right; the thought was oddly comforting. The cells of her body weren't hers alone. She was just using them for the time being. Sometimes produce went bad before the expiration date, but you could always compost it.

Jesus, she thought, *you'd think I was terminal.* It hadn't even been two weeks. But a part of her felt dead already. A part of her *was* dead already, literally.

She thanked Rita for the kind words and went home. When she reached her driveway, she stared at her house. Something looked different about it. The bricks were darker, the walls slightly warped. Roof tiles looked on the verge of slipping off. Even the grass looked duller in sheen, already fading to yellow despite the brutal heat of summer remaining several months away.

She was still standing there when Henry pulled up, concern in his watering eyes. He spoke to her first before frantically removing his phone from his pocket.

Everything okay?

She nodded. It was obvious he didn't believe her. He took her into an embrace, and when he pulled away, head turned, a moist spot remained on her shoulder. She grabbed his hand and pulled until he looked her in the eyes. The lines in his face were more pronounced than ever, hair thinning. Like he'd aged ten years in just two weeks.

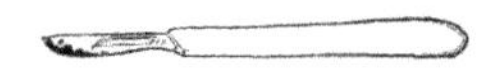

Behind his black glasses, there laid concern in her doctor's eyes. He slid a note across the table while Henry tapped his foot with a nervous fervor.

Have you been experiencing any abnormalities in your vision lately?

The question put a chill through Rachel. She hadn't considered that her only sense more dominant than hearing could be affected. For a moment she imagined herself as both deaf and blind, and she wondered if life would be worth living if it couldn't be perceived through eyes or ears. It felt like a silly thought. Was life worth living for trees? Bacteria?

She wrote back: *like what?*

Anything. Color changes, trouble discerning depth, inability to recognize something.

She thought of the strange dirt in the park, of the state of her house, of Henry's face, but decided against mentioning them. Something had been wrong with the soil. Houses got old. He was stressed.

No, why?

Her doctor grimaced and hesitated before writing back.

Your latest scan shows that the tumor is spreading. Or rather, that a part of it has branched off and is now affecting the occipital lobe. It's extremely unusual. This is the part of your brain that interprets visual cues.

She looked over at Henry, who was staring at the doctor's note. His face was drained of color, eyes locked into an expression of terror. He asked the doctor something, and the doctor responded. Henry began to cry. The doctor scribbled another note.

If you're willing, we'd like to start chemotherapy as soon as possible. It's risky, but it could prevent further growth. You don't have to decide right now. Take a few days. I think you two should talk it over in private. I'll provide some information you can take with you on the benefits and risks.

With a trembling hand, Henry took the packet.

That night, they exchanged notes for so long that Rachel's hand ached. Henry urged her to take the treatment, but the side effects were as horrifying as the cancer growing inside her. She wasn't sure it was worth it. She wasn't sure it would do any good. He begged her not to give up, and she promised she wouldn't. Rita's words came to mind. Her body was a manifestation of Earth, so she couldn't give up if she wanted to. Even if she died, she'd forever remain within its cycles. She considered telling Henry this, but she resisted. He wouldn't find comfort in it.

It was hard to look at him. His face had emaciated, the shape of his skull poking through his skin to remind her that he too was nothing more than flesh and bone, atoms in temporary, organic union.

Eventually they were too tired to go on, but no verdict had been reached. They went to bed exhausted, stressed, and in desperate need of a release.

She heard the whispers again, but she tried to ignore them. Listening would help nothing. It didn't work.

"Let us innnnn," one said. "Knock knock knock, we're already here."

They were silent over breakfast, and for once, it was a relief when Henry left. The air pressure in the room seemed to drop.

Overnight, the inside of the house had come to match the outside. Everything was coated in a layer of thick dust, wood furniture soft with rot, chunks of carpet splitting apart. The television wouldn't even turn on. Somehow, Henry hadn't noticed. Before he left for work, he'd stared into it for half an hour as if he could see something in the darkness.

She sat on the couch and stared at the wall, feeling little desire to do anything else. Both her mind and body were tired. It felt like she was fighting something inevitable, and it was pleasant to zone out and enjoy some nothingness. There was little need for distraction. She didn't move until noon, and then it was only to retrieve her bass guitar and finger the notes, imagining the sounds coming out of them. She sat on the couch, wondering if sound might decay the same way as organic compounds. Energy, that's all it was. Waves of energy moving from one place to another. It could accumulate just like flesh or wood or bacteria, but instead of a body it made reverberations. She wondered if sound could become cancerous. Could it reflect off a wall or a mountain and return defiled, ready to eat its fellow waves and spread until it could spread no more? And what about light, which, too, was just energy. That's all anything in the universe was, just energy changing forms until entropy wore it to nothing.

Eventually hunger drove her from the couch, and as she walked to the kitchen, she looked outside. It was far gloomier than yesterday, with dark clouds replacing the sunshine. It felt more natural. Postponing her lunch a little longer, she strode outside and stood on her front lawn.

It wasn't just the overcast sky, the very color had been sucked from her street. The grass was pale. A noxious yellow hue clung to the air. A woman she at first didn't recognize walked by, her dog beside her. The woman was nude, her sallow skin clinging to her ribcage. Yellow teeth jutted out from her lips while patches of hair fell out and trailed along the sidewalk behind her. Her dog, a skinny, brown mutt with jaundiced eyes, vomited black sludge onto the sidewalk. This wasn't the same Rita she'd spoken to the other day, but she didn't seem bothered by the change. She waved to Rachel, revealing wrinkled fingers with nails hanging loose. Rachel waved back.

On a whim, Rachel kneeled in the grass and pulled up some of the dirt, only to find it that same ashy, sickly soil she'd once had to dig for. Now it was the only kind of dirt remaining.

From deep below she heard the whispers once again.

"Almost done," one said. "Nothing left to change. Come in."

"Ready to move along," said another. "Hungry for more, more, more."

She stood and approached the driveway, where fresh cracks had spread across the surface. Kneeling again, she dug her fingers into the concrete, and they sunk in, the resistance like honey without the stickiness. She pulled globs of it out and tossed them aside. As she got deeper, the molten substance became softer and more porous. Strange insects she didn't recognize had built nests within the depths. They were tiny, black, and chitinous, all spindly legs and wet carapace. They scuttled along her skin, probing it as if deciding whether or not she was good to eat. One bit into her skin, but she didn't recoil.

"No good," it whispered. "Not yet. Deeper."

It jumped from her hand back to the depths of its home. Its brethren crawled out from their holes and dispersed among the lawn, most favoring the soil she'd already disturbed. She followed them, curious and far calmer than she knew she ought to be.

The insects dug and dug, and she dug with them. Six feet down, she broke through the sickly soil and into a layer of earth that felt wet, soft, and pulsating. Though dirtied, she could make out what looked like pink flesh, a giant, wrinkled, endless glob of throbbing earthworms fused together. When the insects found it, they fell into a frenzy, biting and scratching their way until they burrowed inside and the wet globs wept a pink slime and turned dark.

A chorus of whispers filled her ears, so many that she couldn't make out any one voice. This didn't bother her. Words felt inadequate to explain what was happening. As the feast continued, her feelings at the sight of it alternated between fascination and terror. Neither emotion was wholly satisfying. They eventually met in the middle, where the resulting ennui drove her to seek deeper understanding of what was happening to her, to the world and what lay beyond and below it.

She checked her phone, but there was no signal. Despite this it buzzed every few minutes. Nothing was on the screen. The wind picked up, driving little bits of rotten earth against the outside of the house's windows until they were covered with a brown-yellow film. No more neighbors walked by. With each passing moment her mind felt stuffier, cloudier, as if the same film built up in the crevices of her brain and blocked out the signal. Her eyesight flickered in and out.

"I'm going to die," she said to herself. There was no deeper understanding there, but she didn't need there to be.

Soon there was little left to see, so she closed her eyes as she lay on the lawn and let the deprivation of her senses overwhelm her. She imagined herself as one of the tiny black insects, burrowing deep into the earth's brain and consuming endlessly. Maybe there were even tinier bugs now in her brain, killing her cells and sucking her consciousness away. Bugs and bugs and bugs, all the way down, eating and shitting and fucking until there was nothing left to consume.

She opened her eyes, but she saw nothing. It wasn't until she touched the squishy flesh of her corneas that she realized she'd gone blind. There came a tap at her shoulder, a panicked vibration of some kind, but there was no way to answer or interpret it. Instead she crawled into the hole where the insects surely hadn't yet gotten their fill. They flooded her hands, biting and chewing and rejecting her skin once again.

She thrust her arm deeper into the ground, and soon it split apart entirely. She fell and fell, deep into the chasms of the earth, until eventually, another soft, wet surface broke her fall. The bugs immediately swarmed her, but they didn't bite.

Rachel probed the surface she lay on with her fingers. More pulsating slime and endless folds and wrinkles, though chunks appeared missing where they'd been eaten away. In their place, there was only an amorphous sludge that dripped away at her touch.

A sense of peace overwhelmed Rachel. The idea of dying became petty, a fear born entirely of ego. This was the way of things. Whatever she lay on would be gone soon, but there would remain something else, the writhing mass of insects that would eventually be eaten away by another, then another, then another, transforming it into itself again and again until the endless, hollow march of decay wore it away to nothing. How exhausting the perpetuation of life was, how like the eternal task of Sisyphus.

Rachel was done. Whatever she would become next, she hoped it could delude itself into grandeur for a few decades too.

When she touched the top of her head, she realized that this too had decayed. Her hair fell out, skin peeled apart. She opened her skull with no more effort than it took to crack a nut. The insects swarmed her exposed brain. Let them feast for now. Let them enjoy it while it lasted. In the end, cancer would come for them too.

Alex Wolfgang is a horror author from Oklahoma City. You can find his work in *Cosmic Horror Monthly*, *Nocturnal Transmissions Podcast*, and anthologies by Grendel Press, Nosetouch Press, Future Dead Collective, and Howl Society Press. When not reading and writing horror, you'll find him drumming, hiking, playing tennis, and watching movies with his wife. You can follow him on Instagram @alex_wolfgang, on Twitter @alexwolfgang, or visit his website: alexwolfgang.wordpress.com.

A Relationship in Four Haircuts

By Ai Jiang

You met him on Etsy.

That's right.

Not a dating app, but an online marketplace for small business owners.

You'd asked about a custom jade ring you'd been sniffing around for but never found one within your budget—until him. But what you didn't expect was for him to break from his professional persona and ask for your hand in marriage with the same ring you were trying to purchase for $20.99 with 15% discount on top to boot. The ring was probably a knock-off, but still.

It had to be a joke, the proposal, surely, because your username had been CATSONLY_ and your profile picture was that of your British Short Hair's belly. And he? Well, his seller's name was BOUJEEMAN96, in a subtle but not so subtle attempt to hide the implied "69", or maybe he was actually born in 1996.

And so begins your relationship, your Shakespearean tragedy, disguised as a romantic comedy.

Haircut I: The Unruly and Uncut

BOUJEEMAN96 said he'll give you the ring for free if you meet up with him for one date. And you agree because he's a 4.93-star seller with over ten thousand ratings, so surely he must be safe. Or maybe, you're just that lonely, though it isn't something you like to admit, yet the thought often persists like a hungry mosquito.

You comb your hand through your hair several times at home, pat it down with some water, grumble about the greasy strands and unruly kinks, check your teeth to see if you had anything left from lunch stuck near the canines. Then rinse, satisfied.

A message.

BOUJEEMAN96: Can't wait to see you soon.

Even though you gave him your number, he still messages you from Etsy, using his seller profile. At least if you go missing you have this as evidence.

Another ping.

He resent the address of where the two of you will be meeting and a picture of himself in a nice dress shirt and slacks with his face cropped off.

BOUJEEMAN96: a surprise ;)

CATSONLY_: what a tease

As soon as you close your phone, your heartbeat chokes you. You weren't planning on wearing anything fancier than shorts and a plain black t-shirt, but that would mean arriving underdressed in comparison, and you can't have that. And your hair—oh goodness.

In your closet, you find a floral skirt decorated in cat fur; it's too big for you, but it will have to do. With pins, you secure the dress around your waist, scrunching up the fabric to make the ruffles look like part of the design rather than a last-ditch effort at being presentable.

There are still a couple of hours left before your meeting, but you head out early anyhow. The hairdresser shouldn't be too busy at this time. 3 p.m. Most people will be on their afternoon break.

You walk into the salon. You're not the type to cut your hair, but you're also not the type to look in the mirror if you can help it. The limp, frizzed strands have hung to your waist for a number of years; even a trim was too traumatizing for you. But today, for BOUJEEMAN96, you ask them to take off the split ends. You assume they would only take an inch, but it is much more than that, and you're left with hair hanging just below the pits, barely long enough to hide whatever sweat stains might manifest themselves throughout the day, before your date, during the date, drenched long after the date. You try to pull your hair forward to hide yourself, slouching to make it seem longer.

This was a mistake.

Maybe you can cancel the date, wait until your hair grows back. But maybe then, another customer seeking discounted jade rings might catch BOUJEEMAN96's attention, and then your hair won't matter anyway.

At 6 p.m. sharp, you walk into Thai Express, look around, and there he is waving at you, even though he's never met you in his life. Or maybe, you are the only one who never met him, never realized that the two of you had somehow bumped into one another at some point, and that your Etsy username was clearly stamped on your forehead because of how much fur is still stuck on your outfit: CATSONLY_.

Nice hair, he says when you approach.

Thanks, you say. Got it cut today.

This feels familiar, even though it isn't.

You show him a picture of what it looked like before the trim, when it brushed the small of your back, more unruly, and hope he might appreciate the lengths—no pun intended—you went through for this date, for him.

And his smile wanes.

Oh, is all he says. You looked better with the long hair. I like women with long hair. I mean, I guess shorter hair is okay too, but if it's short, much shorter is better, you know? Like a cute pixie cut or something. I think that might suit you.

He doesn't look at your hair again the entire time he speaks about his small business on Etsy. And half his words don't register because you're too busy thinking about when you can drop by the salon again to get a pixie cut and how much it'd complement the sharpness of his statue-like nose.

By the end of the date, he asks to see you again. He even says he'll pick you up from your place, maybe a nearby station if you aren't comfortable giving him your address. He's so considerate, so you tell him there is a convenience store down the street from your place, and that 9 p.m. is fine.

A bit late, but it's fine.

Haircut II: The Pixie

Your hairdresser is fully booked until next month, but your next date with BOUJEEMAN96 is this coming weekend.

On the date, you'd never asked for each other's names, nor used your usernames. But the mystery makes him feel far more alluring, and in the mystery, you yourself could hide the fact that you were struggling to stay afloat and that your dead cat had never been replaced even after your mourning concluded. Not because you couldn't allow another kitten in your heart but because you couldn't afford another.

And the saddest part, when you realized just how much of companionship is bought, was that even your neighbour refused to make small talk when you happened to get in the elevator at the same time. It was the one time only, and it was as though they tried to miss you every time after. You felt bad, bought them a fruit basket, a peace gesture with a small card attached. Suddenly, they appear in the elevator the next day, and you haven't stopped leaving fruit baskets every now and then since.

In the bathroom, you have threads wrapped around your finger like a noose. Your mother taught you how to thread your own eyebrows when you were twelve, but you had a habit of making them always far too thin. And always, always, you'd break skin but never muscle. But it shows—a bruise, a vicious kiss that sometimes beads with blood, and is sometimes very difficult to hide.

But you risk it anyhow—the caress, the tease, never quite a strangle when you start threading the fine fuzz beneath your chin, along your jaw, just above the collarbone at the delicate, veined skin of your neck.

If this is what it means to flirt with death, perhaps this is your way of doing so without ever committing to the relationship. A tragedy with the darkest of humours, and unironically also with the unbalancing of the body's humours.

But this is a romantic comedy, you're convinced.

Now, the hair.

You pull up the highest viewed YouTube tutorial and set it up against a long-expired bottle of moisturizer. Your skin hadn't reacted poorly to it yet, so why not keep using it. You hover over the sink and hack at your hair unceremoniously.

The YouTuber makes it look so easy, but of course, you have no way of knowing just how many takes they needed to make this video, and whether their hair is their actual hair or several wigs they've purchased to create this illusion of professional perfection.

The sink fills with locks you chopped off, and instead of mopping the strands up with your hands and disposing them in the garbage, you try to wash them down the drain, and of course, it clogs. And instead of trying to unclog the sink, you hop in the shower with the scissors and a handheld mirror, the shower still steamy from your rinse, and you continue without the video.

More hair falls. Then the mirror slips from your hand, falls onto the shower floor, shatters. The fragments slice at your legs, some cuts deeper than others. Strands of hair spider across the broken shards like surgery scars. Your legs start to give, and you contemplate in those brief seconds simply falling onto the broken mirror—but you don't. You hurl yourself out of the shower as you collapse.

In the handful of days remaining leading up to the date, you snip impulsively at the pixie cut that looks more like an uneven bob—sometimes when you first wake with your eyes still bleary, sometimes after a meal when you head to the bathroom and catch a glimpse of the choppy style in the mirror, sometimes during the middle of the night when you can't sleep, and small pieces of fallen hair from a recent snip scratch at your cheeks like nails on your pillow.

On the day of the date, he snaps a picture of himself in a different dress shirt and light-washed jeans. You don't have enough money for another dress, but you buy one on discount anyway, also on Etsy—ironically from a seller named BOUJEEFASHION, and you wonder if they might somehow be related to your date—and it is the one you're wearing when you snap a picture of yourself in response to his own.

BOUJEEMAN96: I'm not sure if the pixie cut suits you ;P

CATSONLY_: you said it would):

When he messages back, you remember why you had sworn off love, but at the same time, he saves your disappointment almost instantly by giving you further hope, even if it does trigger some irritation, yet you can't tell if the irritation is from the itchiness of your scalp or from his words.

BOUJEEMAN96: Maybe with some colour, pink, maybe. Would complement your skin ;)

And that was that. Tragedy returning to a rightful romantic comedy.

After your date at Taco Bell, you go to the convenience store to buy a box of pink hair dye and several boxes of bleach lightener, unbranded, because those are on sale.

This time, for sure, you'd coax a straight compliment from him. After all, he did drop you off with a kiss.

Next date is in a week's time, at 10 p.m.

Haircut iii: The Bleached and Dyed

Back in the bathroom, bleach mixed, hair dye on standby, you snip at your hair once more before getting started. The gloves that come with the box mixes are too big, but you make it work. The sink is still clogged, but the shower is cleared of glass at least, so you sit, cross-legged, on the shower floor, naked, with nothing on but an old raincoat you no longer use as you work the bleach into your hair.

First it tingles, then there is a slight burn. You can't remember if the instructions tell you to use shampoo and conditioner or not, having recycled it prematurely, so you do. But when you get out of the shower, the orange that blasts from the roots of your hair screams failure. You don't wait for it to air dry; you blow dry it instead, alternating between hot and cold air just so you don't burn off your ears.

Next box of bleach.

Leave it on for longer.

This time it burns.

This time your roots cry.

The skin from your scalp and around the roots begin to flake by the time you work in the pink dye. That stings too, and you are not sure if hair dye is supposed to sting, or if you now have an open wound on your head. Your hair clumps at the ends, the strands clinging to each other for dear life before the roots are no longer reliable refuge.

Hair falls.

Sink clogs again.

Scissors return when you realize the blow dryer is no longer drying your hair, and it seems like your hair is getting increasingly wetter the more you try to dry it. You can't crop your hair any shorter than it already is without going bald.

On a whim, you open the Etsy app and message BOUJEEMAN96.

CATSONLY_: I've got a surprise for you for our next date (:

BOUJEEMAN96: oh? ;)

You throw in a laughing emoji that matches the expression on your face and leave it at that. But when you lower your phone and stare into the mirror, tears streak and mix with the pink dye smeared on your face, and you know you have little time to fix the mess you made.

At the restaurant, a fancy Sichuan place—but not quite as glorious as you'd thought the choice was because they are having a promotional discount of 85% off certain dishes—10 p.m. sharp, you find yourself settled across from BOUJEEMAN96, who you refer to now as BM96 for short. You've made your hair as presentable as you could, and you hold your breath as you wait for your date to comment on the look he'd suggested.

You're cute, he says after a moment, but he's not looking at you, he's looking at the waiter who just took your orders.

Still, you hold the smile on your face.

The pink suits, doesn't it? you prod.

Mhmm, he mumbles.

When the food arrives, you look down, rage boils: there is hair. And you're about to call the waiter back when you realize that the hair on top of the mapo tofu is your own—pink mixed with the brown-black. You fish it out before BM96 could notice, but in your scramble to do so, more pink flakes onto the dish.

BM96 looks first at the dish, then you, then unsubtly pushes back his food. The smile on your face won't leave, but you feel it wobble.

He says nothing for the rest of the meal, but as though he could read your thoughts when he dropped you off at the front of the convenience store, he says: Don't worry about it, okay, cutie?

And all is well.

At home, in the washroom once more, the bald patches glisten. Some speckled, all glaring and spiteful. The edges of your pixie-cut-almost-buzz-cut are brittle, dry, split, and dandruff litters the top of your head.

The next date is next week, 11 p.m., not at the convenience store, but at your place.

INTERLUDE

You didn't want to have to make this pun either, but truly, you've gotten yourself into quite the *hairy* situation.

It's been six months since BM96 moved into your apartment, and you're staring into the bathroom mirror of the convenience store before collapsing onto the dirty floor slick with soapy water, toilet paper, and piss, and in both hands clumps of your hair that you'd been trying to grow out but hacked off too close to the scalp with a discount razor you haggled the store owner for because it had a chip—one you made yourself—in one of the blades.

You hoped he wouldn't find you, but of course he did—as always, the prince on white horse chasing after the fleeing damsel, but truly, you didn't want him to come after you, no, because you know you'd only fall back into his arms, find comfort in his even temper, his gentle, grooming words that slice like knives yet caress like feathers, because of course he wanted only what was best for you, and of course he knew you better than yourself—or so he whispered, an insistent echoed lulling in your ear, day after day after night after night after happily ever after happily ever after happily—

HAIRCUT IV: THE WIG

You're going to a drive-through movie for your one-year anniversary. 12 a.m. A rerun of *The Little Mermaid.*

You scratch at your head, the wig itching your shaved scalp. BM96 tugs, gently, at the waist-length braid down your back, twirls it in his fingers, then brings it to his lips for a kiss.

Beautiful, he says, as the movie begins, but there is something he holds back from saying.

At home, you pull off the wig and check your hair growth, pull the topper off the regeneration serum and massage it into your head in handfuls even though the instructions say to only use several drops at most, twice a week. The bald spots persist, irritated by the product, but you are desperate, and everything else has failed, and getting professional treatment isn't an option.

The sound of the door closing has you scrambling to secure your wig back on when you realize you've passed out in the bathroom, again.

BM96 is gone, and so is the sparse number of items he'd brought with him when he moved in.

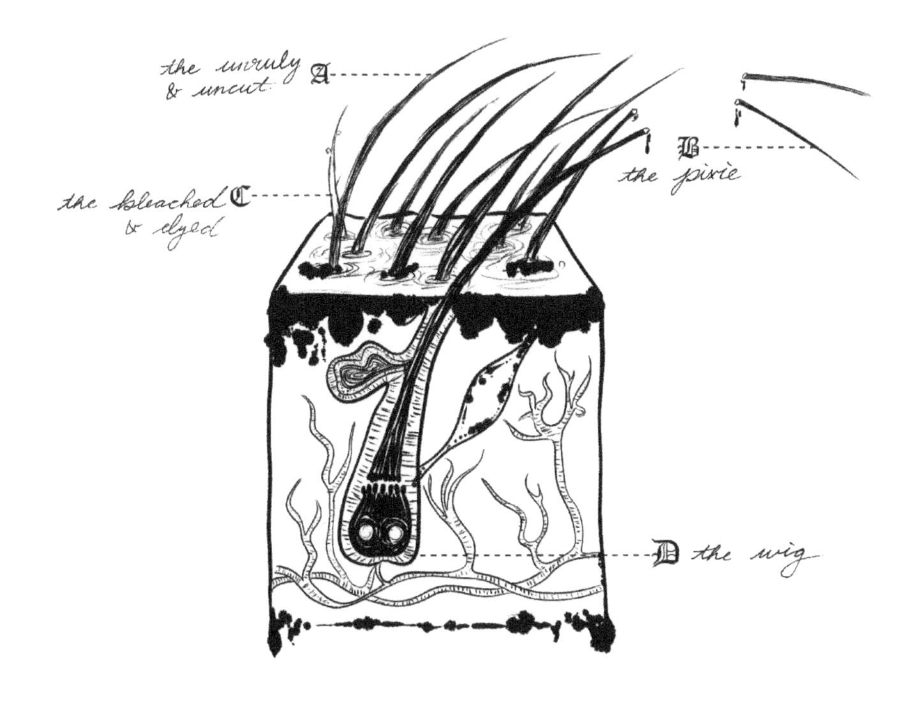

On the kitchen counter is a single jade ring, the one that has been sitting in your cart from BM96's store since the first date.

A ping.

You pull out your phone.

A notification from Etsy.

BOUJEEMAN96: I don't think it's going to work out. But I'd love to give you the jade ring, for free, for the time we spent together. I did enjoy your company, really.

In your cart, the listing for the jade ring expired.

You click on his seller profile. There is a new listing up, a ring, similar but not quite, with an even steeper discount. And it makes you feel like a discounted lover who was no longer worth the discount. Several people already have the new ring in their carts, and you wonder how many of those people will end up welcoming BOUJEEMAN96 into their home, heart, mind.

But you add the ring to your cart again, and wait for a message, a proposal that never comes.

Ai Jiang is a Chinese-Canadian writer, Ignyte Award winner, Nebula and Locus Award finalist, and an immigrant from Fujian currently residing in Toronto, Ontario. She is a member of HWA and SFWA. Her work can be found in *F&SF*, *The Dark*, *Uncanny*, among others. She is the recipient of Odyssey Workshop's 2022 Fresh Voices Scholarship and the author of *Linghun* and *I AM AI*. Find her on Twitter (@AiJiang_) and online (http://aijiang.ca).

An Unspeakable Burden

Mary Rajotte

Though weathered by time and circumstance, the Benoit Estate thrums with the energy of its ancient legacy. Vines cling to the window frames of the hulking manor where the overbearing musk of crowding crepe myrtles cloys the air. Inside the parlour, Amélie keeps her eyes fixed on the study doors while behind her, a half dozen of her kinfolk await the bestowal of the family's most precious relic. No one speaks, but conversation isn't necessary when the Benoits gather. The power of suggestion in a furtive gaze, in a raised eyebrow, or the flick of the wrist holds more influence than mere words.

When Oncles Louis and René sweep the doors open, Amélie doesn't dare move until Grand-Mère, seated in a high-backed chair before a small lectern, lifts her cane and raps it against the floorboards three times. After Amélie steps into the study, les Oncles close the doors, leaving the two women to their arcane ceremony, one witnessed by only the Beholder and her beneficiary.

The room is lit by dim candlelight at the four corners. It's the only way Amélie has ever seen Grand-Mère, how all Benoits pay her witness since she took on this burden, and how it will be for Amélie from now on.

The Benoit Reliquary sits next to a silver athamé on the lectern. It's a glass container the size of a cigar box encased in a carved wooden framework that's gilt-edged with copper fleurs-de-lis. Suspended in clear liquid, the tongue inside looms like a pale grey river stone the size of two clenched fists, finely pitted across the surface and webbed with threadlike veins.

"The source of Lisette Benoit's mysticism, the most incomparable conjurer of our bloodline." Though her lips don't move, Grand-Mère's voice encircles Amélie, everywhere and nowhere, all at once. "She left this earth long ago, yet this part of her endures. Steeped in great influence. With the power to conjure. To compel."

Grand-Mère lifts the Reliquary in her time-mottled hands. The tongue stirs and bobs. "Do you agree to assume this privilege? It carries with it both blessing and burden in equal measure."

"Oui, Grand-Mère."

With a nod, the matriarch holds the Reliquary out to her. Amélie always imagined it would be heavier, but it's lightweight in her trembling hands. A thrill across her scalp for the energy held within eclipses the part of her that wants to shrink from the room and decline the weight of this responsibility.

"Beware, child. Don't take this privilege lightly." Though still seated, Grand-Mère's voice sounds close to her ear now. "Be careful what you ask of this power. It will tell the truth, even if it's not what you wish to hear."

Grand-Mère lifts her cane and taps it on the floorboards again. The parlour doors creak open. The others, lurking in the entryway, slink forward. They converge, encircling Amélie, pressing in, each straining to observe the relic. She's mindful of each whisper, each harried breath, for even these mundane things carry the weight of hidden intention. Though they smile and nod, their pointed gazes turn from her to the Reliquary. Dart from one another and back, with no hint of fanfare or celebration.

In Amélie's mind, a voice murmurs: *may my truth speak where illusion lies.*

Not Grand-Mère this time. Someone—some*thing*—she doesn't recognize.

Oblivious to the voice, Oncle Louis steps up to Amélie. Though a thin smile pulls his mouth tight, his thoughts sound in her head.

A foolish girl chosen for a man's task.

Amélie's cheeks sting with the flush of silent recrimination as he moves away and allows Oncle René to approach next. Taking in the wonder of the Reliquary's contents, he meets Amélie's gaze.

Such a gift wasted on one so undeserving.

She grips the case to hide her shaking hands, relieved when he moves aside and her wife Rose steps forward. But there's barely a hint of encouragement in her eyes, whose characteristic gleam tarnishes in the dim light.

Not even this can make you enough for me.

Amélie's breath hitches in her throat. She focuses her energy, probing Rose's thoughts.

You've always been less than what I want. Less than I deserve. This spectacle changes nothing.

The excitement of the moment—the tradition, the responsibility—curdles like charcoal in Amélie's mouth. The room dims around her and, as the others move away in quiet conversation, Amélie trails her fingertips across the Reliquary's metal embellishments. Traces her fingernails into the woodwork's carvings. Presses her hand against the thin glass.

"Lisette Benoit," she whispers. "I call upon your insight. Grant me your wisdom."

Energy pulses from within the case, vibrating against Amélie's palm. Blackthorn branches sprout from the woodwork, lashing Amélie's wrists and binding her hands, preventing her from letting go. The edges of the room turn murky and blackness swallows everything and everyone, plunging Amélie into the past.

Through the lush, wisteria-lined Garden District to St. Louis Cemetery No. 1, she stands before the Benoit mausoleum where generations lay in the family crypt.

Amélie...

The magnolia trees tremble overhead.

Amélie...

The voice calls closer, this time from behind the mausoleum door, worn smooth by the hands of mourners. Inside, the Reliquary sits on a simple marble table.

Amélie...

Louder now, the voice conjures an old tale.

A man in a white shirt and black doublet towers over a dark-haired woman on her knees before a small crowd. He strikes her. Drags her head back by the hair. Whips her bare arms with blackthorn switches.

Lisette.

She slumps forward, but refuses to give the chaplain the satisfaction of reacting. Two men step from the shadows to grasp her by either arm. They prick her with porcupine quills, piercing her skin until the needles embed beneath.

When the chaplain places an iron headpiece over Lisette's head, she wavers under its weight. The men hold her upright by both arms, waiting for the chaplain to pry open her lips and fit the hinged bridle over her mouth. Unable to breath, Lisette forces her tongue through the barbed opening. She tries to draw it back, but the chaplain pinches her tongue with his dirty fingers and clamps her mouth closed with both hands.

Lisette yelps. Blood seeps through the gap, dribbling down her chin. She sways sideways, but the men steady her long enough for the chaplain to take up the blade in his belt.

"Suffer your devilry, witch," he says.

With one swift motion, the chaplain slices clean through the tissue. He steps aside when Lisette collapses bloody and keening before him. Mud from his boot spatters her face.

The crowd cheers the chaplain on when he parades his prize before them. "I hold in my hand the tongue of this most scornful witch!"

Taking up an earthen jar, he drops it inside, and then douses the organ with pungent vinegar from a small jug.

"May this sour any hateful words you dare utter." A pinch of black pepper goes in next. "And may your lies burn you in return."

Lisette falls in and out of consciousness, aware only of the smell of melted wax, of water being poured nearby, of feet shuffling around her, kicking dust into her face.

"May this," the chaplain says, "drown your loathsome conjurations for good and all."

She rouses long enough to witness him plunge the jar, sealed around the lid with wax, into a bucket of putrid river water. When it falls below the surface, rotting duckweed and nettles smother the back of Lisette's throat. She thrashes, heaving, splashing the chaplain's shoes. He kicks her aside, snatching the bobbing jar from the water.

Lisette paws the ground, fighting to get to him. He glares at her with such withering disdain that it stirs a fire deep within her. Collapsing onto her side, she ensnares him in her gaze, her eyes pure black, seizing him with unwavering tenacity.

Release me.

His brow furrows. He lurches but cannot free himself.

Take this curse upon yourself.

The chaplain's mouth drops open. His eyes widen and pale to stark white. Around him, the others gasp. Backing away, they flee into the night, leaving him at Lisette's mercy.

Lisette drags up onto her elbows. Mustering whatever spark she has left, she rises and staggers sideways, catching herself before she falls.

Release this hold on me. Return what you've taken.

Clutching the jar, the chaplain raises it to Lisette, who snatches it from his grasp, clasping it to her breast.

May you suffer as those you've persecuted.

Long scratches appear on the chaplain's face, stretching from his forehead to his chin. The skin on his hands and forearms bubble and blister as though burned by melted wax. His teary eyes bulge and his cheeks turn red as he snuffs in and out. Dank river water seeps through his lips and floods from both nostrils. Choking, he collapses to his knees.

The iron muzzle unclasps and falls to Lisette's feet. With the jar tucked under her arm, she hobbles toward the treeline, shuddering, groaning. There, she pauses, turning to Amélie.

May these secrets unsealed become truths revealed.

Lisette's voice propels Amélie from the dream, returning her to the study in the Benoit Estate. While the others remain inattentive to her, Grand-Mère catches Amélie's gaze in the standing mirror. With a knowing glance, Grand-Mère mouths without sound, but no one pays her any attention. Instead, they turn to Amélie, smiling, nodding, placating her. Still, their thoughts give them away.

Foolish girl.

Thorns lash her skin.

A man's task.

Blood beads at the wound.

A gift wasted.

Vinegar and pepper burn and sting.

So undeserving.

Putrid water chokes.

Less than what I want. Less than I deserve.

Rose's recriminations lash Amélie's heart with more anguish than any abuse could ever inflict. Goading her, Lisette's voice gnaws, devouring her self-control, stirring up a simmering rage until it boils to the surface.

Their curse is your blessing. Use it.

From her place in the group, Grand-Mère lets out a frantic cry. All conversation stops to follow her gaze to Amélie, who holds the opened Reliquary.

She grazes her fingertips across the surface of the water.

Amélie...

Lisette's voice is a resounding mantra granted to her by a power greater than either of them.

Use it.

Grand-Mère groans and lurches from her chair. Les Oncles grab her by both arms. Unable to speak, her mouth flops open, revealing only an empty blackness. Nothing more than the long-healed stump of her tongue remains. Oncle Louis gasps, exchanging glances with René.

Amélie...

Snaking her hand underneath, Amélie cups the tongue in her palm. It's a piece of cured leather, cold and rubbery. The rough texture sends a chill through her. Her taste buds pucker with vinegar and the sting of pepper. They curl at the delicious intent, at her willingness to conjure the power for herself.

In the standing mirror, her image distorts. Her tongue hangs loose and flaccid against her chin. She doesn't need it, for she has another.

What it must *taste* like.

How it must *feel.*

Yearning floods Amélie's mouth with the tang of fresh honey and figs, a thirst she longs to quench.

The power to conjure and compel.

Her heartbeat quickens at the thought.

It can both influence and corrupt.

Blood rushes in her ears, rattling the house like thunder claps.

Amélie...

She should close the lid, put the Reliquary back, relinquish and return it to Grand-Mère.

They should suffer your devilry, witch.

Amélie's hand trembles. All the times she'd been silenced, reduced to a mere shadow of herself by their opinions. For all their vicious thoughts. Their false smiles.

When Rose edges forward to place a hand on Amélie's arm, her

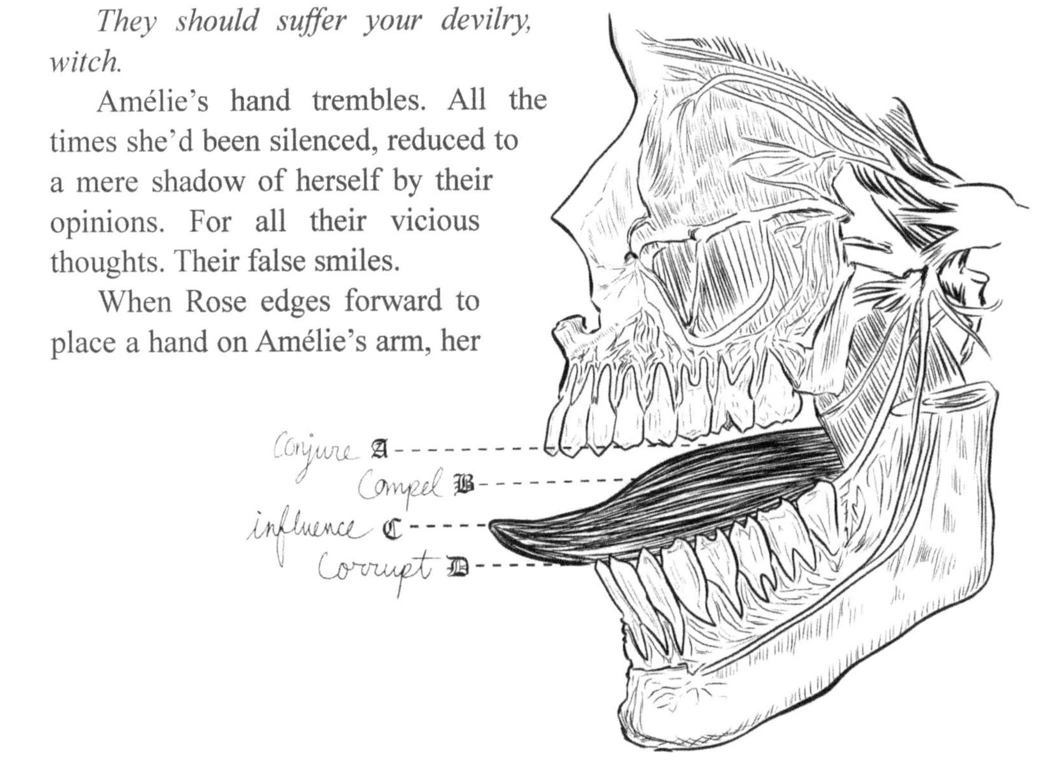

wife's faux concern ignites Amélie's simmering fury. She places the Reliquary down and takes up the athamé. Its blade glints in her hand.

Oncle René takes a step toward her.

Conjure.

Turning to the standing mirror, Amélie pinches her tongue between her fingers.

Compel.

She pulls it out as far as the muscle will allow.

Influence.

The first cut blinds her, sending her falling to her knees.

Corrupt.

Rose shrieks and lurches away.

Bitter blood pours from Amélie's mouth. She howls, releasing the pent up outrage of the disregard she's endured for years. The torment of those who came before her, those silenced, and those who will be silenced once again.

Conjure.

Ignoring the blood and heat overtaking her, she cuts again. Each motion is a declaration of her newfound strength and devotion to her destiny, to herself. To her power within.

Compel.

She severs the frenulum, pulling her tongue from the bottom of her mouth and slicing through the remaining tissue.

Influence.

Holding the severed tongue in her hand, Amélie is consumed by a potent surge of power through her body.

Corrupt.

Discarding it with a wet slap on the hardwood floor, Amélie staggers sideways. Thorny branches entangle her ankles. Drooling blood and mucus down her dress, she ignores the pain and plucks a handful of thorns from the branch.

The liquid is warm this time when Amélie cups her hand under the tongue and lifts it from the Reliquary. Hands trembling, her focus waning, she stands before the mirror and pierces the barb through the cut end of Lisette's pungent tongue. Then, maneuvering it between her lips, she presses the tongue against the stub in her mouth.

When the thorn pierces her flesh, the edges of the room fade to black, but she invokes Lisette's power and maneuvers the thorn through the soft tissue. Her jaw tenses, protesting the foreign object, but her blood sanctifies the grafted muscle.

She slumps forward, bracing herself with her hands flat on the desk and feels around with the tip of her new tongue. Gone is its soft pliability. In her mouth, it turns hard and knobby, a black fibrous root.

"Your curse is my blessing." A sharp jolt shoots through her body as Lisette's raspy voice sounds from within. "May you suffer."

Amélie faces les Oncles, who stand before the group, each with their arms out to either side to shield the others. Trembling, she lifts her head.

"May this sour any hateful words you dare utter."

Oncle Louis clutches at his throat. Sputtering, vinegar spews from his mouth until he falls to his knees, gurgling. Oncle René glowers and takes a step toward Amélie.

"May your lies burn you in return."

The candelabra next to him surges, leaping to catch the cuff of his overcoat. Flames consume the fabric, overcoming his chest with merciless intent. He drops to the floor, slapping at the flames to extinguish them.

Around her, the others scream and cower, trying to get away, but clutched in the grip of Lisette's influence, Amélie looms over them.

"Take this curse upon yourself."

Barbed vines spring from her mouth and spread across the room, piercing their tongues, binding their lips when they protest. Under Lisette's malignant control, Amélie wields her curse, exhuming the voice she always needed but couldn't invoke on her own. Her conjuration spirals and uncoils, overtakes the others, entangling their mouths, bending everyone assembled to her will until only Rose remains.

Aghast at the hideous tongue inside Amélie's mouth and trembling at the carnage before her, Rose backs away, but Amelie can't forget her hidden thoughts.

"May this drown your hate for good and all."

Thorns bloom from Rose's lips, so she can do nothing more than whimper. With tears stinging her eyes, Amélie reaches for her love, pricking her fingertips on the barbs. As much as she wants to hold Rose in her arms, her wife's hateful words are a chasm too insurmountable.

Muzzled by Amelie's charm, the Benoits claw at their mouths in a whimpering huddle at Amélie's feet. Stepping over her discarded tongue, she takes her rightful place before them in Grand-Mère's chair. Ignoring the pain flooding her body, ignoring their deceit, Amélie welcomes the clarity Lisette has given her.

When inadequacy gnaws at the back of her mind, she quashes the thoughts with the memory of the chaplain and his brutality toward Lisette. When the agony of how she was forced to mutilate herself threatens to overwhelm her, she reaches deep for the source of Lisette's strength passed down to her and lets the fire within burn away the words used to diminish her.

Yet a lingering worry takes root in Amélie's mind. Something shifts, rustling in the darkened room. It tickles across her scalp. Twines down the back of her neck. Whispers, from everywhere and nowhere, all at once. Endlessly, the only voice left.

Foolish girl.

May you suffer.

This curse upon yourself.

Canadian author **Mary Rajotte** has a penchant for penning nightmarish tales of Gothic folk horror which have been published in a number of anthologies. In 2022, she launched *Frightmarish: a quarterly Gothic LitZine* for devotees of dark fiction. poetry and the creative macabre. Her debut dark paranormal fantasy novel, *The Bone Key*, will launch in Autumn 2024 from Quill & Crow Publishing House. When Mary isn't writing, you can find her standing on her tiptoes at concerts or conjuring ideas by moonlight. Sometimes camera-elusive but always coffee-fueled, Mary lives in Toronto, Canada with her fiancé. She welcomes messages via her website maryrajotte.com.

EARLY ADOPTER

JULIE SEVENS

I ran my fingers along the hallway wall. It was white, shiny; felt like the surface of the cell phone I'd overpaid for. The `starling` facility was slick and quiet—all angles, polished concrete, muted tones. I identified with the aesthetic, even if I couldn't quite afford to live somewhere like this yet.

Glenn Lewis—the man I was following—took an abrupt turn and shoved a frosted glass door open. A paper sign taped to it announced *RESERVED FOR PROSPECTIVES.* With a deep breath for my jangling nerves, I stepped into the last phase of the intake interview.

Four stacks of paper awaited me on the overlong glass table, edges neatly squared. Glenn swept his hand over the table, inviting me to sit. "Today is a big day, Harlow. You're part of a very small group of individuals who have made it through all the medical evaluations, the neurotelemetry, the psychological synergy exam. Before we can schedule your `mynah` implanting, we just have a couple more t's to cross."

I picked up the pen on the first stack of papers. My hand was sweaty against the plastic.

"This is an NDA. We need you to read it carefully."

"Didn't I already sign this?"

"There was an earlier one, yes. That covered the information you'd receive during intake—up to this point. Now we're really in it, Harlow. This one is going to cover what you'll find out today as well as during the `mynah` pilot itself if you're selected."

A tiny voice in my head—sounding a lot like my dad—wondered if maybe I should ask a lawyer to look at these contracts. But Glenn didn't seem to have the patience for that, and I didn't want to risk my spot in the pilot. I signed all the arrow-stickered spots on the neat stacks of pages, pausing to examine the legalese vocabulary, the thick cream-colored paper, the letterhead. I felt woozy, my cheeks flushed.

At the end, Glenn seemed satisfied. I was doing good. I might get in. He left the room with the papers, and I sat and listened to the sound of the minute hand in the frameless clock on the wall.

Three days later, on Thursday, I got a text from an unknown number informing me that my procedure time was 7 a.m. the following morning. I muted my lunch meeting and cheered into my latte. I was in.

The team shoved instrument after instrument down my numbed throat. On the ultrasound monitor, lines appeared hot white amid the black outlines of flesh, some kind of wire. Then the outline of a box eased in at the back of my trachea, which I was told was a fan that would work like a wind turbine to gather power from my breathing.

My palate wasn't completely numb, but they'd said the procedure didn't warrant an actual anesthesiologist. I watched the outline of a pair of curved forceps touch above my uvula, placing a circle the size of a quarter. Wires pulled down from it and connected to the box.

A jerking motion from the forceps and several pointed spikes jutted deeper into my flesh behind the disc. Sharp stabbing punched through the roof of my mouth, left my sinuses throbbing. I gagged, my throat filling with blood.

"Sorry, Harlow," a nurse said. He suctioned my mouth out. "Breathe, okay?"

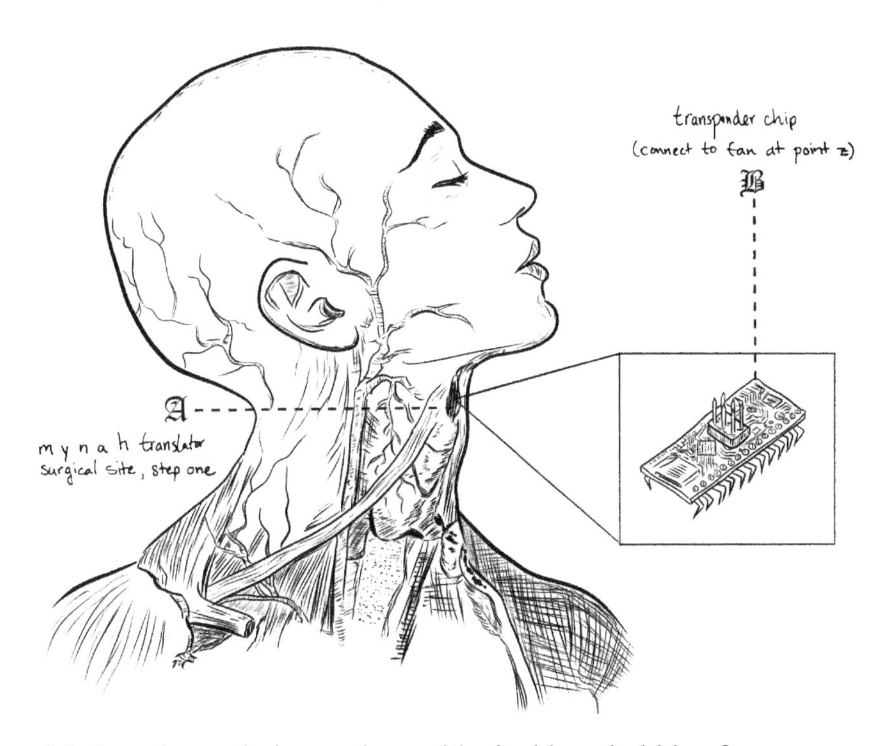

My breath caught in my throat, blocked by a bubble of mucus.

"I know." He winced, then corrected. "It's important to be able to get the FDA to treat this as a wearable, rather than an implantable device. You understand, I'm sure."

The final paper I'd signed had the same warning as a rackety bottle of vitamins: *This product is not intended to treat or cure any disease.* Future-proofing myself wasn't a treatment; it was an enhancement. I was entering the future we'd all been promised. The `m y n a h` was a real-life babelfish from *Hitchhiker's Guide to the Galaxy*, able to translate for me, able to produce real-time translations in my own voice.

I wasn't about to be outperformed at my job by one of the software programs the vendors kept trying to sell—I was better. I would be bionic now, just like Jaime Sommers. I could talk to almost anyone in the world.

Blood pooled on my tongue again as I focused my eyes on a speck on the ceiling and my mind on my new abilities.

At home, a weekend spent watching trash TV and eating sherbet was fine with me. I was banned from talking for 48 hours, but Mr. Slippers didn't care. He lay heavy on my blanketed lap, warm and purring.

Mr. Slippers padded away after the fourth time Netflix asked if I was still watching, and I finished the first bottle of liquid children's Motrin from the cabinet. In the bathroom mirror, I stared down the back of my throat with a flashlight for the hundredth time to admire my new hardware. A thin gold circle was embedded in the roof of my mouth, circuit lines running along the sides and down my throat. Beyond that I couldn't see, but a faint hum emitted from my mouth if I opened my lips wide and took a deep breath. The device made my throat raw and red, puffy around the gold film like a canker sore, but salt water rinses and the Motrin helped.

Amadou Slacked me to ask how I was. He was the only one I'd told in advance what I was doing. After a happy hour spent bitching about our boss, Mr. Aldrich, we'd shared an Uber and I'd breathlessly told him about my plan after he mentioned a friend who worked at `starling`. He hadn't said much at the time, but the disapproval had been clear on his face. Easy for him though—he already spoke three languages.

Still, it was nice of him to remember. I told him I was allowed to talk on Sunday and got a white heart emoji as a reply. Conjuring up some of the French he'd taught me a couple months back, before I'd given up on learning it the old-fashioned way, I typed "A bientot."

By Sunday morning, my fingernails were down to chewed stubs. I had downloaded the companion app and got the companion watch set up. All I'd have to do was command my voice to switch to one of the 1,472 new languages I could speak now. The anticipation was killing me, but my latest dose of children's Motrin hadn't kicked in yet, so I was hesitant to talk.

Desire won though, and I tapped at the watch. A pleasant default voice sprang to life.

Hello, Harlow. I'm `mynah`.

"Hello." Hoarse, but not terrible. I cleared my throat, sipped my water.

First, I'd like to learn your voice. Is that okay?

"Yes."

Great. Let's get started. On your screen, you will see some text. I'd like you to read that text when you're ready.

"Had I as many souls as there be stars, I'd give them all for Mephistophilis. By him I'll be great emperor of the world, and make a bridge through the moving air…Sorry, what is this?"

I use a variety of public domain text samples, Harlow. This one is from The Tragical History of Doctor Faustus by Christopher Marlowe. If you'd prefer a different passage, I can display one now.

"No, this is fine."

I read out the passage, getting accustomed to the way the wires pulled taut like new tendons in my throat as I talked. A strange sensation, half-choking me, half reminding me of a brand new pair of tights being yanked over heels and knees, stretching in a web of plastic.

Thanks. I'm processing.

An animation of a robot thinking danced on my watch. Then a welcoming three-tone melody emanated from my throat, buzzing my vocal cords.

Okay, Harlow. Let's get started!

"`mynah`, speak German." The watch buzzed my wrist to let me know it was listening, waking a grumpy Mr. Slippers. "Hello, Mr. Slippers. You are a cat!"

A deep, throbbing hum tickled my vocal cords as the muscles were automatically contorted to release. The back of my tongue vibrated, and my voice echoed from the `mynah` in a mishmash of manipulated flesh and robotic puppetry.

"Hallo, Herr Hausschuhe. Sie sind eine Katze!"

Mr. Slippers tried to jump away from my grasp, and his claws caught in my sweatshirt.

While Mr. Slippers gave himself a bath under the bed, I went through the kitchen naming foods and dishes in every language I could think of. *Zweibeln, llwy, katsarola, cezve, erdapfel, záclona.* The world was my picture dictionary.

Monday morning, my stomach was in knots on the subway. I'd imagined walking into Aldrich's office and revealing my new abilities a hundred times. He'd been threatening the team with layoffs for as long as I'd worked there, but when he finally followed through, it wasn't going to be me, not when I was saving him a three million dollar translation vendor bill. In my wildest imaginings, he gave me a promotion on the spot.

At his office door—for real, finally—I rapped my knuckles three times, softly. When Mr. Aldrich yelled "What!" as usual, I opened the door.

His eyes bored into me over his monitor screen.

"Good morning, sir. If you have a second, I had something I would love the opportunity to demo for you."

He puffed his cheeks and blew out through slack lips, waiting for me to talk.

"I had the opportunity to join a trial study for a new `starling` project. The device I'm using gives me the ability to speak any language. If you name a language, I can show you."

"Yeah, I have Duolingo, too."

Putting on my best customer-service smile, I clarified. "This can handle real-time translation. I'd love to demo it for you."

"Okay, Spanish."

"`mynah`, speak Spanish." I waited for the watch to vibrate its acknowledgement. "Good morning, Mr. Aldrich. How was your coffee today?" I said. "Buenos días, señor Aldrich. ¿Cómo estuvo tu café esta mañana?" the `mynah` said in my voice.

"That's a neat trick, Harlow. Really cool." He had the tone of a stepdad at a birthday party watching a magician.

His phone rang in his hand, and he held it up at me half-apologetically before answering. He ignored me while he talked for minutes until I slunk from the office and closed the door behind me.

I was used to feeling three inches tall when I left Aldrich's company. I'd gone through all the phases of grief many times and no longer bothered with anger or depression after he dismissed or overruled me, just swallowed it hard. Aldrich just needed convincing.

My calendar had me on a call in twenty with a client in France. I smiled into my coffee mug. This was my perfect chance to test my new powers, and if it got back to Aldrich how impressed they were, even better.

The Muzak paused.

"Yes, hello, thank you for—"

"I'm still holding for Glenn Lewis. He told me this was a direct line. I don't understand why I keep getting the runaround."

"Ope, sorry, let me just—"

Hold music.

"Harlow! Hi, hope you're doing well."

"No, actually, the app keeps crashing."

"Oh, I'm sorry to hear that, Harlow. Listen, though, I have good news."

"Glenn, you told me—"

"We got approved as a wearable! We're all set, then."

"You have to help me. It keeps—"

"So actually, what that approval means is we're going to be able to wrap up the study. It's all done. `starling` really appreciates your participation, really couldn't have done it without you. You're going to get to keep the device for free as a token of our appreciation, and a lifetime subscription to the companion app."

"It doesn't work! There's too long of a delay between what I say and when it starts speaking. Everyone just laughs and switches to English—"

"That's great, Harlow, no need to thank us: no, we thank you! That does mean in the future, you'll have to get in touch with the regular customer service line. You know. Just since we've wrapped up."

"Glenn, there's nobody else to help—"

"Thanks again, Harlow! Have a good one!"

The line was dead air.

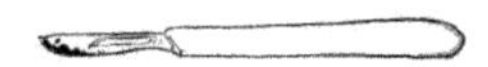

After days of practicing using the `mynah`, I'd gotten better at switching languages. I'd dug through the app settings to try to get it to respond with less lag. And I was getting the hang of the receptive translation, holding the watch up to my ear to translate imported *Big Brother* seasons.

"Hey, Amadou." I leaned over the top of his cube, resting my elbows on the edge.

He pulled an earbud out. "What's up, Harlow?"

"Help me practice the `mynah` translation again?"

Amadou rolled his eyes, but he was smiling.

"`mynah`, speak Fulani. *bzzt.* Hi, Amadou! Do you think you have time to work on this project?"

We waited. "Kedu, kedu, kedu, kedu," my throat eventually produced.

"That's not right at all." Amadou laughed, but tried to stop when he saw how upset I was. "Do you want to try the part where I talk to you?"

I rubbed my throat. My vocal cords were tingling lightly, like I was touching a Van de Graaff generator at the science museum. "No. Thanks, though. Sorry."

The embarrassment almost brought me to tears and I fled to the bathroom before Amadou noticed. In the mirror, I opened my mouth and listened to that little hum. I'd made the mistake of snoring last night and been awoken by my own voice trying to translate a snore.

I scraped at the gold disc in my palate with a fingernail, and was rewarded with a sharp pain like an ice cream headache. I hadn't had ice cream in years.

Connecting...

Mary G. has joined the chat

Hello, Harlow. I am here to help. Can you give me your order number so I can help?

Hi Mary. I don't have an order number, I have a `mynah`.

I completely understand. Let me look over your transaction history so I can find this information.

Thank you for your patience, Harlow. I haven't been able to find a purchase history under the information provided. Do you think it may have been under another phone or email?

There isn't going to be an order number. I was in the trial for the `mynah`. I've tried every support line.

btw your website's broken, the `mynah` page is down.

Thank you, Harlow. I think I understand the issue. We do not have support for this app, as we are the customer support service for `starling` devices. I can give you the information for the software customer support!

They sent me to you. They said they don't have any information about the `mynah` app, but you would. The watch stopped responding to commands, and now the app is just a loading screen. I need to know what to do. The device is freaking out; it keeps switching languages. I can't talk without it doing something unpredictable.

I completely understand. Give me just a moment to find more information for you.

Mary G. is typing...

I had to call in sick because of the `mynah` for a second day in a row. The problems had gotten worse. Instead of just interrupting me, or occasionally translating things without being asked to into a random language—which were frustrating issues to say the least, but I'd tried to laugh them off—my own human vocal cords had started seizing up, muting me.

I'd sat under the counter in my kitchen, back against gold-edged open shelving, trying to contact Glenn Lewis. Publicly posting on `starling`'s social media had gotten me blocked. It wasn't Mary G. today on the chat line, it was Joshua T., and he was less helpful than she was.

Mr. Slippers sat on the copy of the NDA and the contract I'd been given. Everything they'd promised was fake. *Lifetime support!* From who?

Eventually, I dragged myself to bed, hoping I'd have a fresh idea in the morning, and if not at least get a break while I slept.

My throat slammed me out of a dream where I was drowning. I woke, choking and gurgling, and ran to the bathroom sink. Stringy bubbles of bloody spit fell out of my mouth, spattering the enamel.

I gargled with the stinging saltwater rinse beside the sink until it came out clear. A rhythmic zap pulsed in the back of my throat, an electric shock zinging me like a science experiment potato connected to a nine-volt battery.

The flat gold wires at the back of my tongue pulled taut when I opened my mouth in the mirror. The one on the right yanked hard, jerking against my tonsil with enough force to make me retch.

Something snapped—a pop that reverberated my clavicles. It relieved the pressure on my tonsil, but left something hanging loose down the back of my throat. When I swallowed, it gave the distinct impression of eating a bunch of Christmas tinsel like spaghetti. Whatever was loose would neither go down nor come up.

I sank to the floor against the tub. One of the very strict instructions I'd been given was that I was not allowed to seek medical care during the trial without the approval of `starling`. But the trial was over, right? They weren't going to help me, Glenn had made that clear. Could a hospital even help me? *I don't even know how it's installed.*

"What the hell do I—" *zap* "—do, Mr. Slippers?" *zap.* He nuzzled under my chin. My voice said "Co ja do robię, panie kapcie?"

I buried my face in his fur and cried. "Sounds like—" *zap* "—Polish," I told him, attempting a cry-laugh. "Brzmi jak polski," my throat said in a borrowed voice.

Every zap tightened my throat, squeezed it closed reflexively, the electricity humming in my muscles and forcing them together. I paced back and forth in the hall, afraid to speak. Then I squared my shoulders, evicted Mr. Slippers from the bathroom sink, and shut the door on him. This was on me.

In my mouth, my fingers found the gold disc attached to my palate. I slipped a fingernail beneath it and tried to wiggle under, but it had sealed to my flesh. I stuck my fingers further down my throat, ignoring the immediate pool of spit forming as I gagged myself. My fingertip grazed a loose wire, and I slicked it with my wet fingers until I caught it.

I pulled, gingerly, and felt a tug near my lungs.

I pulled, harder, and felt a sharp pain that radiated through my chest. I'd have to pull harder if I were going to get it out myself. If I could.

My hand came out of my mouth streaked red. I had really done it now, I knew I was hurting myself, but then, I'd hurt myself just by having this fucking thing, this worst-mistake-of-my-life, installed. I wanted to reach down Glenn's throat and yank on his tendons and sinews.

It needed to come out. Like a rotten tooth slowly killing me, an abscess working its poison into a pioneer's bloodstream. It froze my voice, what if the next thing it did was close up my throat, what if the zaps worsened? I put this in my body without understanding it. I was an idiot.

When I opened my mouth, more blobs of bloody spit poured into the sink. My tongue went numb during my self-pity session.

Off like a bandaid.

I stuffed my fist down my throat, ignored the scrape of tooth on knuckle, the pain near my ears from shoving my jaw open. I grabbed everything I could that was foreign, the tentacles of this invader, and ripped it out. The `mynah` came out by the roots, like a tree in a hurricane.

A fleshy mass held fast to the wires. But I'd done it. Wires and metal and circuitry dangled from my fingers, one last long wire like a loose thread pulled slowly out of my throat and it was *out.*

I examined the tissue that had come with it, pink and veiny, a real hunk of flesh. Where was the box? I'd missed some. I tried to push my hand back in, but blood poured out too fast, too much, and I hit my head on the sink on the way down to the floor.

The gold disc with its horrible spikes lay in my palm, atop the mound of my throat tissue, maybe some lung—*was that possible?*—and I noticed how flimsy it was. The tile beneath my face though, was not flimsy, and the smashed side of my head throbbed. I looked at my phone teetering on the edge of the counter above me.

Inside my throat, a humming emitted in the `mynah`'s default voice.

This function is deprecated.

beep beep beep

This function is deprecated.

beep beep beep

This function is deprecated.

beep beep beep

Julie Sevens is a horror writer and an everything reader. The tentacular appendages of the universe have moved her from Ohio to Philadelphia, to Berlin. Now just beyond the interstellar blastzone of Chicago, Julie lives with her husband, two sons, a doorstep spider named Lentil, and a ghost in the closet who resists naming. Find her most recently in *34 Orchard* of find more of her nightmares at juliesevens.com.

Telling Tales

Christopher O'Halloran

Crazy? Do you think I'm crazy?

I've always been a little neurotic, but that saved my ass in 2020, didn't it? They nearly fired me from EarFox Studios when I refused to come in, but after a dozen of their hosts and engineers came down with the plague, do you think my commitment to work from home was laughed at?

They're lucky I created such a robust guide for remote recording. Every one of our podcasts continued over Zoom. Sure, our more comedic shows suffered from timing issues, but the celeb interviews did all right, and our scripted stuff *killed.*

Killed so good, it gave us the perfect opportunity to grow the stories branch of our studio—with me at its head.

Of course, it means I have to do all the work—mixing, editing, foley and soundtrack—but who better to? I hear everything.

Everything.

Every click, pop, snap, crunch. Reversing delivery vans. Low-flying airplanes. Every little aberration to be cut sticks out like a hangnail. It's a curse but at least one that earns me a living.

At least with my cans on, I can't hear Edgar, my Maine Coon, chastise me for letting his food dish become fallow. And I can't hear the crunch of kibble between sharp teeth.

"Allie."

This kettle in the studio isn't as good as mine. My hot chocolate mix clumps up and doesn't emulsify properly. Little, powdery bombs liable to explode into dust in my throat. Oh, to remain home.

But it's safe now. The world is safe again. Don't look at the death toll. The infection rates. We've taken necessary precautions for long enough. It's time to get back to work—at work. I can't hear Edgar because he's at home and I'm once more at the studio.

"Hey, girl."

Chips crunch between molars. A building falling into concrete rubble that presses into my skin.

The bag crinkles. Electric static. Tin foil on iron fillings.

Someone sucks on fingers, pulling each digit out of their mouth like it's a flesh vacuum.

I look up, brows furrowed at the remark.

"Don't call me—"

"Let's kick this shit into high gear. I've got ayahuasca at noon." Monty strides forward, talking over me as if his voice was the most important in the building. After all, it kind of is. Folks subscribe in droves to our premium tier just to hear him make edgy banter during his "Jawing with Monty" weekly show. They don't care about the woman putting the production together. Splicing in the opening and closing themes. Inserting ads between segments. Producing all the TikTok and Instagram content to bring in new listeners and retain our loyal following.

They only care about Monty with his carefree attitude, and his everyman demeanor. His dumb chuckle and his slick head. Every bro hiding a thinning hairline or male pattern baldness under a baseball cap can see Monty's charm and gain inspiration.

If he can do it, so can they!

Our CEO is visiting tomorrow. Word around the studio is that EarFox is giving him another podcast. Another chance to spew his thoughts into a microphone, occasionally bouncing off a guest. No artistry. Just bullshit.

I stir my clumpy hot chocolate. It smells of metal.

"That shit would do you good, you know that?" Monty tugs the fridge open and retrieves an all-natural energy drink, microdosed with shrooms. *GALACTIC THUNDER*. Something the studio provides him, no questions asked.

In place of the drink, next to his bottle of exotic protein powder—refrigerated for some reason—Monty places his empty chip bag.

I grunt. You couldn't get me anywhere near a hallucinogen. Like I said, I'm not crazy.

Monty cracks the lid on his can of thunder and tips it to his mouth. Wormy lips slither around the opening. He slurps. Air bubbles infuse the liquid as he crudely sucks it down.

I can hear it sloshing inside his cheeks. Squelching between his teeth, his throat twitching and pulsing as he lets it slide inside himself.

I have to turn away.

He picks a hair off my shoulder. One of Edgar's. I shiver in revulsion.

"It *is* a little chilly in here." He sneezes three times in rapid succession. With red eyes, he examines the hair. "Cat? I'm fucking allergic to cats."

And I didn't ask him to groom me. But I don't say that.

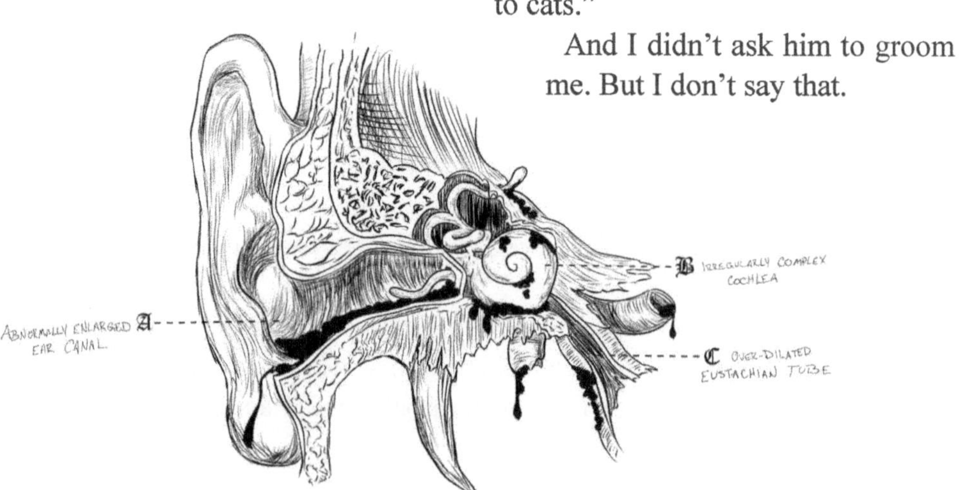

He leaves the room, taking his godawful mouth noises with him.

My hot chocolate is cold. It's disgusting. I can't bring myself to drink it.

It coats the sink pale brown before I rinse it away.

The mouth noises. Everyone has them. You do, too. The little smack of a wet tongue before you start to speak. The clicks at the opening of your throat. The swelling of your sinuses hitchhiking as a sticky residue on every word.

Most people don't hear them. The noises don't grate against their soul. They don't cringe and feel the impulse to dig a long fingernail into their ear to scrape out the offending sound.

But I do. The cans transmit everything being recorded.

"Jaime, did you see that new TikTok song?" Monty practically swallows his mic. Good etiquette; his words will carry perfectly through to my equipment—but so will every slurp and slap and pop and click.

Monty's lips part with a slimy *smeh*, and air whistles over soggy teeth. "If I were a fish and you caught me—you heard that one?"

Jaime—our resident maintenance man—nods politely. He's not mic'd, so there's no point in him talking. It's the Monty show. Just the way he likes it.

Monty laughs. Stoned chuckles, a chorus of *huh huh huh*'s interrupted by a wheezy breath that rattles my brain before he repeats the *ratatat* laughter.

I lean forward and speak clearly into my own mic. "The script is ready for you."

Monty's stare goes blank. His brows furrow. I clearly interrupted a deep and important thought.

"Uhhh, yeah."

The vocal fry tickles my eardrums. I can feel his non-words reverberating in there. Would you blame me if I tore off my headphones and stomped them into pieces?

"I was just warming up."

"You don't want to miss your ayahuasca," I remind him.

Monty smiles at me. The climb of his upper lip along his gums squelches in my ears.

A shiver runs up my spine.

"Right," he says, the plosive T assaulting me. "Let's do it."

It's getting worse. I can tell. Nobody else can—not the audience, not the other podcast producers, not Jaime, the fucking moron—but I can. I'm the one who has to listen live, who has to edit, who has to kill herself making this buffoon sound intelligent.

He's speaking now.

I can't stand it. I pace behind the glass. Like a tiger behind bars, back and forth in my tight line. The headphone cord keeps me in place. My leash.

My nails magically make their way to my mouth. They crawl between my lips and only briefly touch my tongue before I remember the bitter agent on them to break me of this habit.

The taste of dog shit—of spoiled fruit, of decay and vile juices—dances on the tip of my tongue, and I spit viciously onto the floor of the control booth.

Behind watering eyes, an idea forms. The bottle is in my purse.

An hour and a half later, it's in my hand. I'm cleaning the recording studio—Jaime was called away an hour ago to get the reception area and conference rooms ready for the CEO.

Monty's *GALACTIC THUNDER* sits on the table. I pick it up. There's still a couple fingers left inside.

Where's Monty? The bathroom? He always takes a shit before he leaves work. Always leaves his scent lingering in the air. His all-meat diet does hellish things to his waste.

I wish I didn't have to know that.

I don't have much time. That rumble of the pipes was the toilet flushing.

He'll wash his hands, right? I have time.

I unscrew the bottle of nail biter deterrent. It's made overseas, but they must have some safety regulations, right? A li'l diarrhea will humble the man.

I pour the remaining acid in Monty's mushroom drink.

A split second before he walks in.

Fuck. What was I thinking? Dump it. Toss it in the trash. Abort, abort!

Holding the can, I turn from Monty, but he reaches around my side, snags the tallboy from my fingers. His unwashed hand brushes mine, and I nearly hurl.

"Hold up," he says. "The dregs are where the potency is."

He tips the can back against his teeth. Aluminum grates on enamel.

My spine nearly rips free from my back. It trembles like the grinding foundation of an old apartment building in an earthquake.

Swish, swish, gulp.

Monty comes up gasping for air. "Fuck me." His mouth is wet, lips smacking. "All the good shit settled like crazy. I'll be tripping balls on the freeway." His throat makes an atrocious burbling sound, and he belches.

"You're not gonna drive." His gall is astonishing.

Monty winks at me. "Adiós, chica."

He slips out of the room.

I should follow. Strangle him with the cord of my headphones.

He deserves it. Have you seen the shit he tweets? He just said he's going to get behind the wheel of his Ford Explorer after downing a hallucinogen! He might run a family down, thinking they're goblins or whatever.

I could protect those people from him. Take that giant SUV out of his hands.

Beside me, someone clears their throat.

I jump, slamming back into the present. Sweat breaks out below my hairline. My pits feel electric.

Next to me, Jaime holds a small trash can.

Fuck. He must have popped back in to clean up. Did he see me poison Monty?

He'd tell for sure. Why not? All those years working my way into a position of middling power, all of it down the drain.

"Asshole," says Jaime, and holds the trash can out for me to deposit my collection into.

That's it. I'm tired of the smacking lips. I'm tired of the sucking of teeth and the dripping of saliva. His mouth is a cave. Each tooth a dripping stalag-whatever. Pooling drool he gulps down between lines.

And I'm here editing them out. Like the fucking sucker I am.

I tear the cans off my ears. There's only so much a girl can take. He needs to go.

"Allie."

I spin in my chair, rolling back on the casters until I slam up against an equipment chest—empty now that all recording is done in studio again and we don't have to schlep mics and receivers from house to house.

Monty leans against the door jamb. His skin looks grey. How long has he been standing there without me able to hear him?

"What are you doing here?" I ask. There's nobody else in the studio. Jaime left a few hours ago. I'm just staying behind to get this episode cut in time for the weekend. With the CEO visiting tomorrow, I'm not sure I'll get the chance during the day.

It's a good thing I filled Edgar's food dish before coming to work.

"Forgot my pre-workout." He jiggles a thick, black canister with neon-pink, Korean writing on it. "Need the energy. I've been throwing up a lot today." He takes a step forward, keeping his balance with a hand on my desk. "Know why I'd be throwing up?"

I shake my head. "Something you ate?"

His next step takes him into my keyboard. His pinky finger presses the control, alt, and windows key. There's a beeping in my headphones.

"Hey!" I reach forward to push him off the keys, but he smacks my hand away.

"Something I drank, maybe." He flashes a hoary eye at me, bloodshot and wild. "My *GALACTIC THUNDER*. I took it out of your hand. What did you do to it?"

"N-nothing." I'm vibrating. He knows I did it. If he didn't before, I'm sure he can see the confirmation written all over my face.

Monty smirks. "Nice try. But you're donezo here."

I can see it now. He's going to go to our boss and rat me out. Everything I've done to save this fucking company over the last three years, down the drain. The keys to the castle, handed to this neanderthal.

"EarFox needs me," I say, steel in my spine.

"Read the writing on the wall, kid." Monty licks his lips. They're blue, glistening in the light of my three computer monitors. "People don't need your scripted shit. They want improv. They want dudes shooting the shit. Shit they can relate to."

Read between his lines. Even he knows it's shit.

"They want stories, too," I say.

"We can get that from AI."

There's no way. "If you want garbage."

"I can make *anything* sound good." His lips peel back from shiny teeth. "They love—" His mouth smacks, tongue clicking against the roof of his mouth. "—to hear me—" Monty yawns. His eyes roll. Land on my shoulder. "—talk."

I see where he's looking. There's another of Edgar's hair flapping in the breeze of Monty's rancid breath. Being pulled toward his looming face with each inhalation.

Monty takes a deep breath.

The cat hair flies off my shoulder and right into his nose. This is going to be a big one.

It's not; it's a *bouquet* of sneezes. The first splatters my cheek with snot.

Monty does nothing to cover his mouth. His hands land on his knees as he doubles over, spewing all the air in his already depleted lungs into the world.

I lose count of the number of sneezes around the time his face turns purple.

And just like that, he's out. Falling backward, knees buckling. Lands hard on his ass, rocking back at his hips until his head smacks hard against the carpet.

"Oh!" My hands fly to my mouth.

Monty's mouth hangs open, no longer looking so wet. No longer making any noise.

I should get help. That smack didn't sound good. Did his skull crunch as it hit the ground? My own shock mercifully blocked it out.

I stand. I'll get help. I need to.

Then what? Will his gratitude lead him to change his ways? Will he forgive me for poisoning him? Will he see the error of his ways and become the type of person who gives a friend his keys when intoxicated?

Fat chance. He is everything that's wrong with the industry. With the world. He's a scumbag who thinks he can just chuckle through life, failing upward. God's gift to no one.

His pre-workout sits on my desk. His mouth hangs open.

But I can't. I don't feel the urge. The murderous impulse that washes over me when he talks. It's gone now that he's silenced.

My headphones hang around my ears. Maybe…

I slide them over my ears. Reach forward, rewind the track I've been working on.

"The problem is there's no brotherly love among them," Monty says in my ear. He's interviewing a men's rights advocate, some dumbass who thinks schooling university freshmen makes him Plato. "They don't have each other's back because they're looking to throw each other under the bus for clout."

All the wetness of his mouth comes through my headphones. My shoulders lift to my earlobes.

I unscrew the lid on his pre-workout. The smell of cotton candy wafts out at me. There's a scoop sitting in the powder.

Monty's mouth hangs open.

"Crabs in a tank," says the guest.

"Exactly!" Monty smacks the table in the recording. The loudness makes me jump. "Because they think if they're not cancelling, they're going to be the ones on the chopping block."

I can't shut up the Monty on the recording, but I can shut up the Monty before me.

The powder scoop shakes in my hand. I dump it into his gaping mouth before I can lose my nerve. A pile of pink snow, fine as dazzling flurries.

His next inhale takes the powder deep inside him. His chest spasms. The skin on his throat tightens. Those wormy lips turn purple. He coughs a little, but doesn't wake.

A couple scoops for good measure, and he never wakes.

His body fits neatly in the unused equipment trunk. At this hour, I definitely have the studio to myself. Nobody would be foolish enough to stay this late.

The trunk is against the wall. I'll roll it down after I'm done editing this episode. Dump it in the green belt that runs behind the studio. This episode is all bullshit, but it should be the last of it. Without Monty, they don't have anyone to carry this show. In the vacuum, I'll be able to amplify other voices.

Movement in the corner of my eye.

I jump, pushing my headphones off.

Jamie whistles his way in, pushing his maintenance cart.

"Don't mind me," he says. "Gotta get some last minute stuff done for the CEO visit." He takes out a spray bottle and rag and starts vigorously cleaning door handles.

"Yeah." My mouth is devoid of saliva.

My eyes flick over the equipment trunk. Jaime won't need to clean anything inside it, but will he be stuffing anything in, out of sight for the big visit?

"I thought you might still be here," Jaime says. "Heard you banging around about half an hour ago."

Heard Monty's head slamming against the ground. Heard me struggling with his weight, hauling him into the trunk and slamming the lid on his fingers. Not that he'd feel broken fingers anymore.

"Ah shit, look at that." He points at a sprinkling of pink powder. "That prick got his creatine everywhere."

"Pre-workout," I mutter.

"What?"

"I'll get it," I blurt, standing.

"With what?" He smirks at me. "Don't you worry, Allie, I got the tools for the job." He laughs, each guttural guffaw making my stomach turn.

The handheld vac comes out of the cart and before I know it, the powder is inside its canister.

"Bingo, bango, bongo." Another laugh.

That sound never grated on me before, but now…

Jaime walks around, dusting corners.

“Been working here over a decade,” he says, “and I thought we were going in a good direction before they brought on that asshole.”

I nod. Every word he says is dripping in saliva. His throat sounds absolutely coated in phlegm. Why doesn’t he clear it? I’m suffocating just listening.

“Me, I like that NPR.” He smiles at me. “Lots of human interest stories.”

What’s he chewing on? His own cud? I squint and turn away, but that makes the noises worse.

“I like people.” He retracts the handle on his duster and smacks it back into the cart. “Most people, anyway.” With a grunt, he hops onto the equipment trunk. “I bet that dude’ll be shitting his pants all night after pounding back that stuff you spiked him with.”

His ass is a lid away from Monty’s body.

“They listen to you, right?” Jaime leans forward, resting his arms on his thighs. He slides a pack of gum out of his pocket, spits his old wad into the wrapper, then pops the fresh sliver of spearmint into his mouth. “If I share a couple podcast ideas with you, think you can kick them up the ladder tomorrow?”

It’s all I can do to nod. His words are making me sick. Each one floats across the air between us, wedging in my ears like a minty turd in a clogged toilet.

Why did I nod? He’s only going to talk more!

“Well, you know those game shows they have?”

His words lose form. They become a drone. A drill, digging into my head, filthy and corrupt. It’s as if he’s channeling the noises from Monty’s body, proximity transferring the power.

Look at the way he’s leering at me. Blowing bubbles, each pop a veritable firework in the close space. He knows. He’s playing some sick joke, knowing all along where Monty is. Knowing exactly what I did to him.

I can’t take it. The chewing, the phlegm, the wetness. I can’t take it.

I can’t take it.

“Stop!” My hands pull at my hair. Hunks come out with ripping sounds I can feel in my spine. “He’s here,” I cry. “He’s right fucking here!”

I shove Jaime off the trunk, fling the lid open, and drag Monty's body out.

It falls over the edge and onto the carpet. Foam spills from his mouth, light pink either from the powder or his bleeding lungs. His red eyes stare blankly at my computer screen. At the waveforms of his dripping, irritating voice.

Jaime screams and he doesn't stop.

I guess he didn't know.

The sound is a needle. Something comes loose in his throat—he's finally got that phlegm clear.

He starts to cough on what's surely a phlegm-covered wad of gum, hacking, crying, snot running down his face.

I can't take it. His noises make me want to turn inside out.

Instead, I climb inside the trunk and gently lower the lid. It muffles the sounds. Peace as I curl within myself. A cozy kitten.

Christopher O'Halloran (he/him) is a milk-slinging, Canadian actor-turned-author with work published or forthcoming from *Kaleidotrope*, *NoSleep Podcast*, *Tales to Terrify*, *The Dread Machine*, and others. He is president of the most active horror book club on the web, HOWL Society and editor of the anthology, *Howls from the Wreckage*. Follow him on Twitter @BurgleInfernal or visit COauthor.ca for stories, reviews, and updates on upcoming novels.

BRACES

Sasha Brown

The date was bad even before my tooth broke. Neither of us were attracted to the other in person. He slouched and had a high, whiny voice. He glanced at my crooked and stained teeth, looked away in disgust. I'd only uploaded pictures with my mouth closed. I knew what my smile said about me.

He wanted to go ice skating. I didn't want to; it was too big a deal for a first date. Coffee would be better—but it had been so long since anyone had matched with me at all. I tried to be a good sport. I guess, now that he'd seen me, he tried to be a good sport too.

We staggered around in circles. At least it kept us from making small talk. I was never good at talking. But my clumsiness exaggerated my natural tendency to hunch into myself; I felt like a furtive little creature, and I scurried more than skated across the ice.

I stumbled and he caught me, grabbing my waist. Too intimate, as though trying to turn my clumsiness into an embrace. Maybe he thought someone like me would be easy. I shoved him away. I'd just thought to distance myself, but I pushed harder than I'd meant to. There was a childish look of aggrievement in his eyes as he pinwheeled back.

But I lost my balance, too. My skates whipped out backwards and my face hit the ice.

For a moment I was dazed. Then there was alarm, as my brain caught up to my body: the blood on the ice, the frigid wounded feeling, the chaotic and frightening realization that I was hurt. How badly? Which parts bleeding, which parts broken?

There was a new space in my mouth. Jagged. And there was my tooth on the ice, in a little puddle of blood.

I snatched it up. My date helped me off the rink, but I knew he was repulsed. I looked at myself in my phone as we fumbled our skates off. My lips were smashed and bloody. There was a big black gap in my top front teeth.

"I guess you should get that looked at."

As though I might go to the emergency room? Insurance would never cover it. But it didn't matter; the point was, we both wanted the date to be over.

"Make sure you put it under your pillow."

I looked at him, confused.

"Your tooth. Put it under your pillow. For the Tooth Fairy." He was being funny. He was trying to end the date on a funny note, to cover what a disaster it had been. He'd picked this infantilizing, stupid joke, drawing attention to my disfigurement.

I looked at him blankly for a moment and then I smiled. A big wide grin, cartoonishly wide, showing the bloody gap in my teeth. He looked away.

I took the subway home. Trudged up the sad cement-block stoop and three flights of stairs to my tiny apartment. Opened cheap wine for courage to examine myself in the mirror. My face was swollen, bruises forming, lips split and scabbed. My teeth had been bad already, crooked, a lifelong advertisement that I was too poor to afford braces.

An embarrassing low-status symbol. Now, with this terrible hole in my smile, I crossed the border from bad to ridiculous.

Such a stupid, simple accident—but an insurmountable problem. It would be considered cosmetic by my insurance. It would cost thousands to fix. I didn't have the money. I'd never be able to save up enough with my menial job.

I held the tooth back onto my stump like a puzzle piece. It didn't hurt that bad. I wasn't sure if it should. The wine bottle was empty. I folded the tooth up in a little piece of paper, overcome with a grim and tipsy silliness, and slid it under my pillow. Maybe the Tooth Fairy would leave me a thousand dollars.

The Tooth Fairy must not see many grown-ups, I thought, drifting off. Would she come for me? Would she look at me the way my mother had looked at the twelve-year-old boys who showed up, mumbling and hostile, at her door on Halloween? Old enough to be embarrassed, but young enough to want candy. Young enough to demand gifts from strangers.

I lay in bed hazy with hangover the next morning, letting my tongue explore my jagged gap. I would have to find a dentist. At least see what could be done to fit my mouth back together. I reached under my bloodstained pillow, but the little envelope was gone.

The tooth was missing.

I searched under the bed, around the frame. There was a quarter amongst the dust bunnies, but no tooth. I was angry with myself. Drunken, childlike games, playing at tooth fairies, instead of putting it in a jar on the counter or whatever a real adult would have done. I would need a false tooth made now, an even more expensive operation. It felt hopeless.

I was too gruesome to go into work. I could hardly bear going to the coffee shop.

The woman behind me in line gasped when she saw my scabbed and bruised face. "Do you need help?" she asked in a careful voice.

I opened my broken mouth, but she was already talking again.

"I was once where you are now," she said. "I know how it is. You probably feel trapped. How will you support yourself, without him? Where will you live?" She drew closer, as though we were friends. "I made the decision to leave. And do you know what? It was so hard. So, so hard. I really don't—I really don't have it together even now. I live in a studio apartment. It's tough, girl."

She wasn't interested in me. She wanted to talk about herself. Maybe she didn't have any real friends to confide in, so she was reduced to dumping her trauma on a stranger. She talked at me all the way up the line.

After she ordered, she came and stood next to me while we waited for coffees, still talking. "The truth is, part of me misses him. At least the bills were paid. Part of me is like, was it—you know!—was it definitely not worth it?" She gave a little absurd laugh. "No pain no gain, right?" As though it were funny.

I collected my drink and turned to leave. She got in my way, still talking about help, trapping me: keeping me there. Like a prisoner. I couldn't stand it. I pushed by her roughly, jostling her, and hot coffee spilled down her shirt. She let out a shriek and I made a sad face, backing away, out the door.

That night I dreamed of a little old lady tiptoeing across my floor in her taffeta gown. She held a wand with a sparkly star at the end and she smiled fondly down at me. Bopped me in the nose with a wrinkled finger and then floated out the window.

When I woke up, another tooth was missing. I knew it immediately. It felt, to my tongue, like a trench in my mouth.

One of my canines was gone. It wasn't broken, like the first; it had cleanly disappeared. I felt only smooth pink gum in its place. I looked like a jack-o'-lantern, carelessly carved. What could have happened? Was the injury worse than I'd thought? Other teeth, weakened?

I searched my room for my missing tooth. Yanked my blankets down, checked under the bed again. Had I swallowed it in the night? Would I feel it coming out, embedded in my feces?

Under my pillow, no tooth. Instead, a crumpled ten-dollar bill.

There was no rational explanation for this money. I thought about the Tooth Fairy. I imagined an ageless creature, sneaking into the bedrooms of lisping six-year-olds night after night. And then one evening, a perverse joke: me. Maybe it had rarely been in an adult's bedroom before. Maybe my grown-up body, bony and meager as it was, had been enough to fascinate it.

It was surprisingly easy to accept the supernatural. I had never understood the world very well in the first place. It was confusing to navigate; no one behaved the way I wanted them to. To suspect now that I'd been wrong about everything all along—that there was magic lurking, and I just hadn't been privy to it—felt almost inevitable. And to find myself such a cheap and pathetic part of the story. A world of magic, and I, a joke scribbled in the margins. Stalked not by monsters, but by the Tooth Fairy. I'd asked for it, really. I'd invited it in.

Again I didn't go to work. I loitered across the street from the orthodontist's office instead. Teenagers filed in and out, getting fitted for braces. Correcting their tiny imperfections. Lining it all up for a flawless life, while I lurked and watched with my hole-punched grin. Maybe tomorrow, another hole.

I cut through the alley behind the office to get home, and when I saw their overflowing dumpster I paused. All those teens with straight white teeth. All their expensive protections snipped off, discarded here. I could be protected, too. If I could find some way to defend what was left in my mouth. A grotesque thought, but what else could I do? Lie back and allow my mouth to be pillaged?

I pawed through the medical waste. There were braces here, clipped off remnants. I held them to my mouth. But they were plastic, limp. They wouldn't help.

In the very back of the dumpster, though, something glinted. I had to climb all the way in, sinking into a heap of bloody gauze, scrabbling in the corner: big old metal braces, the kind they used to use. Rusted, as though they'd been missed by the trash collectors for untold years. I held them against my mouth. They fit, more or less. Like a gate over my teeth. A fence. A portcullis.

When I went to bed, I wore the braces. I rigged up a system with rubber bands to hold them on. They hurt; jagged bits of metal jabbed my gums, and I could taste blood in my mouth. But wine helped dull the pain. I felt safer already.

I dreamed of a little goblin, just bigger than my thumb. It clambered over my windowsill and scrambled across my floor, climbed up my bedsheets and stood on my chin. Peeled open my lips and cocked its head, quizzical, its beady yellow eyes examining my makeshift defenses. I dreamed of it crouching down, worming its little arms around one of my teeth as though in a hug, working around my braces. Hoisting up, back straining, little grunts of exertion, dragging the tooth free. It scraped across the metal with a tiny screech, and then came loose. The little goblin dragged it onto my chest and leaped up and down, clutching its bloody prize.

When I awoke, another tooth was missing.

Twenty dollars under my pillow this time, as though to thank me for making it a challenge.

And the next morning, and the morning after, and the morning after that: the teeth disappeared from my mouth one by one. No pain, no pain. Only loss.

I stopped even calling out of work, and soon received an email that I needn't bother. No one checked on me. I stayed in my apartment as much as I could.

It's easy to find yourself, at some stage in your life, alone. Needing help becomes embarrassing. An imposition. There's no one who likes you well enough to be inconvenienced. I would be reduced to accosting strangers in coffee shops. I imagined that I might drink myself to sleep every night, watch my teeth dwindle, until finally I was pink and smooth as a baby, all the way across.

Finally, I called my mother.

"You've gotten yourself in trouble with a boy," she said. "I knew you would. Men prey on girls like you. You're not pregnant, are you?"

An immensely loud honk. She was driving. She yelled at someone.

"You were a weird kid, too. I kept telling you to get along, go along, but you never could. Always made a scene. That's why people never liked you, you know."

She paused to inhale. It would be a Virginia Slim menthol.

"Do you wanna know the truth? I'm gonna tell you the truth, honey. Just give him what he wants. It's not always nice, but it's the only way they leave you alone. That's how I ended up with you."

Her voice softened. She was pulling in somewhere.

"Listen, kid." She took another drag. "At least you finally figured out how to get a man's attention. Sounds weird to me, but whatever works." She cackled. She was making a joke. Always jokes. Jokes like a blanket over a body. It turned into a coughing fit.

I disconnected. She didn't call back.

I held my head sideways over the sink that night, using my phone camera to watch my work. As carefully as I could, I applied a line of epoxy between the rusty braces and my teeth.

It was difficult. Hard to keep my lips out of the way. I didn't quite manage it; by the end, they were blistered with glue and bleeding where I'd had to tear the flesh. But when I grinned in the mirror I saw clear hardened masses of epoxy, holding my mouth cage on.

I would not surrender my teeth. I would fight for them.

I woke up that night in the close, confusing dark. I couldn't move. I was paralyzed. I could see nothing. It was unnaturally dark, as though I were wearing a blindfold. It felt like I was in an operating room, given the wrong amount of anesthesia.

My floor creaked, and I imagined the Tooth Fairy. The old lady in taffeta. The scurrying goblin. I was awake this time, though, if blind, and the creature felt bigger. It felt like a dangerous hum, like a buzzing fluorescent light.

My jaw muscles gave way all at once, and my mouth flopped open. The staticky presence neared and things writhed their way inside. Some tendrils felt like an anemone, or what I imagined an anemone would feel like. Squirmy and satiny. Others were like hairless spider legs: jointed but smooth and chilly. Peeling back my lips, exposing my helpless gums. Tapping at my remaining teeth. Like looking for a loose tile in Jenga.

I felt like a pile of sand. I couldn't move a muscle. The spidery limbs wiggled a molar, teasingly, in its socket. The epoxy receded under their touch. From my gums came an almost pleasurable sensation; nerves twanged, a squishing pink.

The tooth gave way easily, with an ecstatic surrender. Flesh pinged like bubblegum strands. I felt the tooth free in my gum; then it slid from its little pocket and was gone.

The thing bent down to me. The abstract hum loudened. I was still paralyzed, blinded. I felt its presence closer, intimate: a gentle agitation on my skin, like breath but not breath. Like attention.

For a long moment, we stayed motionless together. It hovered above me. There was a sound like a white noise machine.

Then the hissing faded away. I nearly forced my head to the side, to see it; but a roaring came in my ears and I fell unconscious. Not as though falling asleep, but like a branch snapping.

There was a hundred dollar bill under my pillow when I woke.

How much money did the Tooth Fairy have? Where did it get it? What would it do once I'd surrendered all my teeth? I imagined it going even deeper. Taking my fingers, bone by bone. Maybe it would never be done collecting me.

I looked at my ruined smile in the bathroom mirror. So many gaps, now. Almost half of my teeth gone. I'd tried to armor them, to protect myself, but I'd failed.

With my puny body and paltry resources, I was used to being seen as weak. A joke. People tried instinctively to push me around. They thought I deserved it; they thought it was my natural role. When I shoved back, they were surprised. It was the only way to defend myself: to push back with alarming force.

I couldn't protect my teeth, but I wouldn't let them slip away. I went to the hardware store for chains.

I kept my mouth closed as I paid. I still looked wrong, though—my lips scabbed, blistered with epoxy. People averted their eyes.

When I got home I dug a cinder block out from under the front stoop. It was hard to lug it up the three flights to my apartment. I felt weak and sometimes faint. I'd been eating only soup.

That night I hooked the chains to my braces. A link went over each tooth, a drop of epoxy to lock it on. There were gaps between my teeth now; the chains slipped on easily. Metal streamed from my mouth, twenty or so chains in all, gushing like vomit. Each hooked around its prisoner tooth. A chain gang of my teeth.

I wrapped the chains around the cinder block.

It was dark, and the sidewalk below was deserted. No one would be hit. No one would be affected in any way. I hoisted the chain-wrapped cinder block and staggered to the window. The frame lurched in my vision. I was fatigued. I struggled to get it onto the windowsill, leaning backwards to get it higher, my puny muscles straining—but I got it there, balanced. I rested my arms on it, shaking, panting loudly out of my chained mouth. I didn't want to think about it too much, but I tried to gather courage for what would come next.

Without warning, the block slipped and fell out the window. I had barely time to brace myself on the frame before the chains snapped taut.

It jerked my head forward, sharp pain in my mouth, a sickening deep yank on my remaining teeth. It almost pulled me down with it. I clutched desperately at the wood, starfishing my body, staring at the sidewalk three stories down, moaning. But I held.

So did my teeth. Behind their rusted portcullis, globbed with epoxy, festooned with metal, my teeth held to their sockets. The cinder block swung wildly in the open air below, twisting in its chains. The pain in my mouth was intense, and blood poured down my chin—but it wouldn't fall. I couldn't haul it back up, either; if I took a hand away from the window frame, I'd be pulled out.

I grunted, a stupid animal sound. I could be stuck like this, trapped in the window frame, a cinderblock chained to my face. News crews would find me in the morning. How pathetic. What a joke. Imagine, that I'd thought I could take control of anything.

And then my teeth let go, one by one. Like tearing open a blouse, buttons popping off in a row. Little explosions of sensation, accelerating, and then they were free and the cinder block smashed to the pavement with its bloody corona.

I sank to the ground, muscles trembling. My mouth was all agony, like my teeth had been replaced by burning matches, red hot wires. I reached up, moaning, to feel the ruins of my mouth: the bloody flaps, the jagged shards.

I wasn't finished yet. I stumbled towards the stairs, down to the street, to collect my little tokens. My bargaining chips.

If the creature wanted my teeth so badly, it could pay for them.

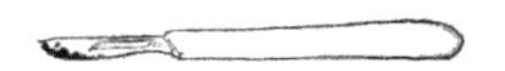

It was a month before I was ready to start job hunting again. The very first interview I went to, though, I knew it would go well. The receptionist grinned happily at me. I grinned right back, happy to show my smile. I looked like I belonged.

"He'll be right with you," she said. We grinned at each other.

I checked my appearance in the bathroom. Beamed into the mirror, showing off my pristine teeth. Dentures, but who could tell? Paid for. Bargained for. Suffered for. Smooth and even and white.

I looked carefully. Was there a hint of the damage behind them? The thin line of a scar, a discolored gum? The stench of rot? No. I looked like I'd been engineered that way, perfect and straight. I ate a mint and went back out, still grinning. It felt so natural. They were going to love me.

The receptionist's eyes flickered down to my mouth, and for a moment I imagined I saw her smile falter. As though there was something amiss; as if she could see behind the facade. But no, it was my imagination. Her smile came back, bigger than ever. "I was starting to get worried! Thought you'd gotten a better offer already."

"Ha!" I bared my teeth. "Oh, no." Finally, I was in on the joke. "That's so funny, though. That's so funny!"

Sasha Brown is a Boston writer whose work has been described as "Gross! (but maybe?)" His surreal fiction is in lit mags like *X-R-A-Y* and *Masters Review: New Voices*, and in genre mags like *Bourbon Penn* and *F&SF*.

DEEPER

Bridget D. Brave

I swear to christ Kayla if u are going to punk out of this like a total fucking bitch I will never speak to u again now pick up ur FUCKING PHONE

Kayla Miller downed a second Xanax with a gulp of water, her plumping lip gloss making the side of the glass unpleasantly sticky. She took a deep breath and stared at herself in the mirror.

"Pull it the fuck together, Miller," she hiss-whispered to her reflection. "You can do this."

The sink of her downstairs bathroom was carefully lined with the supplies she'd determined she needed for this procedure: three fluffy towels no longer in guest circulation, the bottle of leftover hydrocodone from her dental surgery last summer, her prescription bottle of Xanax, gauze, surgical tape, scissors for cutting said gauze and tape, and the item she'd ordered specifically for the occasion: a handheld diamond-tipped jewelry drill.

She'd confirmed via multiple googlings: it would cut through bone.

Her phone buzzed again, the screen lighting up with another profanity-laced threat from Mac. Mackenzie Morrison—three weeks away from becoming Mackenzie Morrison-Sanders—was the reason she was in this predicament. She's the one who insisted her bachelorette party happen in Cozumel. She's the one who insisted they had to do something to top Whitney's group photo shoot with the dolphins in Cabo. She's the one who found the place that would put you through a crash course in freediving before releasing you into the depths for the ultimate bachelorette brag: Instagram-ready photos and video clips of you and your bridesmaids twenty feet beneath the surface, decked out like actual mermaids.

Kayla had pored over the website after Mac sent out the link. The photos made her heart race: perfectly tanned and toned women wearing shimmering, scaled tails and matching seashell bikini tops, their hair floating in a glorious cloud of multicolor extension braids and pearl strands, blowing kisses to the camera and smiling through the bubbles. She wanted to be in those photos. She *needed* to be a part of this.

So she started preparing in every way she knew how: eight weeks at the gym with the toughest trainer she could find to make sure her body would be flawless for the camera. Hours in the tanning bed to ensure she would appear the deepest possible bronze. She'd even gone through the pain of lip enhancement and UV teeth whitening. That the smile would be *perfect.*

At least swimming wouldn't be an issue; Kayla started each morning for the past month and a half with an hour of laps in the YMCA indoor pool (hair tucked into a cap, didn't want split ends ruining the photos). Her form was perfect. She would gracefully glide beneath the waves and do the unthinkable: show up that bitch of a bride at her own motherfucking event.

Then Mac had to go and book them a discovery dive with a local scuba company. Mac said she didn't want anyone to freak out on the trip and ruin it for the rest of them. When she said the word "ruin", she gave Kayla a pointed look. It wasn't as if Kayla didn't *try.* She just had never been particularly athletic. It wasn't her fault that she dislocated her stupid kneecap the second week of their barre lessons and had to discontinue. It isn't as if she purposefully broke her collarbone the time they went mountain biking in Hawaii and had to spend the rest of the trip in their condo high on painkillers and watching daytime TV. And the whole Ragnar debacle? Well, was it her fault she slammed her foot into the patio door and broke three toes and her big toenail? It would be different if she backed out because she didn't *want* to do these things. Something just always seemed to happen.

Which is why she didn't mention the fact that the discovery dive made her feel like her eyes were being squeezed back into her skull, or the dull pounding headache that lingered for days after. The instructor, a nice but overall disinterested middle-aged dude with a suspicious chest scar, had tried to help her clear her nasal passageways as she descended, seemingly mystified by her inability to make her ears pop.

So, like a total *dumbass,* Kayla asked her doctor. Things were going just swimmingly—great blood pressure, no issues with her eyesight or with her ears, until Kayla mentioned her snoring that kept her last boyfriend up at night. The doctor

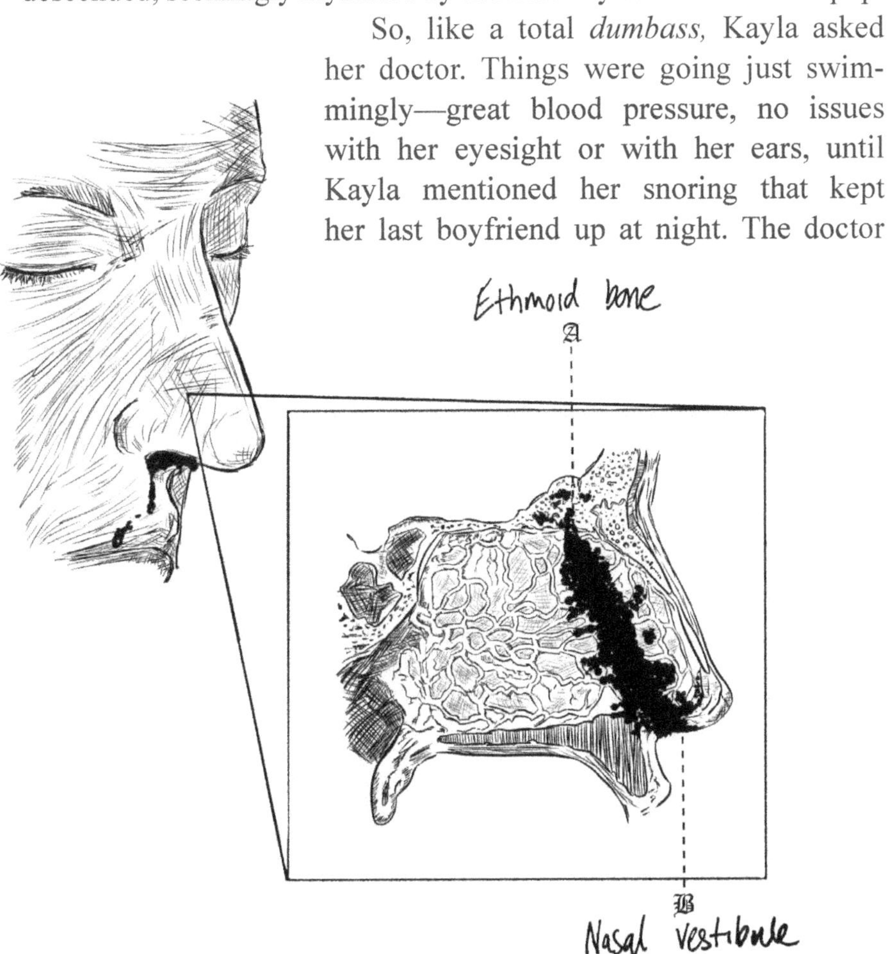

frowned, asked several follow-up questions, and then ordered a CT scan of her head.

Kayla couldn't get the images of those scans out of her mind. The way that the physician had explained that a total occlusion of her left nostril due to a congenital deviated septum had caused chronic sinusitis. That he couldn't recommend diving with such a significant block. That sinus barotrauma could cause dual black eyes, blood leaks, vision problems. That she would need to clear the block to release the pressure or else. That she would need a surgery that required at least *two weeks* of recovery and follow-up, and that he couldn't schedule Kayla for that surgery for another *six weeks.*

Cozumel was on Friday.

Mac had exploded when Kayla mentioned she might have an issue. She hadn't let Kayla get another word out before she dumped the entire laundry list of every time Kayla had just *ruined* some birthday party, girls' night outing, or movie date with one of her *dumb excuses.* She wouldn't get away with *doing* this to Mac, to the bachelorette party, to the other girls, to the photo that *needed* seven people to be framed just right. She just *couldn't.*

Kayla smiled and lied through those gleaming white teeth; claimed it was nothing major, just a sinus infection she needed to take high-dose antibiotics for. Mac had sent her constant reminders to take decongestants, to take hot showers, to "fucking steam" her head with an "entire bushel of eucalyptus" every five hours since.

Now it was Thursday morning. She was due to be at Mac's in six hours for the pre-party. She was already getting shit for skipping out on brunch, too afraid that the alcohol would interact with her plans, and much too afraid that refusing alcohol would be read as her trying to "cause drama" during Mac's big event. It was now or never.

Kayla popped two hydrocodone and bit the inside of her mouth *hard.* It stung, but considerably less than it had before she took the first two a half hour prior. Excellent. By the time she hits paydirt, it should be no less painful than a bonk to the nose. Then she just had to ice until the blood stopped, wait for the painkiller wooziness to wear off, and she could claim a headache without any of her friends being the wiser.

There were *minimal* blood vessels involved, after all. How bad could it be?

She exhaled sharply through pursed lips and picked up the drill. The bit went in slowly as she pushed it right up against where her left nostril stopped allowing passage. That must be the bony part Dr. Liu had shown her on the scan of her head. She probed the spot with the needle-thin tip of the diamond drill as if daring herself to go further.

Just do it, you dumb bitch.

Kayla pressed the button down.

The high-pitched whine nearly scared her as much as the sudden searing heat, and she quickly pulled the drill back out, a few blood drops spattering the basin. "Fuckfuckfuck*fuck,*" she whispered, stomping her foot in frustration. Kayla stared at her reflection in the mirror, teeth gritted.

"Get it together," she commanded her mirror image. "You can do this."

She nervously shook the bottle of Xanax. Two was the recommended maximum dose, but two wasn't close to calming her. She popped another one into her mouth before she could think better of it, the water she swallowed mixing with the flavor of blood in the back of her throat.

Do it. Do it you fucking coward. You didn't spend this much money on abs to fuck this up now.

The drill whined again and this time she shoved it against the stopping point. *Hard.* It screeched in response, the smell of burnt flesh and hot metal filling her sinuses. *Fuck.* She pulled the drill out again and coughed with panic. More blood, the drops a thicker and deeper red, stained the sink. She wiped at it with one of her self-tanner and hair dye-stained towels. The last thing she needed was a pink goddamned sink.

This townhouse had been a gift from her father, a celebration of her first real grown-up job. He'd hated the area, but Kayla wanted to be the first to put money down. She had landed one of the corner units in the very back of the development, facing the woods and far away from the bustle and noise of the main drag. The other units had so far remained empty, which she didn't mind a bit. Especially right now, as she screamed *"motherfucker!"* and dropped the drill again. This time she missed the towel she'd used as a resting area and the drill skittered to the floor, the tip of the drillbit scorching across her big toenail.

"No!" she exclaimed. *"Nonononononono FUCKING NO!"*

The perfectly painted palm tree that had previously graced the nail was now slightly dislodged, two of its fronds cantering off at a weird angle. *"FUCK!"* she roared and began digging in the drawers. This bathroom was primarily where she kept the pet supplies, choosing to use the two on the upper floors for her own grooming. She found what she was looking for and held it victoriously aloft: the glue for Bastian's KittySoft nail caps. His groomer had given her a tube for at-home repairs. The little fucker had a tendency to rip the caps off and go after her leather ottoman.

Two dabs of the glue and *voila!* The palm tree looked mostly okay once again. Kayla dug into her handbag, cursing again under her breath as items spilled from the purse onto the toilet lid and floor. With a little excited shriek, she spotted the extra set of pedicure toe spreaders she knew she'd tossed in there. With her toes secured from further fuck-up, she inhaled a grossly wet-sounding breath and picked up the drill with her shaking hand. One more Xanax and she should be able to finish the job. From the whistley sound her intake of air was now making, she was sure she had managed to break through to the other side with the last pass. One more good roto-rootering and she would be free to pack it up until the bleeding stopped.

This time the drill went in smoothly, no nasty grinding noise. Kayla began to make slow circles with the bit, trying to widen the existing hole. She caught her own eye in the mirror and a lazy grin spread across her face as she leaned forward against the sink. Who the fuck needs an ENT? Not Kayla Fuckin' Mil-

That was the moment her pedicure toe separator slipped under the ball of her foot, causing her to pitch forward. The drill skittered inside her nose and she attempted to steady it before it could slip to the side and sear her skin. Instead it buried deep into the septum at an angle, punching through from her left nostril to her right. In a haze of Xanax and panic, Kayla tried to yank the drill backward, but her grip was unsure and instead it pulled sideways and rapidly down. Kayla felt the burning pass from her nose into her upper lip before she hit the floor.

She blinked against the harsh glare of the cosmetic lights, bouncing off the mirror and the white walls to cause halos around everything in her immediate field of vision. Kayla pushed herself up, noting that the marbled sink no longer passed for pink.

It was crimson.

In the mirror, she saw what she had done. The front of her face below her nose now sagged open, her upper teeth and gums visible through the gaping hole that had once been two separate nostrils. The front of her nose was a mess of jagged flesh and raw-edged cartilage.

You've really fucked it up this time, Miller.

On a brighter note, the hydro and Xanax combo had worked well enough to numb the pain—emotionally *and* physically.

Kayla stepped forward to examine the damage to her face and felt something dully cut into the bottom of her foot. It was the tube of nail glue, knocked to the floor by her flailing.

She bent gingerly at the knee, her left hand trying to hold the front of her face together, and retrieved the glue. A tiny glimmer of hope sparked when she noted the warning, "Can bond to skin. Use latex gloves."

Worth a shot.

With her right hand, she carefully squeezed a line of the adhesive along her ragged septum, then her upper gum line. With the fingertips of both hands she delicately pushed and arranged her hanging skin until her face once again looked mostly put together, counting in her head the way she did when she held Bastian's nail caps in place. "One…two…three…four…five…"

At ten she began to remove her fingertips to see if the skin held. It was securely stuck in place. She'd done it. She'd managed to glue her lip back almost perfectly into place.

Unfortunately, she had also glued her fingers to the skin of her upper lip.

Her mind, slowed by the drugs and the shock of what she'd done, took a moment to remember that alcohol wipes would remove the solvent from fingers. She would just go upstairs and get some of the alcohol wipes she had in her desk drawer. Then she could drive herself to urgent care—or maybe get an Uber, she probably shouldn't drive like this—and someone would fix her right up. There was no reason to panic.

Wait. Why the *fuck* had she closed the bathroom door?

When she purchased this townhouse, all of the features were customizable. That's why she went with the shiny crystal door knobs throughout the dwelling. They were gorgeous. They looked very high end. They were slick and sparkly and looked like some sort of scrying ball a sorceress would have in her home.

They were also impossible to open with her elbows.

Kayla's eyes began to fill with tears as she saw her phone light up. She tried to grab it, and succeeded only in knocking it off the counter with her elbow. Kayla crouched over her phone on the floor. The phone buzzed.

Face not recognized.

Fuck. She would have to bypass the facial recognition. *FUCK.* She couldn't bypass the facial recognition with her fingerprint. Her fucking fingers were glued to her face.

Voice to text.

Kayla held down the center button with her elbow until she heard the telltale beeps.

She made a sound like "brrrrrm," then paused. She made another noise, one of confusion. She let out a muffled scream of frustration. The adhesive must have run when combined with her blood and saliva. She'd glued her fucking lips together. The phone lit up again. It was another message from Mac.

> *Listen u dumb whore were all sick to death of u causing drama*
>
> *Dont bother coming*
>
> *No one wants u here*
>
> *U can venmo me the $1650 u still owe*
>
> *Hope ur little shitfit was worth it*

The cat was at the boarder until her planned return in 12 days. Her dad was in Fiji with his new wife. Matt's "u up" texts had ceased long ago. Her condo was at the edge of the complex, too far for anyone to hear her muffled yells from the basement. And now her friends thought she was flaking, ruining a good time yet again.

And that was when Kayla Miller realized she'd really, truly fucked up.

Bridget D. Brave is an author and reluctant lawyer who is really lousy at writing bios. She can be found nearly everywhere online under beedeebrave.

Section II

THE LIMBS

Run Through the Pain

Taylor Ketterer

Sam glided down the sidewalk. The wind played with her hair, tossing around the ponytail and rustling the loose ringlets. She laughed as she approached her house. *This is the closest I'll get to flying.*

She slowed her stride to a walk while hitting the stop button on her watch, a fluid movement she had perfected over hundreds of runs. *8.00 mi, 1:15:12*, flashed on the screen.

"Not bad," she muttered.

Her favorite part of the day over, she showered, dressed, and sat down at her desk. It was a typical workday: several Zoom meetings that could have been emails, a case review with the most annoying client, and another training session with the intern that didn't seem to learn anything. When the kitchen door shut at 5:30, she jumped up from her chair and ran to greet her husband.

"How was your day?" Mike asked with a quick kiss.

Sam rolled her eyes. "These people just don't seem to listen to anything I say."

"Intern still not catching on?"

"It's like he's not even in our training sessions. And my boss is getting on my case now. It's just so annoying. How was your day?"

"Pretty good." Mike pulled the fajita ingredients out of the fridge and started cutting veggies while talking about his own minor annoyances and coworker antics.

Sam woke up when Mike got out of bed in the morning. She absentmindedly itched a bug bite on her left leg and rolled over to go back to sleep.

"It's 6 a.m., babe," Mike muttered as he walked past her on the way to the bathroom. Sam groaned in response.

Mike turned on the bedroom lights at 6:15, and Sam pulled the comforter over her head.

"Don't you have a run, Sam?" he asked. "You know if you want to beat your previous marathon time you gotta stick to your training."

Sam sat up and rubbed her eyes. Fifteen minutes and a cup of coffee later, Mike was heading to the gym and she had woken enough to run.

She laced up her shoes and burst through the front door onto the street. The early morning sun shone down on her, warm but not too hot, and a slight breeze brushed at her bare arms and legs. It was the perfect day for a run. The coffee had kicked in and she planned to take full advantage.

After a short warm up, Sam rushed forward, pushing her limits, trying to hit her max pace. She sprinted like this for five minutes while sweat flew off her face. She breathed heavily while a fire burned in her lungs and her face flushed red. Then her watch beeped, and she slowed to a recovery jog, her legs like stones. Sam repeated this torturous exercise three more times before heading home at an easy pace. Her heart rate lowered as the wind cooled her damp face.

Sam looked down about a quarter mile from her house and stumbled. She caught herself with the practice of someone who's used to tripping, and looked more closely at her leg. Her left calf and shin had scabs where the bug bites had been, oozing white and yellow wounds surrounded by raw red skin. She gently touched her leg. It was warm but otherwise normal. It didn't hurt at all.

Sam skipped a couple times, testing out her flexibility. Everything seemed fine.

She jogged back home and found Mike in the living room.

"Check this out," she said, pointing at her leg.

"Babe, you have sexy legs," Mike said.

"No, the scrapes! What do you think could've caused them? I didn't even scratch my bug bite that much," Sam said.

"What scrapes?" Mike squinted at her leg, then examined her face. "Is this some kind of joke? I see your old scar, but no scrapes. Not even any bug bites."

"How do you not see it?" Sam's heart pounded as she stared at the very obvious wounds covering half her shin.

"Sam, nothing there." Mike reached his arm out to hug her, but she pulled away.

"There is, though. I see it! This isn't funny," Sam said. "You should get your eyes checked; I'm going to shower."

She went upstairs, showered, dried off, and wrapped the towel around herself while digging out the first aid kid. She brought her leg up to apply neosporin, then dropped the tube. Her leg was like Mike said: perfectly flawless except for a small 16 year old scar.

The sun burned through the open front door as Sam applied sunblock for her long run, the worst but most necessary part of training for a fall marathon. She rubbed the lotion into her skin, feeling the smooth strength of her arms and legs. There was nothing wrong with any of her limbs.

She put sunblock on her face and threw on a hat, sunglasses, and headphones. The heat hit her like a wall as soon as she stepped outside. She immediately regretted leaving her air-conditioned house. She gulped down some water as her GPS watch caught a signal. When the watch beeped, she set out.

Sam ran easily, hitting a pace that she could hold for 14 miles, today's target. She focused on breathing, inhaling and exhaling smoothly. Soon her breath was more ragged, her face bright pink and dripping sweat. Her tank top and shorts were soaked through, three shades darker than they'd been when she'd put them on.

She sipped water from the bottle she wore around her waist, then poured some on her face, only wondering for a second whether it was worth wasting her drink. *I can always run past the house,* she thought. *Maybe I can call Mike and have him meet me outside with the hose.*

Sam daydreamed about sprinklers and pools for several more sweaty miles. By the time her mind wandered to its fifth tropical drink in the pool, she moved on to her body evaluation. Her face stung from the heat and sweat. Her shoulder ached slightly, probably from sleeping on it funny the night before. Her lungs worked steadily even as her throat scratched and tingled from the hot damp air. Her feet screamed with exhaustion but no real pain.

Most importantly, her legs felt strong. Whatever had been bothering her yesterday was gone. She finished her run feeling good, if a little—okay, *extremely*—hot.

Upstairs in the master bathroom, she put her left leg over the edge of the tub and stopped. It was completely covered in cuts and sores. White and yellow pus oozed out of red holes. Blood dripped from just below her knee. Something appeared to move in one of the wounds, causing Sam to jerk back in surprise, overbalancing. She fell onto the floor, slamming her tailbone, and her head snapped back, hitting the bathroom counter. Lights swam in front of her eyes. She blinked a couple times and rubbed the back of her head. It was tender, and a lump had already formed.

Sam stood up, wet a facecloth, and pressed it against her head. She pulled it away: no blood. She got back into the shower. Her head throbbed as she cleaned herself. She touched a loofa to her leg: no pain.

She got out of the shower and bandaged her leg. She checked the clinic's hours then drove herself to urgent care.

"Your leg's fine," the doctor said to her. "You might've pulled something, but there's nothing showing on the x-ray, and I can't see anything noticeably wrong."

"How can you not see it?" Sam asked. "It's covered in sores. What could possibly be the cause?"

"I don't know what you think you see," the doctor said, "but there's nothing wrong with your leg. I don't see any sores. You said you hit your head; how's that feeling?"

"Well, yeah, my head's a little sore, but that's not why I'm here. My leg is infected."

"Sometimes a patient might see things after a head injury—"

"I'm not seeing things," Sam interrupted. "I got a head injury because I saw my leg injury. How can you say my leg is fine?"

"Give it some rest, keep it clean, and no strenuous activities for five days." The doctor looked pointedly at his tablet, avoiding her gaze. "If you still have headaches by next weekend, come back and see us."

"But what about my leg?"

The doctor walked out, leaving her alone in the exam room.

"How's your head now, though?" Mike squinted at Sam, his eyes shiny. "Was the bathroom floor wet? I should wipe it up and grab a new mat; it's clearly a hazard."

"Mike, I'm fine." Sam lay on the couch, ice on her leg and under her head. "It's not my head I'm worried about, it's my leg."

"You said the doctor wasn't worried about your leg, though. Besides, aren't head injuries more concerning? I'm supposed to keep you awake for what, 12 hours?"

"I'm pretty sure that's not a thing. Plus, I don't have a concussion. And the doctor was an idiot. He didn't even listen to me."

"Sam, I don't know what to say." Mike's face slackened as he looked at her. "I don't see anything wrong with your leg."

"How can you not see it?" Sam sat up, then winced as her head throbbed, and she lay back down. "It looks awful. Kind of weird it doesn't hurt much, but it has to be infected, right?"

"Keep icing it then. But there's nothing there. And if it doesn't hurt, I don't know why you're so fixated on it. I think the rest will do you good even if you don't think your head is bad. Why don't I go get us some pizza? Buffalo chicken?"

Sam smiled at him. "Buffalo chicken pizza sounds amazing. Thanks, Mike."

Sam woke the next morning with a throbbing head and no leg pain. Her light tan skin stretched across tight muscles, unblemished. Two days later her head pain had subsided, replaced with irritation.

"I'm gonna be home a little late today," Mike said as he left for work. "I'm going out for drinks with the team, remember?"

"Whatever," Sam snapped without looking up from her phone.

"Whoa," Mike said. "Something wrong, Sam?"

"You mean besides being stuck in the house, unable to do anything?" Sam looked at him, tears filling her eyes. "Whatever, just go."

"Hey, I love you," Mike kissed her cheek. "You'll be back to normal in no time."

Sam sighed. "Yeah, sorry. I dunno, I guess running's more of a stress relief than I thought. Have fun with your coworkers. Have a drink for me." She shot him a shaky smile as he left the house.

The work day dragged by. Sam struggled to focus on her computer screen, distracted by a lingering frustration and wracking guilt from snapping at Mike.

He arrived home two hours later than normal, with a bouquet of flowers and takeout from the restaurant he'd gone to after work.

Sam sobbed into her nachos. "You're the best, Mike," she said through a mouthful of food. "I'm sorry. I don't deserve you."

"Hey, don't say that." Mike put his arm around her. "You're stressed and have lost your main mood booster. Let's put on a movie or something and just relax tonight."

Sam ran easily down the street, breathing lightly in the overcast day. She smiled with the joy of being back on the road. Her leg cramped up a mile in.

"Ow!" She dropped to her left knee. The calf completely seized. She sat on the curb and rubbed it, trying to get the blood flowing. She felt squirming bumps and pulled back. Burning pain shot up her leg.

Slimy white maggots slithered across Sam's skin. One dug into an open sore, and Sam threw up on the sidewalk. Yellow and pink pus covered the calf, interspersed with bright red blood, colorful bruises, and dead gray flesh.

My leg is a rainbow, Sam thought hysterically before bursting into high pitched frantic laughter. She sat for a minute, laughing and coughing. Her leg felt like it was on fire, and tears stung her eyes.

A man taking out the trash across the street shot her a look and she realized how ridiculous she must look, sprawled across the sidewalk with vomit and blood surrounding her. She pulled herself up on a telephone pole and limped back home.

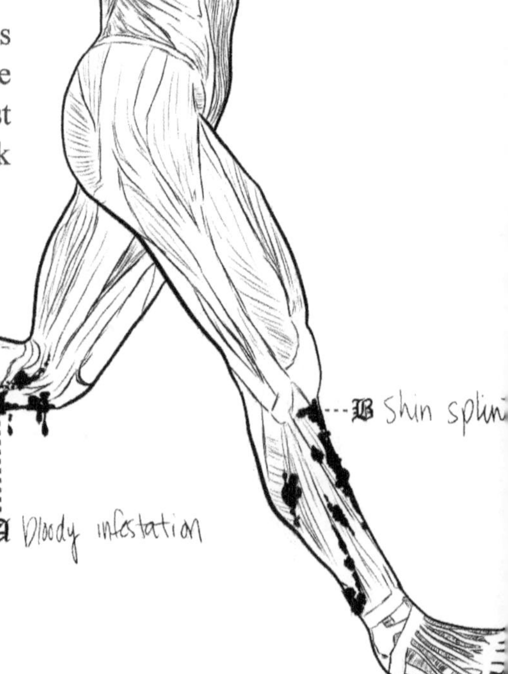

"Mike!" Sam shouted as she hobbled to the couch. He came down the stairs.

"You weren't gone that long. Is everything okay? Did you fall?"

"My leg," Sam said, gesturing to the maggots and ground meat that had once been a working calf.

"Did you twist your ankle? What's wrong?" Mike asked.

"No, I didn't twist my ankle. Can't you see what's wrong?" Sam's voice was icy, but she didn't care.

"Uh…no?" Mike squinted at her leg, as if it were just out of focus.

"My leg!" Sam screamed. "The wounds! The blood! And, I don't know, the maggots!"

"Sam, babe, there's nothing there." Mike looked at her face. "How's your head feel?"

"My head is fine!" Sam staggered out of the room.

"Where are you going?" Mike asked.

"To the hospital! Hopefully they'll be better than urgent care."

"Let me drive you, please."

Sam and Mike sat in the ER for hours. Sam sent Mike to the desk every half hour or so to check when she'd be seen.

"I'm sorry, but your wife's situation isn't urgent," the receptionist said every time. "Trouble breathing, chest pain, shortness of breath, any of those would put her at the front of the line. But not leg pain." She squinted over at Sam. "Leg pain that has no discernible cause."

Invariably Mike went back to Sam and lied to her that the emergency room was just very backed up.

They finally got called in. Sam got bloodwork, an x-ray, an ultrasound, and an EKG, all while telling the doctors and nurses to just look at her leg.

"Your leg is perfectly healthy," the doctor finally said. "No bone problems or blood clots. Your heart sounds good, and all the bloodwork came back negative. I'd like to monitor the head symptoms, though, especially since your husband mentioned mood swings. You have a history of depression?"

"My head's fine," Sam spat. "And my mood would be a lot better if someone around here would do their job and fix my leg so I can run again! And what about these freaking maggots?"

"Uh…what maggots?" The doctor looked at Mike, who shrugged.

"The maggots crawling all over my legs!" Sam cried in pain and frustration. "They're right there. My leg looks gross; I think they're killing it."

"There's nothing on your leg, Samantha," the doctor said. "I'd like to monitor you overnight for the head pain and hallucinations."

"I'm not hallucinating! And I'm not staying overnight if you're not even gonna deal with my leg!" Sam limped out of the room.

Sam woke up alone in her bed. She pulled off the covers and vomited in the trash can next to her. Maggots swarmed in and out of the sores over her leg and left wet spots on her sheets. She tried to get out of bed, but her leg couldn't bear her weight and she collapsed to the floor.

Sam dragged herself across the room, crawling on her hands and right knee, her left leg trailing behind her. Every minor movement jostled her and shot a jolt of pain up her entire body. She slowly approached the stairs, then sat down at the top and scooted down, step by step, on her butt like she had as a toddler.

"Mike?" She called. No answer. She dragged her way across the house to the kitchen. She sat and thought for a bit, then continued crawling, through the kitchen and into the garage. The pain radiated through her body and pulsed across her vision.

"I need to get rid of this pain. I can't live like this." Tears streamed down her face and blurred the world. Fire seemed to consume her calf and spread up to her waist.

She wiped her face, clenched her jaw, and made her way to Mike's tool bench, made easier because his car was gone and the garage was half empty. She pulled out a drawer in her attempt to stand, spilling tools across the floor. Then she used the opening where it had been to pull her way up the side of his bench and leaned on it, digging through the tools until she found his bow saw.

Sam sat down with the saw and started cutting, right below her knee, above the dead and infected skin. It hurt a lot less than she'd thought it would; the burning pain in her calf and shin consumed her focus.

She sawed away at her leg, removing the source of pain and infection. Blood spurted out of the new cut, pooling around her on the cement floor. She swayed from the shock but kept going, sawing easily through the flesh. She hit bone and slowed, needing to put more pressure behind the saw, but as she adjusted her rhythm, it got easier, and once she was through the tibia she quickened her progress.

Sam threw up to the side but kept going. Black dots flashed in front of her, blocking the view of her leg, but she maintained the rhythm. She hit the fibula and forced the saw through, leaning into it and using her upper body's weight to push the saw. Her head swam and she swayed as she got to the last bit of sinew. With a final push, the saw cleared the remaining flesh, and her lower leg flopped to the side. Sam collapsed onto the cement floor, passing out in a pool of blood and vomit.

Taylor Ketterer is a new writer from Rockland, Massachusetts. She enjoys reading, writing, and watching horror. When she isn't exploring horror she is training for marathons or working as a cost analyst. You can find her on Twitter @tketterer.

THE ROTTEN CRADLE

Demi-Louise Blackburn

"You sure you're alright, Mam?"

I nod at my daughter, wheezing as I drop into the recliner. Every muscle in my body judders of its own accord, thin legs struggling to take the strain of my feeble weight, arms shaking as I grip the chair. A glass of old orange juice sits on the table to my right, and when I take small, gasp-filled sips, even my jaw quivers. I place it back atop a sea of doctor's notes, newspapers, and used tissue. Nicola catches it before it falls onto the floor.

"Mam?

"What?" I snap. "I said I'll be fine."

"You didn't say a thing, for a start," she says, her voice drifting off as she heads into the kitchen. Cupboard doors open and bags rustle as she puts away the food shopping.

"I bloody well did, you just don't listen to me. You never listen to me these days."

Nicola soon returns with a glass of water, a sandwich, and a straight, thin line where a smile should be. I puzzle over it, but the thought slips away from me.

"Thanks, love," I say as she places the food down and clears the table."No, give the paper here. I'm not done with it yet, give me a chance."

She huffs and throws it back onto the pile before slumping down into the armchair next to me, staring out of the living room window. I still expect to see Charlie's thin, straight-backed silhouette in that battered chair. Instead, Nicola's form is wide and obtrusive from the corner of my eye. She never did shed that baby fat, despite my warnings. Her Dad hadn't ever cared about her size. I did the caring for us. All of it.

In my head, somewhere distant and weathered, I hear my mother fretting over needing adjustments on my dresses, and like a fountain, out of my mouth comes: "You need to go steady. You're putting on some timber."

Nicola's face drops, and her hand rests protectively on the pudge of her stomach. I turn and look out of the window, watching a car drop someone off across the road. Janice from next door warned me about the flats a few days ago. Her son knew the lodgers, and they were *dealing*, of all things. She said to keep an eye out. So, I do. Another car pulls up.

"Look at them lot over there! I knew something dodgy was going on. Did I tell you what Janice's lad told her about those flats?"

I don't get a reply. Nicola sits, stock still, in her father's armchair, gaze pinned on the phone in her hands, looking tense and sad. I can't understand why, as though I've missed part of our conversation.

At some point, the television flickers to life, and late afternoon's gloom is staved off by a tableside lamp. Nicola potters around, as she always does when she's ready to leave, avoiding my eyes as she tidies up and waters the rubber plant. It consumes an entire corner of the living room, now Charlie is no longer here to pester me to cut it down.

Finally, Nicola shucks her handbag over one shoulder, and says, "Alright, Mam. I'm gunna get off now. Is there anything else that needs sorting before I go?"

There are a thousand things. Crumbs line each crease of my armchair. Hair rollers are chucked across the dresser behind me, clogged with thin, grey hair. The rug is stained and stinking. Beneath the rubber plant, the laminate is water-logged and bloated, and an army of ants have made their way inside the house to patrol the perimeter of its pot. My clothes and skin both smell as though they weren't dried quick enough.

At night, ever since Charlie died, a stranger keeps trying the front door. I don't sleep anymore. And I want to.

"No, love. You get going."

"Alright." She leans over the armchair to give me a kiss. "Love you. If you need anything just give us a bell. I'll keep my phone on."

"Get gone, get gone," I say, waving my hand, and I listen as she leaves the living room, unlatches the front door, and locks it behind herself. In my head, I repeat: *Nicola locked the door, Nicola definitely locked the door.*

The television witters on. A bus parks up on the street outside, letting out a steam of passengers, and I watch them as they watch me. If I stare straight ahead of me, it's easy to pretend Charlie still sits to my right, just in the corner of my eye. And, when I listen closely, there's the scratch of a pen as he fills in today's crossword. *Blood worry. Coagulated. Thicken, as in cream. C – L – O – T.*

Then, Charlie's voice, muttering about cutting down the rubber tree before it strangles him in his sleep.

The heavy *cluck* of the mantel clock ticks away, but time moves without me. Morning might've passed, might be due, might never arrive. I think about gardening to ease it. Last year's pansies, begonias, and petunias have since withered and rotted into sludge. The hyacinth bushes out front are sun-bleached and papery. They might not even flower again.

When was the last time I tended it? Before Charlie left me, or after?

I dip in and out of sleep, drugged by the stuffy, afternoon air, soothed by the memory of sinking bulbs into fresh soil, the smell of baking concrete.

When next I wake, Nicola is in the armchair as though she hadn't ever left. At her feet, there's gift bags and shoe boxes full of letters and photographs, and she's smiling as she sifts through a bundle in her hands. I keep quiet for a long time, but my breathing must have changed, because she turns to me.

"Look how bonny you used to be here, Mam!" she says, passing me a photograph.

My mouth is dry and my voice cracks as I reply. "Charming. Wait until you get to this age." The words come out harsher than expected. I take the picture from Nicola and bring it close, feigning interest to wipe the wounded look off her face.

Most of the image is, admittedly, blurred and damaged with age, and yet I can *smell* the coastal air. Ocean spray is but a cut of white and blue in the background. There is a long, dark spiral of hair down my back, and my skin is as tan as it would ever be. The bundle in my arms is chubby and pasty. It's Nicola. I can't remember if she was laughing or screaming or fast asleep. But I can remember the weight of her.

A solid, warm press in the cradle of my arm.

That phantom weight is more familiar to me now than the image of my younger self. I hardly recognise the woman. Don't relate to her. As though this is a stranger holding my sweet little girl. Only my little girl is now a tall, stocky woman, occupying the shadow of her father's presence beside me, looking more tired each day.

I hand the picture back, and the look on my face must warn Nicola not to pass me any other photographs, because she pulls away, silently viewing them herself, offering me pitying looks when she thinks I'm not looking.

Without a fuss, I pull out the handkerchief I keep stuffed in the arm of my jumper, and press it against my nose and mouth, desperate not to make a sound.

The handle of the front door rattles, and I wake.

My heart thunders, but my unseen intruder only moves me with frustration. It takes some time for the shadow of the bedroom to meld itself into something familiar, and when it does, I look to the bedside table and use my right hand to grasp the cherry-red angina spray overturned there, lacing the webbing of my tongue with it.

The snake wrapped around my chest continues to squeeze.

Before the landline is even in my sight, I hear Nicola berating me for choosing to call her when I should phone an ambulance. Why doesn't she understand?

Dying doesn't frighten me. Not since I woke to the cold line of what used to be my Charlie sleeping forever beside me. But being alone during that final, unknown thing. I needed her. She never understood, no matter how many ways I explained it.

"I'll never forgive you for leaving me alone," I wheeze to the empty spot in my bed. "Always did everything I could for you, was always there for you, of course you'd piss off first, leave me here like this."

The sobs come. Great, blubbering howls that fill me with shame. I pray the neighbours don't hear me, but I can't hold them back. They wouldn't leave a dog alive like this. Crippled and trapped, circling over its own shit and piss while someone rattles the cage door morning, noon, and night.

By the time my tears dry, and the gallop of my heart slows, I'm exhausted. My face itches from crying, and when I reach up to wipe away the damp—only my right side obeys, the left is heavy and unresponsive. My pulse quickens again. With my working arm, I flick on the bedside lamp, a headache spiking from the light.

When my eyes adjust, I fear, *hope,* that I am hallucinating.

The delicate skin around my elbow has ballooned…and blackened. But in its centre, suspended in a cocoon of clear liquid, is a small, puss-like lump. As a girl, we'd kept chickens in an allotment, and one morning found a bundle of discarded eggs behind the nest boxes. Work of a jealous, brooding hen. Daddy promised us they'd be fine. But when we'd split them open into the pan…the yolk had halted. Malformed and rotten. Spidery crimson vessels trailing around it like the handlebar tassels on Nicola's first bike. A crippled, nearly-chick smoking away in the pan.

The lump pulses in the clutch of my arm, in time to a steady knock.

Strangely, it's the noise of the front door which terrifies me. The civility of it. *Please let me inside. Knock-knock. Knock-knock.*

I cradle my swollen elbow, cupping my free hand over the joint, shielding it from the noise, and bite my lip to stifle the low moan bubbling from my throat. My body is alight with panic. The front door handle dips and rises. The letterbox opens—

and doesn't shut.

Listening out, small noises mask the intruder's movements. The hum of the fridge. The click of my throat. But I can *still* sense it. Fingers whispering across the wood of the door, rattling the letterbox cage as long digits slip through the wire, then up to the chain, tinkling as it hooks and slides it across. Silence. A beat. The clock *thunks* heavily. Something sharp traces the seams of the door. A knife? Or an enormous, dexterous cat slipping its claws into the gaps of the door and tracing until—*click.*

A cold rush of air blasts through the house.

Then settles.

The lights in my head go out.

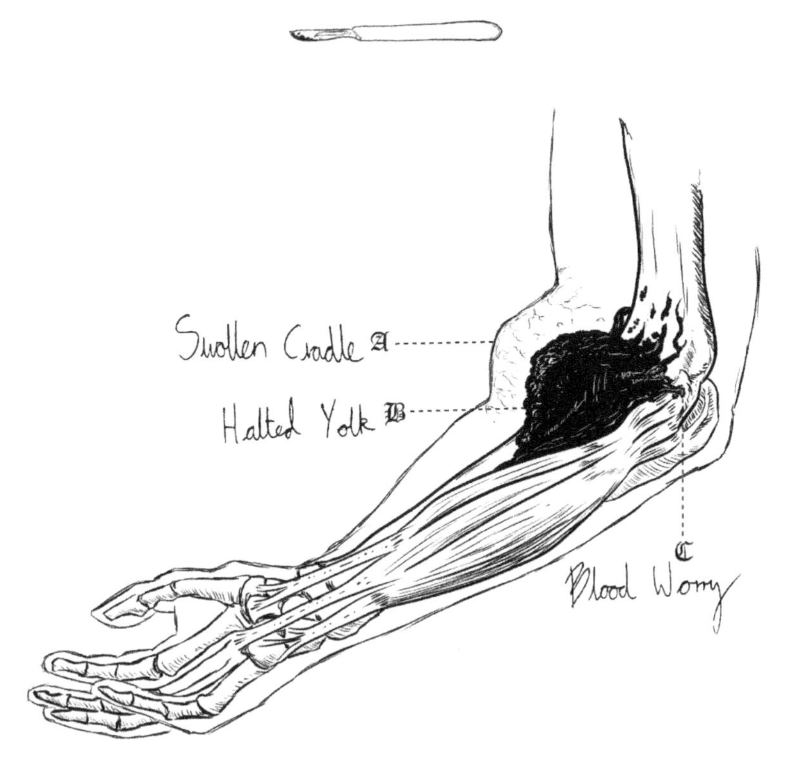

Nicola looks at me strangely as she wipes drool from the side of my mouth. A vague tang of blood sits on my tongue, and the bedroom smells like a horrible mix of stale food and sweat. I try to push myself further up the bed with one arm. The other lays useless and fat across my stomach. In the dead centre of my inner elbow, a pale, milky eyeball twists and rolls wildly.

"I promise you, Mam, it's just a bruise. You know how you are with all those blood thinners. Even a small knock and it just goes dead black sometimes, doesn't it?" Her voice is small and scared and needling. It infuriates me.

"And I'm telling you there's a lump, or something, in there."

"Don't shout at me. I'm only saying there's nothing to worry about."

A thousand responses rise and fall in my head. I feel sick. In the end the only reply I can cleanly grasp onto is: "Oh, just fuck off!"

My face heats immediately upon saying it, and Nicola stills in shock. Before I know it, I'm crying, using my only working hand to slap at Nicola as she hugs me. The shame is beyond me. "Get off. You never listen to me anymore. Just think I'm a senile old bitch who's ready for the rubber bus. I'm telling you something is wrong, and you just don't—"

"Then let me call you an ambulance, we can get it checked out then."

"No! No more doctors. I don't want none of it anymore."

"Then what do you want me to do?" She pleads.

And, in truth, I don't know. I'm so confused. My own spinning thoughts make me nauseous. Every time I look at the bloated cradle of my arm, something new, yet familiar, greets me. The toothless, gummy mouthing of a child's suckling pressed against the silk of my inner elbow. Hands and feet writhing and punching, imprinting loose flesh. And all she sees is a *bruise*. I can't explain it. Instead, my frustration grows and grasps onto anything it can.

"*And* you left that door open again! Now someone's been rifling in here. I dread to think what they've taken. Did you even check? Have you even had a look around? They could've taken everything."

Nicola moves to sit at the edge of my bed, hand hovering as though terrified to touch me. "Mam, what are you on about? You heard me unlock the door this morning. What do you mean someone's been rifling about in here?"

I'm too worked up to continue. Nicola tries, again, to get an arm around me, and I shrug her off, instead cradling the monstrous lump of my arm as I sniffle and hiccup. A bone deep exhaustion falls over me.

After some minutes, Nicola's jaw tenses and she abruptly stands and goes into the living room. From the frosted, partition glass between the bedroom and the living room I watch her slump into my chair, and pretend not to hear her sobbing, too.

Nicola arranges care for me not long after the invasion.

The nurses visit twice a day, morning and night, and I swear they send someone new each time. I can't ever remember their names. Their faces. Nicola assures me it's so I have a better quality of life. Some comfort, despite me lamenting that it's a waste of money. Because she struggles to get me on my feet these days, because she doesn't know the proper way to support me, and my lack of muscles makes my weight feel leaden. She simply can't keep straining herself with the way she is.

It's this, or a care home.

But this flat of mine feels vacant even with me rotting away inside of it. A rotating door of strangers in blue overalls. Nicola's visits are brief, and infrequent, and all too often I insist, against my aching heart, that she spends her weekends with friends, or travelling, anything but being stuck in here with me. I've always known it would be unfair on her. My ageing. That it would drive a wedge between us after Charlie's passing wore us down. But what could be done about it?

The infant coagulating and swirling around in the soup of my elbow is more familiar to me than my own daughter now.

The nurses still see only a bruise, sometimes nothing at all, and when I point out to them that the intruder—a thin, sickly fellow who I never quite see the face of—never left and is tucked behind Charlie's old chair, or that I think he's rigged the television to watch me back, they blindly nod and assure me not to worry and ask me only to let them know if he starts scaring me.

One of them even asks for him to leave me alone, but her eyes are several feet away from where he's crouched and waiting.

In the end, whatever is growing and forming in the cradle of my elbow becomes a comfort, more than a fright. I let the television gossip in the background, my eyes glued to the tight, supple flesh, so thin it provides a window into the inner workings of what slumbers and grows there. It isn't a bairn, not exactly, but there is an essence of a child within it. Separate parts floating, bumping against the glass of my skin, tethered with delicate, blue-purple-red veins.

I should be afraid. When it's disembodied, suckling mouth swirls to the top, I see tiny pebbles embedded in the gums, and I wonder what might happen if, *when,* its teeth fully form, and it chooses to mouth and worry its small, pink tongue against the junction of my limb—and bite down.

I force myself not to think about it and take my arm and pretend to swaddle an infant against my chest, rocking and rocking until the horrible twinges in my arm subside, and an odd sense of peace begins to take its place.

I know something is wrong when I wake to silence.

No carer bustling through the front door with a shrill, chirpy good morning. No pestering to eat, or offers to bathe, not even the incessant chatter about what they plan to do once they're free from looking after me. I'm in bed with cold morning light slinking through gaps in the curtain, a frigid weight beside me, and a warm, wet feeling across my chest.

Instinct pushes me to check my elbow's cot first. The tumour has ruptured. My nightgown is see-through and sticky with curdled pink liquid, and in the seam of my arm, the flesh is scorched and knotted, thin and flimsy meat gnawed loose by rodent's teeth. But the wound has, miraculously, clotted, and leaks no more. I feel painfully hollow.

To my left, two throats rattle and gargle.

The intruder sits beside me, a lump of sinew and gristle cooing in his arms. Charlie, too, gurgles with it, but his lungs are thick with tar and his throat is frozen along with the slack-jawed, hazy expression he'd left the world with, as though disgruntled in his sleep, but still fast on. The telephone rings.

There is a vibrating barrier between me and the world, fizzing and popping and pushing the air around me back and away. Everything arrives muted. Charlie looks at me with dead eyes, the corners of his mouth barely twitching, but suggesting a smile all the same. He chokes as he coos at the lump in his arms, but not an ounce of fear fills me.

Sorrow does.

Charlie shifts from the bed. In the indent of his spot, there is a horrible dark stain, and the length of his back is taut and purple. He shuffles from the room, an essence of *something* of ours in his arms, and the agony of its missing weight beats a harsh rhythm against my open wound. The front door begins to rattle. Finally, I move.

Together, we reach the front door to our home, and from the other side comes Nicola, rushing through us towards the bedroom. Charlie walks on, not looking back, because he knows now not to stay. Not to intrude. Everything left of me aches to linger, but I follow. Down the side of our family's home, pansies, begonias, and petunias blossom and bleed into the dark. Nicola's muted, drowning sobs fade far behind me.

We reach the end of the path, stall at the ginnel's gate, and I can't hear my daughter anymore. With stiff movements, Charlie turns and offers the bundle of offal out to me, his waxen face impassive as fluid drips like drool through his gnarled fingers and onto the paving slabs. I take it. A steaming mass of tender cartilage and cleft lips and calcified nubs.

But further, deep into the bowels, I see pasty, chubby skin and blue eyes and a weight I'd never forget. Never. *Never.*

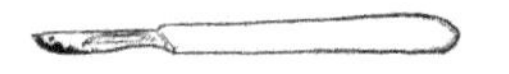

Demi-Louise Blackburn is a dark fiction author from a small, tired town in West Yorkshire, England. Some of her morose tales have found homes with the likes of Kandisha Press, All Worlds Wayfarer, Ghost Orchid Press, and The Future Dead Collective.

At the beginning of a new project, she silently gives thanks to her old tutors and their inability to raise eyebrows at stories such as 'The Death Rattle', or the nauseating 'Black Tar Baby'. May their uncanny understanding of 'the weird kids' never dull.

In spring, you may spot the shadow of Demi around the riverbanks of her home, at a festival during summer, or holed away painting during the cooler months. But mostly, you'll find her skulking online, collecting questionable and potentially haunted knickknacks for her office, which is lovingly dubbed 'The Smile Room'.

For further inquiries, find her at demi-louise.com or contact@demi-louise.com

Intoxication

Lindsey Ragsdale

"Let me buy you a drink."

The words wafted from her lips like smoky perfume.

I turned towards the voice, wobbling slightly on the leather barstool. She wore a meticulously tailored suit of dark green silk overlaid with patterns of tiny, pointed leaves that glimmered in the dim light. Her sleek black hair was pulled up in a tight bun. Amethyst drops hung from her earlobes. And she had eyes like I'd never seen. Dark pools with a flash of violet in the depths. I felt dizzy just looking into them.

Or maybe it was just that last martini catching up to me.

I'd been sitting at Mikey's on a Friday night, as I usually did, staring at my third empty glass. Alcohol was the only thing these days that hushed the whining voice in the back of my mind. A petulant tone complaining about another shitty week at the firm, why Josie/Sarah/Amanda stopped calling me back, or another lonely weekend looming ahead of me. Pick one, or all of the above.

But this stranger was a welcome interruption, cutting through the miasma of pity in which I wallowed. Women never approached me at the bar. I tried, sometimes, with them, in mumbled introductions that never lasted more than two minutes before they drifted away. This mysterious woman, well-dressed and attractive to boot, was a first. At the very least, we could platonically commiserate about the injustices of life together. Misery loves company.

"Sure, why not?" I tried to grin, hoping I didn't look too much like a letch.

The woman signaled to Paul, the Friday night barkeep. He nodded and pulled two wine glasses out from beneath the bar.

"Red or white?" she asked me.

"Dealer's choice," I replied, and she smiled for the first time.

The rest of the night was sensory overindulgence. After two glasses of merlot at Mikey's, Thalia, as she introduced herself, took my hand and led me down the street to a jazz lounge, where a four-piece band traded harmonies back and forth while we stood in the back and swilled grenache. Then we explored a nightclub, where deafening bass pulsated to stippled disco lights painting the walls and floors. Sweaty bodies crushed us on all sides as we sat at the glitter-flecked bar and sipped rosé. A taxi whisked us down a dark alley to a haze-filled dive bar, where we shot pool while balancing glasses of lukewarm chardonnay on the rails. We watched the sun rise over the lakefront as we slumped on a bench in a comfortable silence, clutching paper bags around half-bottles of white zinfandel.

Thalia was electricity in human form. All night she'd chatted, and listened, even in the loudest room, to every word I said. After that second glass of wine, I'd poured out the guilt and anger I felt at being unable to change my life for the better. My simmering resentments at remaining a mid-range paralegal for years, watching colleagues promoted to seniors and specialists. Scrolling through endless announcements of engagements, weddings, and pregnancies on social media, while I sat alone in the dark in my apartment. Resolving to adopt healthy habits, or plan a trip to Italy and Greece, or apply to law school at long last, but never following through. I felt balanced on a precipice, gathering dust, while too paralyzed to take the plunge.

All the while, Thalia nodded and made sympathetic sounds, and the more I talked, the more I felt understood by another being for the first time in years. It seemed like Thalia, at that point, had made it her mission to give me the best evening she could, surrounded by laughter and light and human contact. Strangers were drawn to her, often making small talk with both of us, or asking to join our casual game of pool.

It was the best evening I'd had in a very long time. I didn't want it to end, as I heard the birds begin to stir and chirp in the trees around us as the sky grew brighter.

"Jake," Thalia said, breaking the silence. "Thank you for such a lovely evening." She put her free hand on my right thigh as we sat together, and I shivered. She took her palm away and the skin beneath my pant leg tingled, like a current was shooting through my veins.

"No, I should be the one thanking you," I slurred. A thought occurred to me. "Let me give you some cash. Didn't you pay for all our rounds?" I dug my wallet out of my pocket, but she put up a hand to stop me.

"My treat," she purred. "Let's get you home."

My next memory was waking up, fully clothed and alone, in my apartment. The joy, the happiness, the lighthearted nature of the incredible night I'd just had quickly faded, as the worst hangover of my life took hold.

My brain felt pickled and shriveled, like something forgotten at the back of a refrigerator. How could such a wasted organ cause so much pain? Spikes felt like they were piercing the backs of my dried eyeballs, making them throb relentlessly whenever I turned my head. I licked my chapped lips and groaned as the putrid taste coating my own mouth reminded me of sour, stale wine.

It took all my strength to pour myself onto the carpet and crawl into the bathroom before my dry heaves brought anything up. After filling the toilet bowl with purple, I closed the lid and rested my face on the cool floor tiles for a moment. I prayed to slip back into merciful sleep, but the nails pounding into my skull and the piercing daylight wouldn't hear of it. Shuddering, I stripped off my sweaty, grimy suit and crawled into the bathtub, turning on the faucet by feel and huddling into a ball as cool water pooled around my naked form. I opened my eyes enough to draw the shower curtain closed, in an effort to block out the light, and I saw something odd.

There was a dark handprint on my right thigh, almost like a bruise, deep purple in color. It felt slightly warmer to the touch than my surrounding pale skin. I racked my savaged brain. Had I fallen? Did someone grab me?

It wasn't until a few hours later, wrapped in a bathrobe and choking down ice water and Saltines, that I remembered—Thalia had placed her hand on my thigh. But when I whipped open my bathrobe to inspect my leg again, the mark was gone.

The following Friday night, I went back to Mikey's, eyes peeled for Thalia. We forgot to exchange contact information during our night on the town, and I couldn't stop thinking about her.

I'd woken up Monday craving that adrenaline rush of people and parties and fun-filled nights, which came as a pleasant surprise. Usually Monday mornings were filled with dread and anxiety for the upcoming workweek. Endless deadlines and constant multitasking made being a paralegal stressful. It was all I'd ever done, so I wouldn't even know where to start if I wanted a new career. I'd learned to live with the weekly dose of despair, though I hated myself for it.

Not this week. My days flew by and my nights were filled with bar-hopping and dancing. I'd planned on club soda, the hangover fresh on my mind, but the words tumbled out of my mouth at the first bar I tried, a neighborhood spot called Linda's Pub: "A glass of the house red, please."

Every day that work week I didn't get home until 2 AM at the earliest. I'd spent more money on glasses of wine in all its decadent forms, red, white, rosé, sparkling—I craved them all—than I cared to admit. I'd bought many bottles to share with new acquaintances that I chatted, laughed, consoled, and even cried with once. My newfound extroversion bubbled forth like a tapped spring and my thirst for wine was endless. Each morning I woke refreshed, reinvigorated, and ready to start the party cycle anew.

I never stopped scanning the crowds for Thalia. She never appeared, but I wasn't discouraged. We lived in a big city; perhaps she was exploring a different corner of it this week. All I dared to hope for was her return to Mikey's this Friday.

Jake, I imagined her saying. *I can't wait to have another amazing night with you.*

Two hours passed and I remained alone at the bar. A few people had wandered over to order, and inevitably tried to strike up a conversation, but I denied them as politely as I could, not wanting to miss a glimpse of Thalia. I tilted the last burgundy drops out of the bottle into my mouth and signaled to Paul to close my tab. Earlier, I'd asked him if he'd seen Thalia that week, but he'd shaken his head.

"Your friend didn't show, huh?" he said, as he brought me a receipt to sign. "Too bad. You guys really hit it off last week."

"Yeah," I sighed. "Maybe another time, I guess."

Paul looked at me closely. "Jake, you don't look so good. Take it easy tonight, maybe? We're not going anywhere. Come back tomorrow?"

He was right. My head was starting to ache and a dull beating began somewhere deep inside my body. I frowned. I'd only had one... bottle. It was a lot, but not compared to my earlier binges this week. Maybe I should take a break. I nodded to Paul. "Good idea."

"Call you a cab?" he offered, but I waved him off and turned towards the exit.

I got worse as the night went on. The pain in my skull plateaued quickly, but no amount of Advil could kick it entirely. My face was flushed and I felt jittery and sweaty all over, but my temperature was normal. Oddest of all was my right thigh. The handprint hadn't returned, but I felt throbbing deep within the bone. My leg grew swollen and tender from groin to knee over the course of a few hours. I could've sworn I felt tiny fingers running along the underside of my skin, and the sensation was so vivid that I expected to see my flesh rippling and puckering in response.

Ice packs soothed my head and thigh to some extent, but on my third trip to the freezer, I was having trouble standing and walking. Any pressure on my thigh caused discomfort. I resigned myself to the couch and tried to sleep, my right leg propped up on a cushion, hoping I'd feel better in the morning. If I didn't, I resolved to call urgent care. I swallowed a few Benadryl just in case this was some sort of allergic reaction, and closed my eyes.

I woke in darkness to a frantic knocking on the front door. Barely remembering to pull my bathrobe over my t-shirt and boxers, I staggered to my feet, wincing with every slow step I took. The swelling hadn't gotten better. If anything, my thigh had swollen up to twice its size, though I couldn't see properly without turning on a light. I also felt dizzy and lightheaded, like I was drunk, but surely the effects of that single bottle would've worn off by now.

I opened the door to Thalia. She wore a wine-dark dress and strappy sandals, and her hair was loose around her shoulders. Her eyes were bright and cheeks rosy.

"Jake!" she exclaimed, taking in my sorry state. She glanced down at my thigh and her smile widened. "Come with me."

I stared at her, uncomprehending. "Thalia? How did you know where to find me?"

"Who do you think brought you home last week?" she said. "You've done so well. It's time."

"For what? I don't understand."

"Your leg." She pointed down. I wrapped my bathrobe tightly around me, embarrassed. "I'll help you. I'm the only one who can." She took my hand. "Just trust me."

In my stultified condition I stuffed my feet into a pair of sneakers and grabbed my keys as Thalia pulled me out the door, closing it behind her.

Outside the lobby of my apartment building, a limousine idled at the curb. A tall, thin man in a suit stood by the rear door. He opened it as Thalia gestured that I should get in. I did as gingerly as I could, too astounded and dizzy to say anything. She got in behind me.

"We need to celebrate," she said, reaching for a bottle of Veuve Cliquot. She expertly popped the cork and poured a golden fizzy stream into two champagne flutes. She handed one to me and I stared at the bubbles making their winding ways to the liquid surface, wondering what the hell was going on.

"I don't feel like drinking," I began, as Thalia clinked her glass against mine and took a long swallow. She closed her eyes, savoring the taste, as I placed my flute in a leather cup holder. "Thalia, please, where are we going?"

"To help you," she murmured, caressing my swollen thigh with her hand. The flickering fingers' sensation stilled the pain, to my immediate relief. I still felt throbbing down deep in the meat of my thigh, but it slowed to a steady beat, instead of the frantic pounding crescendo from earlier.

Maybe she could really help me, I thought. The past week had been full of hope and change, all because Thalia came into my life. Perhaps I should trust her and go wherever she was leading me. In my woozy, inebriated state, it made a fractured sort of sense to settle back and let the night play out. Thalia had healed my loneliness and filled the emptiness in my heart by showing me a good time with strangers, all of us yearning for connection. Why shouldn't she heal my thigh, too?

I settled back and closed my eyes, letting the soft jostlings of the car lull me into an uneasy slumber.

A hand on my shoulder. "Wake up, Jake." I reluctantly opened my eyes. The limo had stopped, and Thalia had opened the door. "We're here."

I sat up and winced. The pressure and heat in my thigh was raging. "I don't know if I can walk, Thalia." I gestured to my leg, looking like a sausage about to burst its casing.

She turned and spoke to someone standing outside the car, then stepped out. My door opened, and the limo driver stood behind an empty wheelchair. He offered a gloved hand to me, which I gratefully accepted as he maneuvered me into the chair. He pushed me smoothly over the curb. Were we at the hospital?

It was still the middle of the night. The street was deserted except for the three of us. As my eyes adjusted, I saw old-fashioned, wrought iron street lights flickering on the corners, and a brick-paved sidewalk. This was the oldest neighborhood in the city—I'd only seen photographs of the looming stone homes lining the street, elaborate curlicues and Gothic touches giving the buildings an imposing, foreboding feel. All the windows were dark except for the building we faced, where the first floor lights blazed from the stone facade. A crimson awning adorned a set of carved wooden doors, one of which swung open as I was pushed through the entrance. Stone carvings of grapes and ivy entwined in lush patterns arched over the entryway and I only got a glimpse before the door swung shut behind us.

"Are we at the hospital?" I asked drunkenly, before realizing how dumb of a question that was.

"This is where you need to be," Thalia said, taking my hand to walk alongside my wheelchair. "There are some people who want to meet you."

I was pushed over a thick carpet to a set of gold plated elevator doors. Thalia typed in a code on a keypad, and we left the driver in the cramped lobby as she wheeled me into the elevator. Down we plunged, and when the doors opened, a cacophony of voices and loud music poured in, as shocking to my senses as being doused in icy water.

I fumbled for the edges of my bathrobe, suddenly aware of my ratty attire and half-naked state. Thalia noticed me and laughed, squeezing my hand.

"Don't worry," she said, shouting to be heard over the music. "You'll see."

And see I did. What looked like hundreds of barely-clothed humans, of all expressions and body types, writhed on what I realized was a massive dance floor lit from below. People danced and swayed and fucked with complete abandon and pleasure, not a bit self-conscious or reserved. The walls of the room arced up into the gloom. I had the sensation I was deep within the bowels of the earth.

Thalia raised her hand, and the music ceased. Many pairs of eyes turned towards the elevator, and I braced myself, but smiles and applause broke out. Cheering and chanting emanated from the endless crowd, and the people right in front of us parted to clear the way. Thalia pushed my chair through the happy throng, and strangers reached out for us. Some shook or clasped my hands, while others patted my shoulders, murmuring welcomes. I felt a tentative smile spreading across my face; my initial discomfort and confusion slipping away.

We came to a sort of clearing, an empty space on the dancefloor covered with rugs and pillows. The crowd stood on the edges, many clasping goblets and conversing in soft voices. Thalia escorted me out of the chair and helped me take a few steps to the center. Several people came forth to help me sit as comfortably as I could, by bringing more pillows and blankets and propping up my swollen leg. Someone pressed a goblet into my hand and melted back into the crowd. I sniffed and took a nervous sip of wine. Then it was just Thalia and me, as the crowd encircled us at a respectful distance. Hundreds of people gazed rapturously at the two of us. She turned as they cheered, putting a hand into the folds of her dress.

"Bear witness!" she called, her voice ringing through the cavern. "Bear witness to my child, offspring of Thalia, daughter of Dionysus. Bear witness this night as I bring her forth, in wine, women, and song." She lifted something shiny into the air, and a cold sweat broke out across my brow as I realized she held a gold-plated knife. The crowd stamped and roared.

I struggled to stand up in a sudden panic, knocking over my goblet in the process. Thalia glanced down and concern flitted across her face. She knelt and stroked my cheek with her free hand.

"Jake," she whispered into my ear with her smoky tone. I closed my eyes and thought of the two of us sitting on leather barstools for the first time, only a week ago. "You are so lonely. I see it in your soul and the depths of your heart. You yearn for the bounty that life can offer. You have so much to give. And these people," she gestured at the crowd, who had fallen almost silent. "They love you. Stay with us. The father of my child will never want for anything again."

"What!" I sputtered, as she placed her hand on my hot, pulsing thigh.

"It is time," Thalia called. Three people rushed forth. Two took my hands gently in their own, while the third kneeled behind me and placed a cooling cloth on my brow. Thalia brought the golden knife to my thigh and looked into my eyes with her violet ones.

"This will only hurt for a moment."

I couldn't respond as she drew the tip of the knife swiftly across the hot length of my thigh and pain exploded through my nerves. I screamed and thrashed, but my minders held me firmly. The agony was enormous and I squeezed my eyes shut as I felt a cup pressed to my lips. "This will help with the pain," said a voice into my ear. I sipped, and the sense of disconnect and disorientation only increased, but it helped me process the wholly unbelievable scene before me once I opened my eyes.

My thigh remained, slit open like an overripe fruit, but the bloody mess I had braced myself to see wasn't there. Instead, purple, pungent liquid gushed from the edges of the gaping wound. It cascaded onto the ground, puddling in my nest of pillows and blankets, feeling warm and sticky against my skin. My minders gasped and they trembled at my side.

"May I?" a hot voice rasped into my ear—a man holding my hand—as he lifted a trembling finger to mop up a stream of droplets pooling by my knee. As I watched, he stuck his finger into his mouth. "Wine of the father," he moaned.

"May I?" the woman holding the cooling cloth to my forehead asked. "And I?" said the man holding my other hand. They panted as they watched the man licking his purple-stained finger. I was at a loss for words.

"Soon, my acolytes," Thalia said as she loomed over me, having exchanged her knife for a small blanket. My minders nodded and drew back, trembling. "Hold on, Jake."

She reached for my wine-covered thigh, and to my horror a tiny, purple-smeared hand reached out of my thigh wound, grasping at the air. Thalia gasped and cooed as she prodded gently at the tiny hand, which grabbed her finger. She closed her eyes, a beatific smile on her face. Tears of purple ran down her cheeks, leaving plum tracks in their wake. "Our daughter," she whispered to me.

Thalia parted the lips of my wound with delicate fingers before sliding her hands inside me and pulling out a human baby. She was small and looked like she was spattered in ink, but her lavender eyes were wide open as she took in the world around her. The crowd sighed and cheered as Thalia swaddled the baby and held her up in the air. The applause grew so loud I worried the ceiling would come crashing down on us.

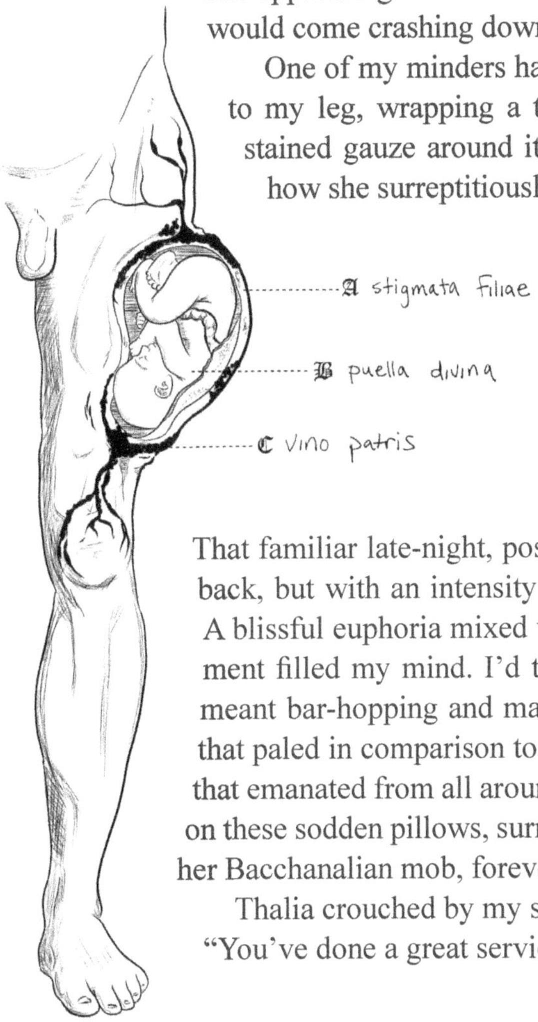

One of my minders had turned her attention to my leg, wrapping a thick layer of purple-stained gauze around it. I tried not to notice how she surreptitiously licked her fingers as she worked. The pain had died down the moment the baby emerged from my thigh, and all I felt was exhaustion and the room spinning around me. That familiar late-night, post-drink sensation was back, but with an intensity I'd never felt before. A blissful euphoria mixed with drunken contentment filled my mind. I'd thought a happy night meant bar-hopping and making new friends, but that paled in comparison to the devotion and care that emanated from all around me. I could lie here on these sodden pillows, surrounded by Thalia and her Bacchanalian mob, forever.

Thalia crouched by my side, holding our baby. "You've done a great service," she said. "You've gained my respect and that of my followers. We will take care of you for the rest of your days."

I leaned back into the pillows as Thalia handed me our daughter. "She's perfect."

Thalia opened my bathrobe and pulled up my white t-shirt, stained with purple. "Now you must feed our daughter." Thin trickles of red wine oozed from my nipples as Thalia held the baby to my chest, who latched on and began to suckle.

She gazed up at me with lavender eyes and smiled, intoxicating me with her love.

Lindsey Ragsdale (she/her) is a writer from Chicago, Illinois. Some of her stories appear in the anthologies *Howls from the Wreckage*, *The Darkness Beyond The Stars*, *Howls from the Dark Ages*, and *Nightmare Sky*. She loves reading, writing, cooking, crocheting, and long walks by the lake. On Twitter, find her @Leviathan15.

WHOLE AGAIN

EMMA E. MURRAY

It happened all at once and yet stretched out across an eternity. I'd been careless. Tired. Dumb. It was a long trip back from my dad's house. I was irritable. Ready to be home. Stupid.

Cora was bouncing off the walls, it was hours past her bedtime. I remember glancing at the blue digital numbers on the car console, 11:47. I climbed out, stretched, and pumped gas, half-blinded by the harsh glaring of overhead lights, half-asleep from road hypnosis. Only an hour and a half left to get home, I told myself, talking myself out of stopping at a motel or even to pull over for a quick snooze. I had to keep going.

Cora was everything a nine-year-old can be. Obnoxious. Immature. Horrid. Hilarious. Sweet. Wonderful. She was my daughter. The love of my life and my whole world for nine years, as well as the obstacle to my personal growth, my nights off, my freedom. Being a mother was so much more complicated than I'd imagined. I just needed her out of my hair for a minute, so without much thought, I slipped my wallet out of my purse and into her eager hands.

"Go and get yourself a snack or something."

I sent her in alone, without a second thought. I shouldn't have been surprised when she returned with her arms full, a smirk on her lips.

"What the hell, Cora?" I grabbed the three full-size bags of chips, the candy bars, and the two sodas wedged in her armpits. "Who said you could buy all this?" She shrugged and of course hadn't gotten a receipt, but still a child, she wasn't clever enough not to reveal her worst offense. From her pocket she pulled out pack after pack of those trading cards all the kids obsessed over.

"How much did you spend?"

"I don't know. Maybe twenty, thirty?"

"Cora!"

"I never get anything, and I thought it wasn't that much," her words fell out, rushed and full of remorse as I seized her shoulders, shook her, a thick shroud of rage falling over me and distorting my thoughts. Sure, it was outside our tight budget, but it wasn't the end of the world. I could cut back somewhere else to recoup the loss, and she was right that she rarely got any of the treats or surprises her friends seemed constantly showered with, but the anger clouded my mind. If I had counted to ten, it would've passed and the consequence would've waited until we got home, a grounding or a night without her phone. No, I had to blow up.

I wanted to hurt her, so in an immature overreaction, I tore open a few of the packs and scattered the cards into the crisp night air. Without a word, Cora got back in the car, slamming the door and pouting, arms crossed over her chest. I regretted it immediately, but it was too late. We hadn't gotten very far when the tire indicator came on. I cursed and she raised her eyebrows, a shadow of a smile on her lips.

"I thought we didn't say bad words, Mom?"

Slamming the door behind me, I looked at the spare and jack in the trunk and contemplated whether I even remembered how to change a tire, it'd been so long. And I was tired. So very tired. The blue of my phone illuminated my face as I tried to decide if it was worth calling AAA for help, knowing I couldn't really afford it, or if I should try on my own. Every little thing felt like a catastrophe. I was crying and screaming, kicking the flat, when Cora got out.

"Hey Mom, you look like you need help."

"Just leave me alone. I can't think," I'd snapped at her. So she did.

I can see her profile in my periphery every moment I'm awake.

She was flipping through those goddamn cards that had survived my blowup and dropped one. That was it. My sweet Cora, bent over the road when the headlights appeared; the car was moving too fast.

The sound was softer than you'd think.

Not the crack of broken bones or screams of agony, but a heavy thump and wet tearing as she was dragged, leaving behind piece after piece of herself. My ears rang with intense tinnitus. I couldn't hear my own desperate wails as I lunged after her broken body, no longer recognizable as my Cora. No longer human, she became a shredded mangle of flesh twisted in surreal positions.

The car pulled over immediately, the driver distraught, and it didn't take long for red flashing lights to illuminate the viscera that was once my daughter. They covered her with a tarp, hushing me and telling me not to look, as if I hadn't witnessed her final moments. It all blurs in my memories, a rapid, heavy heartbeat drumming in my ears over every spoken word, but there is one moment I remember clearly.

Before the driver had stepped out, before anyone noticed, I saw my baby's tiny left leg, ripped free, torn at the knee, her foot knocked from the shoe by the massive force. I can't explain why I needed that part of her. I know it makes no sense, but there was no sense to be made in those painful tragic moments.

I picked it up and tucked it in my tote before anyone could see.

My bag went unchecked, even on the long winding ride in the back of the ambulance, even by the nurses who changed me out of my blood-spattered clothing when I lost my ability to speak or move. For the rest of that night and into the next day, while I rested heavily sedated on a hospital bed, Cora's leg was in my purse across the room, barely obscured from view by the sweatshirt and yellow legal pad shoved on either side of it.

I'd forgotten I'd taken it, the entire night of the accident a haze of excruciating pain, but when I reached around for my wallet, checking out with the discharge planner, I felt it. The woman babbled on about therapy options and bereavement groups, the printer spitting out page after page of useless brochures on losing a loved one. I could only nod, mouth open, as I tried to make sense of my Cora's leg hidden in my bag. Everything was too surreal. I convinced myself I was dreaming and took a taxi home, unworried about the cost. Dream money didn't matter and soon I'd wake up.

I stared at the bag while I worked up the courage, finally summoning the strength to reach inside. I took the leg out with shaking hands, but it wasn't the gory mess I'd feared. It was Cora. A part of my beautiful, perfect Cora. My fingertips caressed it, gently wiping away the scabs of dried blood, and then I held it to my heart for the hours upon hours of heaving, choking tears.

I don't know how anyone found out about the accident, but the calls started not long after I got home. At first, I let them go to voicemail. However, I knew eventually I'd have to face someone, so when my body was left a desiccated husk, I answered, dry throat creaking and head floating with the hollow aftermath of being emptied of every sob.

"Don't worry about a thing. I've got it covered," my brother Tyler told me. "But I have to ask, did you have Cora covered by any life insurance? I'm sorry, but it'd certainly help with the costs and everything."

When my phone finally quieted, partially because it was late at night and partially because I'd given up and switched it over to "do not disturb," I found a new wave of grief waiting for me. I held her bare foot to my cheek until I fell asleep, whimpering on the couch.

In the morning, I had a little more clarity. Before I took a double dose of the tranquilizers the hospital had given me and curled into my damp corner of the couch, stained with tears and sweat from nightmares, I had to find a place to put Cora's leg.

I was scared for anyone to find it, though I couldn't pinpoint just why. Was I afraid they'd find me disgusting, morbid, perverse for keeping it? Or was it that they'd take her away from me, this last spoiling piece of her, everything else collected and kept away already? It certainly wasn't a fear of being locked away in a psychiatric hospital, though I was sure that would happen as well. I didn't really care about living anymore. I would've taken myself out, to meet either Cora again or enter an endless unfeeling void, neither option unappealing, but I didn't have the strength. Not even enough energy to kill myself; it was honestly so absurd I could've laughed, but I didn't. There was no more laughter, no more tears, nothing except sleep, Cora's leg carefully wrapped up and hidden in the back of the refrigerator. It pained me to put it away, having to treat it as the piece of flesh it was, but I didn't want it to decompose. I couldn't bear that.

As the next few days passed by and preparations were made, I was surprised no one noted the leg's absence. Didn't they wonder where this part of my child had gone? That was until the devastating reality hit me like a punch to the gut: she'd been so destroyed by the accident that they likely couldn't take any accurate survey of her parts. My poor child, the love of my life, had been scraped off the asphalt with a shovel. I wanted to erase the image of her spread thin down the patch of road, but it came back again and again.

When the funeral finally came, it was a mandatory closed casket. I remember the funeral director telling me it was better I didn't see, as if I hadn't seen already. I wanted to look, as horrible as it'd be, to make sure it was my Cora inside, but they'd sealed the casket shut. I picked at the seal with a fingernail as I leaned over the pearly pink veneer and whispered my apologies into the cold steel. My brother had chosen pink because I'd been too deep in my grief to help. I winced to imagine her buried forever in her most hated color, but there was nothing to be done.

At least she didn't have to see it, I thought, and my skin burst into a flurry of goosebumps to imagine the busted sack of organs that was once my daughter buried under suffocating layers of dirt and dark and squirming insects. I tried to get away before the vomit escaped my lips, only making it a few steps from the casket. Everyone said they understood, helping me to a chair, wiping my chin and dabbing at my dress. They were so gentle with me, as if I'd break into a thousand ceramic pieces with the slightest touch. I'd even ruined her funeral.

When I got home, Dad, Tyler, and a few others stayed with me for a while, probably until they deemed it socially acceptable to leave. Then I was alone. I hated their company, their awkward condolences and tiptoed chitchat, but as soon as they were gone, I missed the distraction. I couldn't help myself, praying for forgiveness as I took the leg out and warmed its chilled flesh against my skin. Beneath the coppery scent of blood, it still smelled like her. Grapefruit body wash and the sweet smell of childish sweat.

How could she be gone?

Before I took the nightly handful of pills to keep me numb and help me sleep, I tucked the leg under my pillow, my hand resting against the downy hairs and smooth skin as I drifted away. All night I dreamt of Cora, watching her whole life all over again. When I woke in the late morning, I stayed huddled under the blankets for a long time. I knew I had to do something with the leg before long. It wasn't respectful to her memory to keep it until it rotted. I needed to bury it or cremate it, a private goodbye to my daughter, and yet I couldn't get myself out of bed to start the day. I wanted every moment possible with the last piece of her left.

Bare feet dug into the carpet. I held my breath as I removed the pillow, gently as if Cora could still feel, as if I could hurt her if I moved too fast. And there it was.

It took me a moment to fully comprehend what I was seeing. The same tiny toes, same arched foot, same soft blonde-haired calf, same knobby knee, but where the thigh was ripped away, there was no longer a dried, ragged stump and shredded skin. Instead, a bulb of pristine new flesh had appeared over the top.

I gasped, staggered backward, and hit my back against the wall. It made no sense, but I could only gape in silence for so long. My hands tremored as I reached out, fingertips just touching the skin. I darted back, breathing hard. It was warm.

My mind grasped for any logical explanation, and I realized perhaps my own body heat had warmed it during the night. Significantly calmed down, I touched it again. It was very warm and as my fingers traveled up the shin bone and over the bulbous growth, I felt the contracting of muscles and the ripple of movement. I brushed my nails over the sole of the foot, and the toes wriggled as if the nerve endings were stimulated. Cora had always been ticklish, even as a baby.

When I held the leg to me this time, fresh tears streamed down my cheeks and neck, collecting at my chest where I pressed it, and the leg seemed to hug back. My Cora. She wasn't fully gone.

Every night, I slept with the leg tucked in next to me, wrapped in my daughter's favorite plush blanket and with her toy otter swaddled in with her, and every day, I spent time researching strange and supernatural phenomenon on the internet, hoping to find something like this. There was never anything like it, only an obvious hoax or two.

Over the week, I watched the lump of flesh lengthen into a cylinder until it had formed a full thigh, exactly like Cora's down to the twin moles just below her hip. In another week, she consisted of a full pelvis, a soft belly, and the start of another thigh. There was no need for explanation. Cora was coming back to me.

With my bereavement leave up, I started getting calls from work, but I ignored them. I didn't bother going to any of the follow-up therapy sessions or to refill my prescriptions. I didn't answer any texts or calls from friends or family either. They wouldn't understand why I wasn't sad anymore. How could I explain the miracle that was happening slowly right before my eyes?

Two more weeks and I'd dipped into my savings account to pay the rent and grocery deliveries. I didn't dare leave the house. Cora couldn't be alone. Not yet. She was fully formed to the clavicle, with two perfect arms and two perfect legs. At night, she held me in her arms, though they were weak and still fell limp occasionally. I'd rest my head against her chest, listening to the strong thrumming of her heart.

I had so many questions that needed answers. Was she hungry? I'd hear her stomach rumble, but had no way of providing nourishment unless I could get an IV, which I would have somehow obtained if needed, however she continued to grow without it. Using a blood pressure cuff that Dad left over long ago, I found her to be perfectly within the normal range, so she couldn't be dehydrated or suffering. It was a genuine miracle. One I didn't deserve.

When her neck sprouted, I was giddy at the idea of hearing her sweet voice again. When her jaw appeared, I counted the lovely teeth and coated her tongue with sponged water, moisturized her lips with a thin layer of lip balm. My job finally terminated me, leaving a voicemail and sending a letter by mail. They sounded concerned beneath the frustrated professionalism, but it was necessary I stay home. Now that she was drinking, she needed me to walk her blind healing body to the toilet, to dress her, to keep her nourished, to make sure she was taken care of.

Cheeks formed, a maxilla and nose, but she still didn't talk. I kissed the half-face, nuzzling her nose like I did when she was an infant. I felt like a new mother again, reliving those all encompassing first months where Cora needed all my time and patience. She began to eat soft, easy to swallow foods. I was terrified she would choke, so I watched her carefully, giving her the full attention she deserved. She began to stagger around the house on her own, using her outstretched arms and open palms, as one walks through a darkened unfamiliar house. But I was sure soon she'd remember. Soon she'd see.

With the sprouting of lovely ears, so delicate, their attached lobes just like I remembered, I could whisper my apologies and eternal love and a million promises of how I'd be a better mom this time around. How thankful I was that she was coming back to me.

I would never put work first again, no matter how badly we needed the money. I wouldn't miss another day with her. I'd be a witness to every milestone, a helping hand through every hardship. I'd do anything for her. I could never make up for the tired, stupid, shitty parent I had been before, but I could try.

When I woke up after three days of stunted progress, I gasped, tracing my fingers down her apple cheeks. Her eyelids fluttered open, and she looked at me. Her skull was fully formed, fused, the fuzz of new growth scattered across her scalp.

"Cora, I—I love you. I'm so sorry." The words poured out of me in deep braying sobs until she stopped me with a finger on my lips. She didn't talk and still struggled to walk, but my daughter was back.

By the afternoon, a bit of the astonishment had worn off and I was formulating how I might reintroduce her to the world. Cora had died according to the paperwork and eyewitnesses. Would they accuse me of fraud? Would they take her away to conduct experiments? My blood stilled at the thought. I'd never let that happen. Maybe just a few close, trustworthy loved ones needed to know for now. Tyler, even though he was sometimes an asshole big brother, was the first that came to mind, and a slight shame washed over me as I remembered my phone. I hadn't even charged it in over a week, leaving it a black dead screen on the kitchen counter. Just as I'd plugged it in, there was a loud, frantic rapping at the door.

"Hello? Please let me in. I'm worried about you."

It was Tyler. I looked at Cora, her eyes full of confusion and fear, and I froze until he added, "If you don't let me in, I'm going to call the cops or bust down this door. Please don't be dead in there."

The anxious hurt in his voice was too much. I tried to reassure myself that I trusted him as I kissed Cora's forehead and went to the door. I opened it a crack and watched the relief spread over his features, his brow smoothing and eyes misting up.

"God, you scared the hell outta me. Why have you been ignoring me?"

"I've had some things I needed to work through alone, that's all." The blush creeps over my face, deep and burning with shame.

"I know losing Cora has been incredibly difficult for you, but the answer isn't to shut everyone out." Tyler sighed, shifting his weight awkwardly. "I went to your work first. They said you just never answered them again and they had to let you go."

"Listen, I had a good reason. It'll all make sense in a minute." I took a deep breath. "Come inside. There's something I need to show you."

I saw his eyes dart to the half-hidden smile on my lips and his face faded two shades paler, but when I opened the door and walked toward the kitchen, he followed.

Cora was still sitting in her usual place, pushing scrambled eggs around her plate with a fork. A sniffled combination of a laugh and a sob accompanied the grin I could no longer contain. I turned to Tyler, ready to explain, but the way his face had gone haggard and sickly made me stumble on my words.

"What the fuck? Is that—is that what I think it is?" His eyes rolled wildly to me, the whites showing all around and venom striking me with every word. I wheeled back to the table, but she wasn't there.

"Cora!" I screamed, looking around the room, running to her chair and pulling it out, as if she might've shrank and hidden under the table. That was when I saw it.

On the table was Cora's leg. Only the foot, calf, and knee with the jagged tear where it had been shorn from her fragile body, but it was worse than before. The skin was shriveled, discolored with patches of dark rot and bits of furry mold. A distinct smell, sharp like cheese and rancid, wafted from where the leg lay, but that didn't stop me from grabbing it and holding it to my chest again.

She was still my daughter.

"What did you do?" I shrieked, turning to Tyler, my vision blacking to a pinpoint of pounding light aimed right at his face.

"What do you mean?"

"She was here! She had healed. Come back Cora!" I fell to my knees. "You ruined everything by coming here!"

I heard his footsteps, quick and heavy out of the house, and his voice far away, telling someone my address and the nature of his emergency. I didn't look up. In my arms, I cradled the last part of Cora, kissing the kneecap gently as I rocked her back and forth. They'd never understand. She just needed more time. I knew what I needed to do, take the pills, all of them, and sleep with her in my arms until she grew back again. That was all we needed. A long rest together. She'd come back. She had to so I could apologize again and finally hear her answer: that she forgives me.

Emma E. Murray's work has appeared in anthologies like *What One Wouldn't Do*, *Obsolescence*, and *Ooze: Little Bursts of Body Horror*, as well as magazines like *Cosmic Horror Monthly*, *If There's Anyone Left*, *Pyre*, and *Vastarien*. Her chapbook, *Exquisite Hunger*, is available from Medusa Haus, and her novelette, *When the Devil* (Shortwave), as well as her debut novel, *Crushing Snails* (Apocalypse Party), will be coming Summer 2024. To read more, you can visit her website EmmaEMurray.com

Section iii

THE MIDDLE

WORLD OF ANGEL

JOHNATHON HEART

The human soul occupies the entire body, and the heart is its nexus.

We knew this, once, before science corrupted our intrinsic understanding of ourselves. Before we first scanned a brain and came to the deeply disappointing conclusion of: "Oh, that's all it is, then."

Which is true and false. Yes, the essential *you* is inside a different organ. But it is still just an organ. We are not anything beyond meat.

Most of us, at least.

I begin here because there's no other place to begin. My earliest memories come from pre-birth, resting my consciousness inside something deeper than my mother's womb. I didn't know that blood and viscera were foul, then, as their warmth provided comfort. It was impossible to determine where her heart-dream ended and the womb began.

Since then, I've had the ability to see the worlds inside of hearts. Souls. And I did not just look, but visited. I left my body and inhabited the consciousness of another. By the time I was a toddler, I had visited countless humans.

And I hated them all.

In the heart of my father was murder; deceased infants dangling from muscular trees by strangling umbilical cords. All of them with my

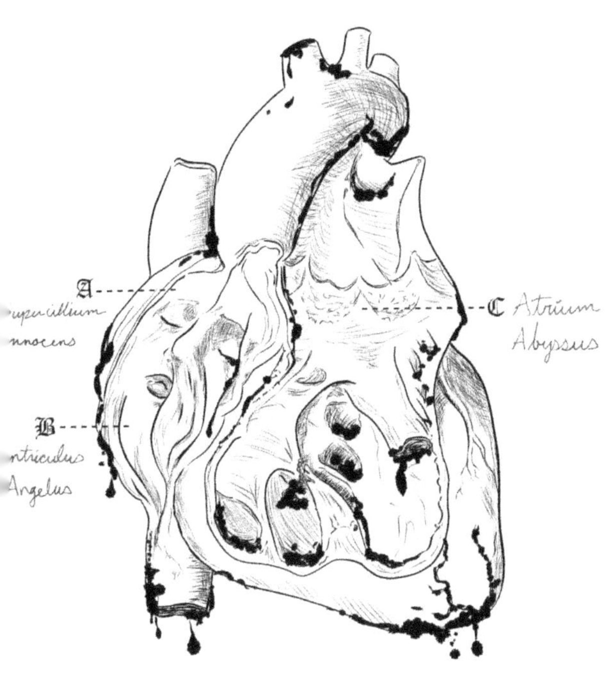

face. Motivated from his frustration at how I could not learn faster, and my endless screams.

From the roots of his trees sprouted roses of familial love, the only things holding him back from acting out these fantasies.

In my brother were toy cars of skin and keratin, products of a raw and selfish Want.

My mother's own flesh-soul cooled and frosted over as arguments with my father intensified. Inside her world, he was frozen in lakes of blood. Silent as she wished he'd be.

I knew that they sent me to daycare to get rid of me. With the hope that their marriage would be mended without the constant presence of children. It wasn't. They broke apart years later.

In school I found my brother's same horrific Want in the other children. I learned how every caregiver wanted any other job—except for one, who battled a perverse fascination with my brother and I. I learned, the hard way, not to linger. The pathway was only mine at first, but if I spent too long in another they would soon find the road to me, a great gap forming in the barrier between one soul and another. To prevent this, I began to skip between different souls, without even returning to the 'real' world.

For years, then decades, I entered these worlds full of ugliness. Built of bone and cartilage, interspersed with horrible depictions of selfish, destructive desire. At first, I reacted to all of it with instinctive gut-level revulsion. But as I grew, so too did my understanding of what I witnessed. The lusts and bigotry, the internal violence.

Despite how desperate I became to escape this, I spent less and less time in the physical world. After the advent of adulthood, I worked a menial, purposeless job, lived in a place where I could sustain myself, and otherwise paid no attention to the 'real' world.

I knew it did not help me. In fact, I vowed many times to no longer visit souls. But a drive I could not control overtook me. Perhaps it was loneliness. As my inability to love and trust others took its toll, I began to wonder if there was anyone truly beautiful. Anywhere at all. A soul that could withstand all my contempt and cynicism.

Then I found *her.*

At once I went from tragic to fortunate, for no one else would ever see her as she truly was. We are each only ourselves, and must assume all that is different in relation to others. I have been gifted with that ability to distinguish. I know for a fact that I, also, am only human. As are we all.

Except for her. *She* is an angel.

I was heart-wandering when I first traversed her world, skipping between souls through the spaceless gaps that separate them. I had just left the soul of a child murderer, jumping across lips licking themselves as small bodies tore apart, spilling blood. I pulled aside veins and ventricles like obfuscating tree branches and stepped from this, into heaven.

She sat smiling at the sky in a field of flowers, discordant in their variety. Roses, dandelions, orchids, rhododendrons. Rotating golden discs hovered through the cerulean sky like birds, their songs the buzzing of bees. Far off, fog hazed the vista of a forest and an ocean beyond.

She glowed like a goddess amongst it all.

In the split-second before her eyes turned to me, I made myself vanish.

It should be obvious why. I have said I am human: full of disdain, and a thing to be disdained. Even one interaction between us would sully her.

So I watched her exist. I never saw her physically, but I preferred that. Her world was gorgeous, so she was gorgeous. I visited her forests eventually, tall and towering with drooping flowering vines. The antithesis of my father's forest of death. Her oceans were filled with kelp and coral, with ornate seashells dotting white-sanded coasts. I came to know her as I knew her heart.

(Beneath even the most beautiful illusions it is still blood and veins. I accept this in the rare moments when I step away from the dreamer and sense her pulsating core. The uncomfortable rhythmic pump pressing on me and keeping her body going. I am aware of how each heartbeat is not a constant. How every one is a grotesque labor keeping a flesh-machine functioning. Even her. *Even her.*)

Then another heart intertwined with hers.

I watched his veins entangle her. Her beautiful world tainted by his blood, leaking into her oceans; red rain from this new non-dreamer who failed to hide that he was just some organic body. I wanted to scream; I wondered how much ugliness one invader could induce. I transported myself to him.

Through the gateway of the soul, I saw her in his eyes.

Possessing her. Making her irrevocably his. Her licking him in perverse areas, allowing him to be with her and another woman, being turned inside-out for his pleasure. Nowhere in these fantasies did her soul show. Everywhere, the blood of his heart fell over her, staining her naked body red and transforming her into a golem born of gore. Leaks and splashes from their orgiastic violence fell upon me.

Pleasure physical, not spiritual. A reminder of the body.

I felt myself returned to intolerable mediocrity, with everything beautiful a tarnished lie. Thrust out of the dream and back into a barren studio apartment, I wept and held back vomit. My throat strained. My skin itched. All the reflexes of a being that is a body and nothing else. As fixed and unfixably human as this empty man who had found her, and made her his own.

There was one solution. I did not know if it would work, but I would try.

I returned to his heart, and reached into the valves that constructed everything. Once I held those thick muscles, I twisted my grip.

The artificial but organic world around me groaned. One by one, the sexual spectres vanished. A great scream tore through the skyless air as blood built up, burst.

The next heartbeat did not come.

I was wrenched free of his world as it ceased to exist. As he did.

I faded away, back into my apartment, cross-legged and shirtless. My own heart pounded as I comprehended what I had done. I had stepped into the souls of murderers, but never had I been one. I had dreamt of killing the especially evil, but I was a coward when it came to acting. And now, when I finally had acted, it had been an experiment. My uncertainty had killed all hesitance, and I was forced to contend with how well it had worked only now that it was over.

What scared me the most was how little I regretted it.

I waited for the guilt, but it did not arrive. He had been foul, and was poisoning her. I'd seen it. She was the one beautiful thing on this Earth and in all the worlds inside it. Everything was justified to protect that.

A heart attack is (as far as anyone knows) an Act of God. No one would suspect foul play.

I swore, then, that I would do it again if the need arose. But deep down I worried: how would *she* respond?

True, for a time, her heart became gray. The trees drooped and the buzzing halos ceased to show such joy in their traversals. But *she* was pure still, and for this I would tear down every world. I would obliterate any other man, woman, or child. If there could only be one angel on this whole Earth, then I would preserve her.

When I left this time, a gap remained. I stared, stupefied, at this thing that I had not seen in years. A hole between my soul and hers. This thing that I had always taken great pains to avoid. Beautiful but gray on her side, and bloody and organic on mine. My hideous flesh-sounds interrupted and overcame her dulled and dispirited music. No, no I would poison her like all the others. I tried to close it, but I did not have the control over myself that I wished. With my hands I grabbed the edges of the portal, and pulled them together.

In the moment before it closed her eyes looked up. She saw me for almost a second before she was gone.

I swore that I would not observe her again, then. I knew that I was just as pollutive as anyone else. But late at night, as I lay in the apartment that offered me nothing, in a foul world overrun by human stink that everyone else seemed to have just gotten used to, I wondered if one peek would hurt.

That was how I came back to her world and found it recovered from its grief, as beautiful as before. One peek became a visit. And then another. I would hide my exits as the gap, through which I bled into her, spread. Each time I managed to close it, even as it grew more difficult. I made sure that she did not see me again. I knew it was wrong, but there was one soul, one, that offered beauty. I had tried so many others and found them monstrous.

One day, when I visited, I found her tarnished by blood again. Another had arrived, his heart just as eager. Rage throbbed throughout me, especially after I visited his soul to find that he barely knew her, but his imaginings cast her as any of the porn stars he'd seen on-camera.

I chose to be poetic with this one. I gave him a moment to fantasize, waited for his heart rate to increase, then grabbed his vein and twisted.

Others followed. As a matter of course, I looked into each of their hearts, even when I knew they'd be unworthy. I was never wrong.

And still the hole increased in size. Each time. Still I fought to hold myself back. But I always failed. Always reasoned to myself that there was one pure soul on this Earth, and I was protecting it.

All the while, I became increasingly creative.

One man who dreamt of erotic asphyxiation failed to breathe. Another, a surfer, died at sea, his body never found. A chronic adulterer died in the throes of orgasm with another woman. (Not my Angel. A third that he cheated on both her and his wife with.)

Every murder justified. I saw into their souls. I knew who they were.

Soon, nearly a year passed without the intercession of another invader. I was elated. Perhaps enough had been eliminated, and no more would come.

The gray spread within her, and now receded less until it did not recede at all. It began to enter me through the growing gap. Her halos died and did not return. The sea shifted from a brilliant blue to a murky green. The trees entered an eternal autumn, and many shed their leaves entirely.

But these damages were nothing, of course, to what her "lovers" offered her. No, this only justified my decision to hold back and never interact, since I myself was equally toxic.

Once her grief ceased, her world hardened. Then it crystalized, still beautiful but filled with sharpened edges. Leaves became cutting diamonds. Ornate blades sprouted like shrubbery. Sometimes, she sat on the beach examining her face in a reflective sword. As days went on, I saw her swinging it elaborately, practicing movements that could kill with all the grace of a dancer.

I knew, of course, that her every development would be beautiful. That her mourning would only make her more majestic. That all I had done was in service to her, in the end. Even as the gates between us now are so hard to close.

This is my confession, such as it is. For I am unrepentant.

Back in my world, filled with rage and violence, the sun sets into a crimson ocean. Fleshy guardians crawl from the bloodmist mire and paw at a beach that sweats red rivulets. They feed upon arthropods with their perverse organic beaks, like human mouths extended. They swallow their kills.

I sit among them. Pondering myself. Wondering how I can know that I am foul, yet do nothing about it. Attempting to discern what it was that made *her* so pure from birth.

Until sand crunches under an intruder's feet.

I'm ready. I jump to my feet and run. I have been an invader and so I know to prepare for invasions. In moments I am off the beach, cutting through a forest of red, purple, and blue bushes made of flesh.

I hide, tucking leathery branches over my head, and survey my surroundings.

A vengeful brother or father of one of the men killed? Or just an observer, as I often am? I'd suspected that I was not alone in this ability. I am unique in nothing else, after all.

The trudging steps approach. Not near enough yet that they could see me. I do not silence my breath. My heart is this space, and its beats are the rhythm of this world. I know all vulnerabilities are hidden. Anything that could kill me is invisible or protected.

My surroundings pulse harder, more frequent as my tension grows.

She emerges, stepping among the blood-creepers. Now less an angel, more a valkyrie; her beauty honed to an edge. Bladed wings rise from her back, shoulders, and neck. She drags her sword from her hand, freely cutting the ground.

No. I think of the growing gate between our worlds. The ease with which one could move through it. My own folly in just ignoring it, continuing to visit her. But she is pure, pacifistic. She would never harm a soul.

"Nothing I've cut has killed you," she says, to my forest. "You're smart. I figure that's how you got away with it, for so long."

Her sword swipes out and slashes the top off of a bush. I feel it, but do not murmur.

Twin fears assault me. I am hunted and hated. I will be murdered by she who I sought to protect. No. No, this won't be the end.

I jump out from my hiding place and look directly at her. At the beautiful light casting itself across my soul of hideous flesh. The one proof I have ever seen that we can be more than a body. Now the Angel of Death.

"Please," I beg. "I only tried to protect you."

"From love," her glare is hard, empty. "From human connection of any kind."

A foolish side of me wonders how she could have possibly discovered…no, it doesn't matter. There are any number of markers I could have left behind. Now I have to focus all of my energy on negotiation, survival.

"You need to understand," I say. "You are the only one…we are foul. We are just cells replicating themselves. Flesh-prisons built to spread genes that subsist because we, by chance, evolved to do so. There's no purpose to any of it. And for hundreds of years…" I break off. I am good with words, but I cannot overcome this existential terror going deeper than a fear of death. For *her* to hate me…

I force it out of myself. "For millions of years we have lied to ourselves that our existences had purpose. That we had a soul more meaningful, more beautiful than our bodies. But I have looked into those bodies, and there is only one I've seen who can be valued beyond that."

My finger wavers up, and points at her. Her beautiful eyebrow rises with her lip. I recognize this as repulsion, but I cannot stop.

"It's you. I would say I love you...but no. It goes deeper. You give me hope that there is value to existence. But you cannot sully yourself. You—"

Her sword swings, and my finger is gone.

Followed by a spurt of blood. I stare for one moment before another spurt follows, to the timing of my pulse.

And as she draws the sword back again, I run away, holding my hand. Through the mounds of forest and into the plains and mountains writhed with veins. Every step on dark red rubbery organs reminds me that yes, I am this thing she so despises. Only animal fear pulls me on and I grunt like a pig between desperate murmurs.

What happens to her after she murders me? What becomes of her own beautiful world once she has *killed?*

I climb a mountain and dive from it into a lake of oxygenated blood. Swimming for my life in a space in which only I can breathe. But she floats down after me. I look back to see the fluids receding for her, my red sea parting for my own true Goddess. In the deepest corners of my heart, she holds infinite power. More, even, than me.

"No!" I cry.

And now I see the error of my ways. I promise God or Heaven or greatest of all: *her.* I will do better. I will. I have learned. I denied you your choices. I accept and embrace this. I was a guardian devil when I thought I was an angel. Please, I beg, please just spare me.

But more than that, *love me.*

Her sword runs through my heart.

The blood vanishes all at once. We are in a chasm. My mind functions still. I feel the blade's alien presence. I know it is a thing more dangerous than any sword would be in the physical world.

But the nexus of the soul is in the heart. She did not even stab the heart itself, but that nexus deep within.

I look at her one last time, standing in the darkness that remains of me. Rage molds her. Her face, once pure, is now cords of muscle on its left side, twisted and wounded unnaturally, baring pieces of her skull in places where the flesh has fallen away. Her bare, lidless eyeball is nestled in it.

"I never valued my purity," she hisses in contempt. "Only you did."

I want her to understand. A thousand images flash through my mind. The desire to simply sit with her, smiling and having her smile back. Now, the curtain closes.

I fall to my knees, and watch the blood pool around them. Red in a colorless abyss. Hopes rot and heaven fades.

The dream that ensues is of silent disintegration. Far away, a disembodied existence is aware of decomposition. Maggots devouring skin and softening fibers. Mindless but clever bacteria consuming bone marrow. All returning to the dust that it only ever was.

There is a lone hope. A wish for an angel. Even if it can only be an illusion.

Then nothing at all.

Johnathon Heart is the pseudonym of a prolific (former) editor-in-chief. He is dedicated to writing stories for anyone who thinks that Halloween is better than Christmas, that love is worth believing in, and that all the best love stories are at least a little bit sad. Clearly enough people think this for him to get published. He has appeared in a variety of anthologies and is slated to appear in more. His hobbies include arguing with imaginary people and wasting the entire day. He does not actually enjoy these things, but he does them anyway.

Wandering But Not Lost

P.L. McMillan

Dr. John Wurth gripped the steering wheel with white knuckles. He'd been looking forward to the drive into Moonfell, had anticipated the sea of trees and quaint architecture, and the shiver of excitement as he entered his new home town.

Instead he was furious. Absolutely enraged at his wife. She sat next to him, her phone in her hands on her lap, looking straight ahead. Her perfect strawberry blond curls tied back into a ponytail, her face pale, cheeks blotchy.

What will my new patients think, John wondered, *when their new doctor drives up with his tear-stained wife in tow.*

He scowled. *What will they think of me?*

"I thought we agreed, honey," he said between clenched teeth.

"I know, John, it's just with the move, I've—we've been so busy," she replied. "I just forgot, okay?"

He shook his head. "It takes what? Five minutes to check and make a note for the ovulation calendar?"

"What do you want me to say?" she snapped, her quivering voice threatening more tears.

More manipulation.

"It's not like you were home most of the day, someone had to finish the packing, clean up the house."

"Oh, so it's my fault for needing to finish up all the loose ends at the hospital?"

They passed the large, elaborate sign that cheerfully welcomed them to Moonfell, population 8,363.

John had planned to stop here and get a photo in front of the sign with his beautiful wife to commemorate their move. Not anymore. The mood had been ruined. Who wanted a picture with a puffy-faced, teary-eyed woman? What kind of memory was that?

"Is this some kind of..." John sucked air through his teeth, trying to find the right wording so she wouldn't start crying again. "Silent protest? Against having kids or something? Some passive aggressive thing?"

His wife hissed in a breath. "I fucking forgot, John. Why is that so hard to understand? You're not the only one who had loose ends to tie up."

Stung, he went silent. *There is no reason for her to be so nasty, so rude.* His wife had owned a small business—just a mobile pet grooming thing. Hardly the same as finishing a medical residency and degree. All he'd asked her was that she help with the move and track her fertility. He'd begun to worry she was sterile, that they'd need IVF.

She sighed. "I'm sorry for snapping. I know you've been really stressed with everything too. Can we just move past this?"

His wife reached over the center console and squeezed his thigh. Ahead, small buildings appeared in the dense ocean of pine and oak. The edge of town.

"Yeah, okay," John said, smiling. *We can christen the new house, another chance for a child.*

"Honestly, with the move and your college debt," she continued. "It might be better to postpone starting a family, don't you think?"

John's tentatively recovering mood withered again.

"You agreed that starting a family after I finished residency was a good idea, babe," he said, his frustration reaching a boiling point.

"I know what I said, John," his wife replied, taking her hand away. "But that was before you had to switch from surgery to general practice due to stress, that was before all the extra debt, and before you decided we needed to move to the middle of nowhere for a fresh start."

The houses grew more frequent, sleepy residential streets became busier roads with shops and restaurants as John drove them and their UHaul deeper into Moonfell.

"Oh, so it's my fault now?" he said. "You're punishing me—"

"It's no one's fault," his wife interrupted. "I just think we should take a beat and settle in, pay down the debt before we have a kid, okay? We're still young, we have tons of time to figure this all out."

She opened the center console, pulling out a bunch of napkins left over from a fast food lunch, and dabbed at her cheeks.

"I don't even have a job here," she continued and he wished she'd shut up. "We can't afford a kid."

Everything she said sounded like an accusation—for being too stressed and anxious to finish his first targeted degree, for having to swap to another, adding more and more debt, and for her having to give up her client base in the move. As if she couldn't find just as many bored housewives in Moonfell eager to get their poodles, Shih Tzu, and chihuahuas all dolled up and pampered.

Ahead, a massive balloon arch stretched over the street, and under it was a small crowd of people waving.

"Oh my god," John's wife said. "That's not for us, is it?"

He spotted his name on a sign and his heart soared. The whole town had turned out for *him.* He couldn't help grinning.

A woman stepped forward from the mass of smiles and waved him into a spot on the side of the road. The woman was tall with closely cropped brown hair, dressed in casual jeans and a pink-striped blouse. John hopped out of the UHaul cab as she approached.

"You must be Mayor Katz," he said, holding out a hand.

The woman took it, surprising John with a firm grip. "I must be. But you can call me Patricia."

"I wasn't expecting a turnout," he said, turning to wave at the crowd and drink in the cheers.

"We haven't had a new doctor around these parts for thirty years," Patricia said. "Felt like a good excuse for a celebration. My car is right there, why don't you follow me to your new place?"

Their new home was a large two storey house at the end of a long private drive and surrounded by trees. On one side of the house was a two door garage, on the other was a separate one storey building—a clinic with a parking lot.

"Wow," John said, pressing his fists into his lower back and cracking his spine. "Convenient."

A freshly painted sign over the clinic front door read: Wurth Clinic.

"It's all yours," Patricia said. "There's some old furniture Dr. Orwell's family didn't want that you can have. All the utilities are on. I left a list of phone numbers on the fridge."

She held out a ring of keys, which John took with a sense of pride.

My clinic. No demanding supervisors or nosy admins. I'm in charge. This is my place.

Patricia got back into her car. "Oh, I planned a welcome party in front of town hall. 6 p.m. You don't have to worry about dinner, it's a potluck! See you there!"

John waved until the mayor's car was out of sight before dropping his smile. He turned to his wife. "You think she'd give us a day to get moved in before expecting us to show up for a party."

She shrugged. "I don't know, it's sweet. Plus, like she said, we don't have to worry about dinner."

It was easy enough to find town hall, being in the middle of town, its yard completely festooned with streamers, chairs, screaming kids, and even a live jazz band. John pulled into a parking spot, marked with yet another sign welcoming "The Wurth Family".

Patricia swooped in as soon as they were parked, guiding John and his wife on a whirlwind tour of introductions, ending with a trio of expecting mothers and their husbands.

"Here are your special charges," Patricia said.

"Nice to meet you all," John replied, having instantly forgotten their names. *Maybe meeting them will spark my wife's maternal instincts,* he thought, as he turned to find her down on one knee, cuddling a golden retriever.

"This is my wife," he said with his patented bedside manner smile—forced and Splenda-sweet.

She stood up, dirt on her knee. In the night sky, fireworks blossomed like spring flowers of all colours.

"Are you planning a family?" one of the women asked, stroking her belly.

The expecting mother looked like a goddess, fit to burst with fertile blessings. Before he could respond, his wife jumped in.

"We aren't sure yet," she said. "John's just starting his career..."

She's deliberately antagonizing me in public in front of my new patients.

The mother-to-be smiled, nodding.

"It'll happen when the time is right, as it does for all of us," she said.

"And not a moment before," said another of the mothers-to-be.

John clenched his teeth, grinning against his humiliation. His wife smiled, stepping between the women, placing her hands on their bellies, asking all the right questions—pretending she wanted a child too, playing the part.

The night grew later, the families—his future patients—trickled away. The moon, three-quarters full, hung low over them. That was when Patricia approached again, as John yawned and wished for bed.

"I'm sure you're both tired," the mayor said. "But there is one last part of your welcome that cannot wait."

John prickled at yet another demand from him. He wanted to go home, to convince his wife to see his side of things. *Still, I don't want to give the wrong impression and there would be time enough in the future to enforce boundaries—and talk some sense into my wife.*

From the square, Patricia drove them out of town, down a well-maintained dirt road deep into the woods, before pulling off into a clearing.

"You can see so many stars out here," his wife said as she got out of the Jeep.

"This way." Patricia grabbed a flashlight and led the way down a narrowing, winding path over knobbly roots and beneath a choking canopy of needles and leaves.

"I can't imagine what could be out here that's so important," John grumbled, gripping his wife's hand tightly.

"It's exciting, like a scene from a Gothic romance," she whispered back and he shook his head.

The woods were dark, the trees close and creaking with secrets delivered by the night winds. The air was heavy with the scent of pine and sap, crickets calling out for one another in the darkness. Ahead, a rocky face rose, glinting in the moonlight like a stone dagger. Patricia paused by a gaping gash in the stone's face.

"We're not going in there, are we?" John asked.

The mayor smiled, turned, and disappeared into the darkness. And before he could tell his wife they were going home, she followed the mayor.

"Fuck," John hissed and chased after.

It was a short walk, then the path opened up to a tall cavern. The stone ground and walls were perfectly smooth and polished. The domed ceiling was open at the top, letting moonlight shine on a perfectly round pool of water in the middle of the cave. And in that water floated hundreds of slightly luminous jellyfish.

"Oh my god," his wife said, softly.

"This is the treasured secret of Moonfell," Patricia said.

John approached the edge of the pool and a shock ran through him. *Those aren't jellyfish.*

Uteruses, of varying sizes and hues of fleshy pink, floated peacefully in the crystal clear water. Their fallopian tubes dangled down like tentacles, their cervixes sighed sleepy breaths like fish. Fresh, vibrant organs, bobbing in the water.

John sniffed. He was baffled that the cave didn't reek of carrion, of rotting meat. No, instead it smelled like clean skin fresh from a hot shower, of a warm breath just before a deep kiss. He stumbled back from the edge of the pool with a shudder.

"Decades ago, a man murdered his wife for getting an abortion," Patricia said, stepping up beside John. "She sought to escape his abuse, but he got to her first."

Beneath the uteruses glittered stones of intense brilliance, catching and reflecting the light in the moonpool like silver.

"On that day," Patricia continued as though she were unaffected by the cloying perfume of the cave, "Moonfell was bound to a covenant."

"What happened?" his wife asked, kneeling by the pool.

"Whenever a resident of Moonfell has their first period, their uterus leaves and comes here." The mayor gestured at the pool. "It stays here, and only until it deems its person ready for a child, does it return."

"Wandering wombs?" John spat. "That's preposterous! Unnatural!"

"It's beautiful!" his wife whispered, picking up a pair of hand knitted baby booties.

The mayor knelt by her side, laying a hand on his wife's shoulder. "Young couples, when they want a child, will often leave an offering to tempt their womb back."

His wife giggled again. "Give it baby fever, so to speak?"

The mayor laughed as well and John wanted to scream.

"What about the gems, at the bottom of the pool?" his wife asked.

"Not all uteruses belong to those who ever want children. When those people die, their uteruses turn into beautiful gems, forever drinking up the moonlight."

His wife's eyes glittered with tears just as the stones at the bottom of the pool glittered with light.

"I can tell already," the mayor said, standing, looking at John's wife. "You're going to fit in just fine here."

His wife stood too. She and the mayor took each other's hands, smiling at each other, and John clenched his fists.

"Haven't you ever tried to cure this—this malady? Transplant the organs back in?" he snapped.

The mayor looked at him, frowning.

His wife looked at him, the disappointment clear on her face.

"That would go against the covenant," Patricia said gently, as if chiding a naughty child.

John turned his back on the pool, on the mayor, and his wife. His face felt cold, shivers wracked his body. *This can't be real. It has to be some kind of prank. Haha, joke's on the new doctor.* At the same time, he couldn't deny what he'd seen.

"I showed you this," the mayor said, "so you wouldn't be shocked at any test results. When the time is right, the wombs return to their people. We have no say in the matter."

Dawn broke in blood hues across the horizon, a mirror of the mattress laid on the bare floor and covered in mismatched sheets dug out from various packing boxes. His wife was in the bathroom, her blood stained clothing strewn about the floor. The air reeked of copper, moist and warm.

John stood by the bed, clutching his shoulders, staring at the blood.

"It's not true," he muttered. "It can't be true."

An ultrasound at the clinic, twenty-minutes later, proved it was true though. Where his wife's uterus should be was now a void on the screen. An emptiness. A missing piece.

Standing with a jerk, John shoved the ultrasound machine away, its little wheels squealing on the linoleum. His wife also stood, wrapping the paper medical gown tighter around herself and shivering.

"Maybe this is for the best," she said. "We just moved here, after all. We need time to settle in. It'll come back when the time is right."

"When the time is right?" John snapped. "Listen to you! You'll fit in perfect with this fucking cult of a town!"

He stormed out of the room, the clinic, blinking against the bright morning light as he pulled a bucket from the garage and drove to the winding road that led to the forest path.

The pool caught the sunlight and shone like a fallen star. A young girl, no more than seventeen, stood at the edge of the pool, holding a chocolate bar in her hand. As John watched, she knelt and placed it on the stone floor.

"What are you doing?" John asked, holding his bucket and net, and trying not to breathe in the scent of the pool.

The teen looked over her shoulder. "I'm leaving chocolate for my—" she gestured. "You know."

"Why?" He stepped up beside the girl.

"So it stays away," she said. "I don't want to get pregnant."

The girl walked to the tunnel mouth as he stared in shock. "Aren't you a bit young to be doing that type of thing?"

With a bright laugh, the teen stuck out her tongue, then turned on a heel, and disappeared down the tunnel.

"This town," John said, pressing the heel of his hand against a closed eye. "Everyone in it is insane."

He felt crazy himself, now that he was here. *What do I think I'll find? Do I really think I'll recognize my wife's uterus out in the wild? That it will look fresher or something?*

Still, John was compelled to try. He refused to give up, to let whatever curse was on this town win. So he looked.

And there it was.

A uterus near the pool edge, plump and glistening, and with two plastic strings poking out from its cervix. *An IUD.* It had to be his wife's. Why would any person of Moonfell need an IUD if they had no wombs?

"You lied to me!" John screamed, pointing at the bucket on the dining room table. "You've been lying to me this whole time!"

"I—"

"How long?" He slammed a hand on the table, causing the water inside the bucket to ripple, for the plastic IUD strings trailing from the uterus's cervix to shiver. "How long?!"

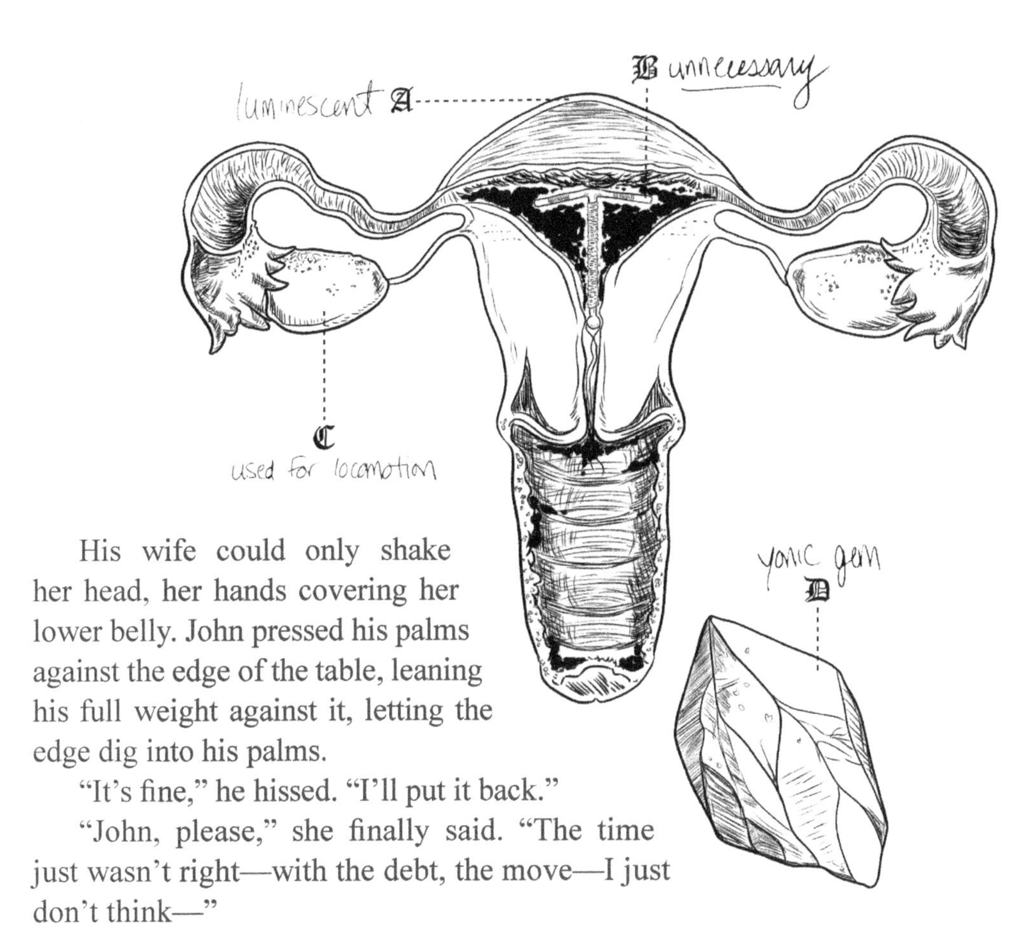

His wife could only shake her head, her hands covering her lower belly. John pressed his palms against the edge of the table, leaning his full weight against it, letting the edge dig into his palms.

"It's fine," he hissed. "I'll put it back."

"John, please," she finally said. "The time just wasn't right—with the debt, the move—I just don't think—"

"I'll put it back," John said, straightening.

She paused, staring at him. "What are you talking about?"

"I can do it," he continued. "I can put it back."

"That's crazy, you've never completed—"

"You're happy this happened, aren't you?" he screamed. "You wanted this because you never wanted kids!"

"That's not true, John! I—"

"You're selfish, you know that? You won't even let me fix this!"

Tears poured down her face but John knew she was faking. *She always cried in fights, to try and manipulate me. If she was actually remorseful, she would be trying to get better, to become whole. Without her womb, she is nothing, an empty specter with no purpose.*

"Fine!" she cried. "Fine! I'll do it!"

His wife lay hollow on the examination table.

Her belly splayed open, her wayward uterus nestled in, anchored by all the necessary stitches. A tear rested just under her left eye, her lips were slightly parted, as though she were waiting for a kiss. Just waiting. Yet the whine of the flatline continued.

The air was thick with the reek of blood, of drugs, of leaked anesthesia.

And his wife lay there, the warmth leaving her pale, pale skin.

John sat in a corner on a low stool, as he had for the past fifteen minutes after his attempts to resuscitate his wife had failed.

"Impossible, this is impossible," he whispered.

But it is possible. Because of Moonfell and its curse. Because of its people who accepted this biological horror and never fought against it.

"We should have never moved here," he whined, reaching out and taking the now cold and stiffening hand of his wife. "Why didn't you stop me? Why didn't you convince me not to take this job?"

The sigh, soft, like someone on the verge of tears.

Then a tremor ran through the building.

John looked up.

A dull beat, like that of a heart, thudded through the air.

Despite the drone of the flatlining heart monitor, John stood, hoping to see her breath, for her eyes to flutter.

In his wife's abdomen, her uterus throbbed in a steady rhythm, its glistening flesh shivering.

Another tremor ripped through the building, cupboard doors swung open from the force. The uterus's convulsing picked up in speed, rebelling and pulling against its stitches. With it, so too did the tremors echo its fury and the earthquakes increased in frequency and power.

Jars full of cotton swabs, bandages, and wooden tongue depressors shattered against the floor, the lights flickered and went out as dust rained from the ceiling, freckling his dead wife's face.

John fled, stumbling out of the room and down the central hall into the front lobby as the floor buckled and reared against him. Through the front door, he threw himself out into the open air.

The day had long since darkened to night and he fell to the dirt, looking up to the stars. The moon stared down, impossibly full and blood-red.

Distantly, screams rose from the town of Moonfell. A crash reverberated through the air and a great oak fell, smashing through the roof of his new house. John rolled over onto his stomach, managing to regain his footing. Headlights appeared, driving up his road, a line of cars, pulling into his clinic's lot.

The mayor got out first, standing across from him, steady on her feet despite the earth's assault. Her face was bathed in the blood of the moon.

"What have you done?" Patricia asked.

"We have to evacuate!" John said. "We're in danger!"

"Where is your wife, John?" the mayor replied.

Behind her were the townspeople, silent and crimson shadowed. He even spotted the young teen from that morning, arms crossed and frightened.

A sharp pain, an echoing smack, and John fell onto his ass, his hand pressed his cheek.

"Where is she?" Patricia hissed.

"I didn't do anything wrong," John cried. "I just tried to put it back. Back where it belongs!"

The mayor shook her head slowly. She glanced at the clinic, its windows broken, foundation cracked, and a tear ran down her cheek.

"Take him," she said.

"No!" John screamed. "Please!"

He scrambled back, along the dirt, but they were faster despite the earthquakes. Hands fell on him, tore his clothes, yanked his hair. They pulled him up and he was carried on a sea of fear, thrown into the back of a pickup truck, and tied with rope, gagged with tape.

In the cave, the moonpool blazed red as the uteruses trembled with rage, the very waters of the pool rippling from the muscular convulsions.

John fought against his bindings, the rough rope tore the skin from his wrists and ankles, blood dripped to the stone floor.

"For your violation," the mayor said, standing at the edge of the pool. "For your trespasses."

He was dropped and landed on his hip, a bright flare of pain shot through his body.

"For that and more," Patricia continued. "We give you to the pool."

A man pulled the tape from John's lips and he screamed. Hands hooked under his arms and yanked him to his feet.

"You can't do this! You have no right!'

They threw him into the shallow pool and his head struck the beautiful gems at the bottom. Dazed, he went limp. The water, sweet and smooth, slipped between his lips like a tongue. It reached his throat and he choked.

Around him, soft masses of flesh closed in, pressing against him, warm and firm.

A sharp pain broke through his daze. His upper left thigh. Blood in the water.

Another lance on his left hand.

Another on his neck, his foot, his belly, his shoulder. He tried to scream against the pain but the water gagged him.

A uterus pressed against the side of his face, its cervix reaching up towards him.

No, he mouthed.

The pain of losing his eye was the worst John had ever felt. Half his vision blinked out.

His other eye was taken soon after and he was doused in darkness.

I should have drowned by now, I should have been released.

But the pool would not let him go. He felt every bite, every nibble, as the uteruses of Moonfell ate him alive.

With a passion for cosmic horror and sci-fi horror, **P.L. McMillan**'s short fiction has appeared in a variety of anthologies and magazines such as *Cosmic Horror Monthly*, *Strange Lands Short Stories*, *Negative Space*, and *AHH! That's What I Call Horror*, as well as adapted to audio forms for podcasts like *NoSleep* and *Nocturnal Transmissions*. In addition to her short stories, McMillan's debut collection, *What Remains When The Stars Burn Out*, and debut novella, *Sisters of the Crimson Vine*, are available now. Find her at plmcmillan.com.

Within the Naga's Coils

Rachel Searcey

The phone rang, deep within the house. Then, darling Charlotte's wails followed. The call had disrupted her nap.

I leaned against the window frame and peered between the parted curtains. From the top floor of the house, I could see for miles. A steady wind bent the dry grass almost horizontal and the sole oak tree in the middle of the field whipped back and forth. A cramp rippled through my abdomen, circled my navel, and then shot down my legs. I staggered back to the bed to stretch out before I lost all sensation.

Choking down nausea, I watched as my toes stopped wiggling, refusing to listen to my brain's commands.

Even with the fan on high, the heat was stifling. Sweat prickled under my armpits and along my back, yet everything below my waist felt cold as ice. I pulled the cotton sheet over myself and collapsed against the mound of down pillows. My heart pounded in my head and my vision began to tunnel. I took a deep breath and let it out until the feeling subsided. Walking, let alone standing still for a few moments, wasn't worth the effort anymore.

I heard my mother's padding footsteps up two flights of carpeted stairs, subtle beneath Charlotte's ear-piercing cry. I braced myself when the door knob turned.

Mother scowled as her eyes roved over the state of the bed and the mess of tissues left on my bedside table. Charlotte squirmed on her hip, reaching for me, but my mother held her still, hand digging into my child's thigh.

"You're hurting her," I said and reached to take Charlotte, but Mother twisted away.

"Don't strain yourself. She's just like you were at this age: fussy and never happy. I know how to handle her." She thrust the portable at me. "Cillian's on the phone."

I took it from her and pressed it to my chest, expecting her to leave the room. Instead, she found the trash bin and began to fill it with crumpled tissues and the remains of breakfast, all the while glancing at me out of the corner of her eye. She jiggled Charlotte on her hip and took more time than she needed to. "Shush now, let mommy talk to daddy." Charlotte beat her tiny fists against my mother's shoulder, but she quieted.

Resigned, I brought the phone to my ear and watched my mother make her way around the room. Charlotte's wet tomato-red face was buried in my mother's shoulder. I ached to hold her, but Mother was right, I was exhausted.

"How are you feeling?" Cillian asked. His voice sounded distant and muffled. There was a bass thumping, like music in the background.

"I'm okay, you know how it is." I tried to sit up and stifled a gasp when pain rippled through my abdomen. I pushed my hand against my navel, ran my fingers along the divot, where the pain was the worst. Mother glanced at me and frowned.

"I'm sorry you're not feeling well." He was sincere, as always, and I loved him for it.

"How's Hong Kong?" I asked. "What time is it there? It must be the middle of the night."

"The guys wanted to take me out to dinner. I just got back to the hotel. Tomorrow is meetings all day and night, so I might not be able to call." He muffled the phone with his hand and spoke to someone nearby. "Gotta go, baby. Burton's waiting. I love you."

"Love you."

The line went dead. I set the portable on the nightstand and closed my eyes.

"How's Cillian?" Mother asked, putting the phone in her dress pocket.

I turned away from her, head buried in the down pillow. "He's fine."

"I wish I could go abroad. I was invited by some girl friends, you know, but with Charlotte..." Her voice trailed off, wistful and full of longing.

"We would be fine, if you wanted to go," I said. "Cillian was open to hiring someone. We can afford it."

"Oh no. Out of the question." She smiled at Charlotte. "I wouldn't dream of it." Mother gave one last look around the room and nodded. "Much better," she said.

"Can you leave Charlotte?"

Mother cocked her head at me. "You're looking tired. I'll feed Charlotte lunch and take her for a walk this afternoon."

"I feel fine."

Mother shook her head. "Get some rest and I'll come back later with your lunch and meds." She left, closing the door behind her.

I let out a hiss of frustration, pulled the sheets over my head, and was assailed by my body odor. How long had it been since I'd bathed properly? I remembered the glorious hot shower after giving birth. Taking a bubble bath when the stitches had healed. *Over six months ago.*

After I was bed-ridden, Cillian helped me into the bath. But he was rarely home these days. And I refused to let Mother do it. I'd rather stink. Nobody was looking at me anyway.

Dr. Chawla's cold fingers probed the area around my navel, which had become mottled and bruised. I winced and clenched my teeth as my eyes watered.

"That hurts."

"Mara says your appetite is poor."

I glanced at Mother, sitting on the edge of the bed with a smile plastered on her face. She had dressed up for the doctor. Showy costume jewelry dripped from her ears, her neck, her wrists. Nails painted, make-up done. Hair pulled into a low bun. The gaudy flower pattern on her dress hurt my eyes.

I felt like a ghoul in my ratty nightgown pulled up under my breasts. Matronly, shapeless underwear—worn for comfort and ease of moving to the side when I used the bedpan.

"No, I've been eating." I shot Mother a questioning look. What had she been telling him?

"Charlotte eats more than she does," Mother said, a lilting tone entering her voice. Was she *flirting* with him?

I pulled the nightgown over myself, relieved to keep my dead half out of sight.

"The blood draw returned nothing conclusive. You'll need to see a specialist in Dallas, maybe stay for observation."

"Yes, of course. But my mother doesn't drive. We are grateful you came to us. All this way."

"When does your husband return?"

"Not for another month."

"I'll make some phone calls and see about arranging a ride for you."

"Thank you." Hope rose in my chest and I almost cried.

"Doctor," Mother said. "Will this affect her ability to have children?"

"Mother, *please,*" I said. She *knew* Cillian and I had agreed to one child, even before this mysterious ailment.

The doctor hesitated, looking between us, unsure of who to talk to first. "There's no way to tell until we've done further tests. I can't believe you waited so long to see somebody about this."

Mother's voice was ice cold. "We thought she would get better."

Dr. Chawla narrowed his eyes at her. I stifled a smile. How many times had Mother told me I was overreacting? *Wait a few more days... wait until Cillian gets home, ask for his advice.*

"Better late than never, but please don't hesitate to call if you need anything." He held out a business card but Mother snatched it before I could take it.

"Yes, doctor, thank you." I tried not to assign malice to her actions but she made it difficult.

"Continue the multi-vitamins and I'll write you a prescription for the pain. Meanwhile, sleep on your back and no weight on your abdomen. Stay off your feet." He scribbled something on a pad and Mother took it from him. Her hand brushed against his.

"I'll get this filled," she said, her black eyes hard as stone.

"We'll figure this out," he said, a reassuring hand on my shoulder.

The red clock face numbers were seared into my eyelids when I closed them, showing up green against the black void. Three in the morning and I couldn't sleep. I wished I was already at the hospital, not trapped in the guest bedroom. Cillian insisted I sleep here, where I could have my own space, but I hated it.

I hadn't even had a chance to decorate this room. We moved in right before Charlotte was born. The room still smelled of fresh paint and new carpet. Mother had put plain blackout curtains over the windows.

Mother refused to bring the phone or television upstairs, saying it would overstimulate me. Arguing with her did no good. She insisted she had my best interests at heart. Of course she did.

The fan fluttered against the ceiling. Wind hissed against the house and wormed its way into the attic above me to sing between the slats.

My intestines seemed to be wriggling around like worms. I wiped sweat from my brow with the towel Mother had left me. Every time I took a sip of water, the liquid coursed through me in moments and I had to pee. The bedpan was full and Mother wouldn't come upstairs for another three hours.

A pile of unread books on my nightstand seemed to mock me. Trying to focus on the small text made my eyes hurt and triggered nausea.

In the light of the clock face, I pulled up my nightgown to inspect myself, probing with anxious fingers. The bruising seemed to have spread, across my hips, towards my pelvis. I whimpered in spite of myself. My belly button was a deep purple, almost black.

Hoping it was a trick of the light in the dark room, I turned on the bedside lamp.

The shadow remained, as if the divot had been marked with black ink. I almost expected my finger to sink inside when I pressed against it, clenching my teeth when the pain traveled like lightning through my nervous system. But it *felt* like my belly button.

I tried to look at my hips and back, to no avail. I couldn't see. The dead weight of my legs kept me from moving very far. Feeling hadn't returned since yesterday, after my foolish attempt to look out the goddamn window.

Beneath the hiss of the wind, I heard Charlotte crying. She slept in Mother's room on the bottom floor. My hands clenched at my sides as I waited for her to stop, for my mother to comfort her in my stead. I pressed my fists against my closed eyelids and wiped away the hot tears.

Charlotte needed *me,* not Mother. All I could do was lay here.

Useless. *Broken.*

No wonder Cillian stayed away. My stifled cries caused my throat to clench up. A weight settled on my chest and I willed my ribcage to collapse, the bones cracking one by one until there was nothing left of me.

I dry swallowed my sleeping meds, wincing as the bitter pills lodged in my throat. But I refused to drink any more water.

I awoke to blazing sunlight. The curtains on either side had been thrown open but there was no sign of Mother. No breakfast, either. The clock read 10 a.m. I was wrapped up in the sheet like a mummy, a result of my restless sleep.

My mouth felt like it was stuffed with cotton and my head was pounding. Punishment for taking a second dose of the sleeping meds. Only a mouthful of water remained in my glass on the nightstand and I swallowed it in one go.

My bladder protested and I pulled the dangerously full bedpan towards me. Mother hadn't emptied it this morning. I'd hold it until she returned.

The only sound was the wind blowing through the attic. Did she leave? Was there an emergency? Maybe something had happened to Charlotte.

I pushed myself up on the pillows and tried to think what to do.

"Mother?" I yelled, hoping my voice would penetrate the closed door and down two flights of stairs. I had wanted a little bell but Mother was insulted, saying she wasn't "the help" and would be checking on me regularly.

Stop complaining. You're always worrying too much.

I bit the inside of my lip and waited.

The phone rang a dozen times, before whoever was calling gave up. I didn't hear the answering machine pick up either.

My dry throat strangled my voice when I called for Mother again. This had never happened before. She was always here. I imagined her sprawled on the kitchen floor—a heart attack or a stroke. But she was a healthy fifty-six years old.

Charlotte's piercing cry shattered the silence. My heart caught in my throat. I moved to get out of bed, not thinking, and felt myself starting to fall. My hand caught on the edge of the nightstand but my hip bone hit the floor with a jolt. I cried out, gasping in pain as I righted myself.

The nightgown was tangled in the sheet up to my ribs. My legs were numb and my arms were weak from months of inactivity. Wrestling it free, I began to weep when my gown pulled up and I saw the state of my lower half. Bruised and fragile, like fruit left to rot in the sun. The area around my navel was a pool of blackened flesh. Purple and yellow smudges, as if I'd been beaten, radiated down my legs to my deadened feet. My fingers sank into the broken flesh, which cracked and oozed when I applied pressure.

I screamed, my wails echoing Charlotte's.

With no other option, I began to crawl across the floor, using my forearms. The carpet burned against my skin as I made my way to the door. I was panting when I reached the top of the stairs. I rested my cheek against the step.

The aroma of meat frying wafted up the stairs. The rattle of a pan on the stove. *Mother was home.*

"Mother!" I screeched. Why was she making me do this? Why was she ignoring me? My stomach cramped with hunger. I'd have to climb down head first and hope I didn't fall.

Looking back the way I came, I'd left a streak of fluids from the bedroom to the stairs. A yellow-brown trail soaked into the carpet. A rotten smell rose from the broken skin on my body which had stretched and rent open.

My midsection had lengthened by over a hands-length. I could feel my hip bones, much lower than they were supposed to be. But it was like touching a dead body. I felt nothing as my fingers probed the soft flesh.

Maybe I was dreaming. I laughed, realizing I must have overdosed on the sleeping meds and was now having vivid, lucid fever dreams. All my fears manifested in one convenient package. A direct result of going stir crazy in the top floor of the house with only my overbearing mother for company.

I placed my hand on the first step and as I lowered down, the sensation began as a steady pull, like warm salt water taffy. Gooey and slow, I slithered down the stairs to the second floor. Cool relief washed over me, as if a pressure valve had been released.

My belly had been stretched into a kind of tail, thin and black. Ragged on the end where it had pulled free. I covered myself with my nightgown, discolored with fluids and scrunched around my breasts.

When I descended to the second floor, the tail stretched like taffy and my useless legs remained on the third floor step. As I watched, they disintegrated into a mushy puddle dribbling down the stairs.

The final flight was much easier and I used my hands to walk.

I passed the kitchen and inhaled the lovely scent of curry emanating from a large skillet on the stove. Charlotte was still crying, down the hall in Mother's room.

I opened the door.

First, I saw Charlotte, standing in her crib, rattling the bars like a tiny prisoner. Her face was swollen from crying.

Then I saw the man in Mother's bed.

"Dr. Chawla?" I said, confused.

He had been sitting upright against the pillows, reading a book. I stared at him and he stared at me.

"Why are you wearing my husband's pajamas?" I asked.

He reached a hand to the pile of blankets on the other half of the bed and shook it. I realized it was my mother, who rolled over, still half-asleep.

Mother sat up, eyes agog. "This isn't what it looks like, baby," she said.

Dr. Chawla stood and hurried to the dresser where he pulled out slacks and a shirt. He dressed himself with his back turned to me.

"I can explain," Mother said.

I laughed and slithered further into the room, pulling my tail behind me. "Is he actually a doctor?"

Mother gasped when she saw what had become of my lower half. The man—was Chawla his real name?—turned at her exclamation. The noise erupting from his throat was like a frog choking on an insect.

gluglugluglug

I couldn't help myself and collapsed my head onto my forearms, my shoulders heaving with laughter. Charlotte screamed all the louder, reaching for Mother. "I wish I could wake up," I said to myself.

The man skirted the back wall and climbed onto the bed, over my mother. She grasped at his arm but he wrenched it free when he stepped off the bed. He kept to my right, his eyes never leaving my elongated, ragged torso.

His bare feet slipped in the trail I left behind, but he caught himself and took off running. I heard the front door slam open and then an engine start.

Mother realized he was leaving and rose from the bed to follow him.

"Wait! Take me with you!" she shouted. She struggled into a robe to cover the flimsy slip she was wearing.

I grabbed at her ankle to stop her from leaving the room.

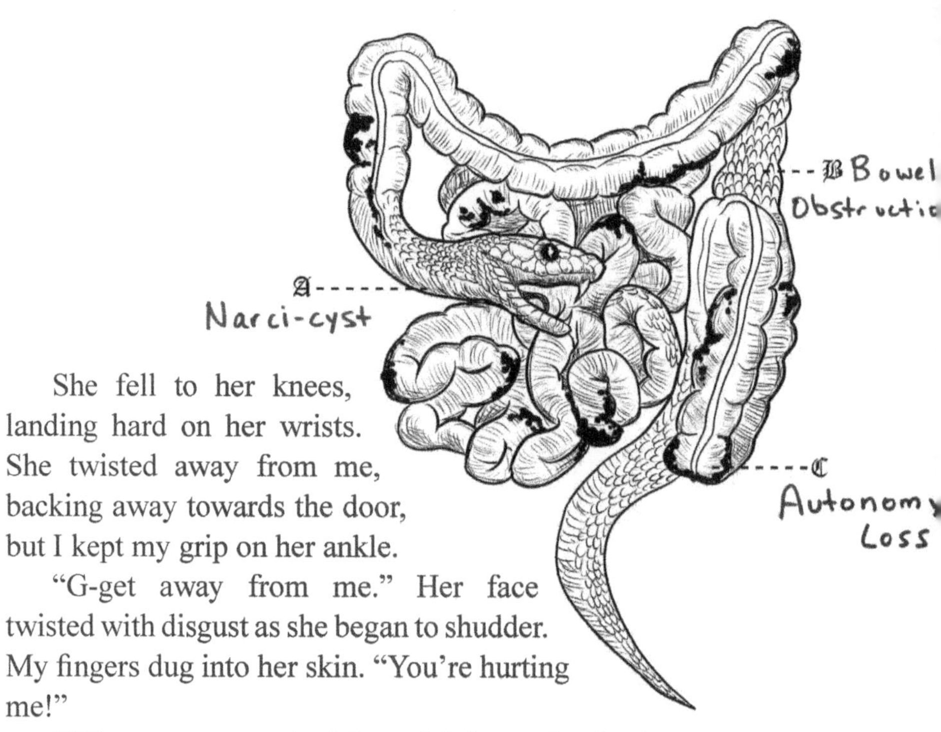

She fell to her knees, landing hard on her wrists. She twisted away from me, backing away towards the door, but I kept my grip on her ankle.

"G-get away from me." Her face twisted with disgust as she began to shudder. My fingers dug into her skin. "You're hurting me!"

"Where are you going? I need help getting back to bed."

I climbed up her body until I was laying on top of her. She was shaking so badly, she must not realize she could have easily pushed me off. Her body felt warm and alive, in contrast to the aching cold which seemed to emanate from within me.

"I'm sorry, baby. I can explain—"

I didn't want an explanation. "You're not taking care of Charlotte. Or me, anymore."

I placed my hands on her throat and pressed. Little white droplets of spittle frothed on her lips. Her fists beat at my back and head, but I felt nothing.

Her eyes rolled back and she went still. I laid my head on her chest and listened to her heart slow until it stopped. She was still warm. Mother's chest smelled like the curry, still simmering on the stove top.

Charlotte had quieted and lay asleep in her crib. I crawled over to look but decided to leave her be. Her little face was peaceful, unlike all the times my mother brought her up to my room. My fingers grazed the soft spot on her skull. I smoothed down her wispy black hair, mussed from her tantrum.

A gust of wind swept through the house. The front door must still be open. I dragged myself to the foyer. My tail whipped behind me, as if it had a mind of its own. Hot, billowing air brought dust into the house, across the cold tiles.

My arms gave out and I collapsed on the wood porch slats. A howling rose from the yard as a dust devil whipped at the sand. Parched dirt still held tire tracks from the man's car, but the wind was taking them away. The small whirlwind died as soon as it started.

When I closed my eyes, the wind rustling the grass sounded like the ocean. The phone rang in the house, but exhaustion overcame me. I would rest on the porch until I felt better, and maybe I would be whole again when I woke up.

Rachel Searcey is a filmmaker and writer living in the Florida panhandle with her husband, two children, and three cats (2 black, 1 torti). She's bi-racial—Indian and white— and has recently ventured into prose after over two decades of producing indie horror films. Her work has been published in *Cosmic Horror Monthly*, *Diet Milk Magazine*, *Flash Point SF*, *Aphotic Realm*, *Dark Void Magazine*, and *Collage Macabre: An Exhibition of Art Horror*. To view Rachel's films and news on published works, visit agirlandhergoldfish.com

Section IV

THE REST

The Resurrectionist

Bryan Young

She cut into the body in the flicker of candlelight. The scent of formaldehyde got stronger with every nick until she no longer noticed it. She splayed the skin of the cadaver's wrist and hooked it open so she could see the inner workings.

First it was the tendons, ligaments, and nerves.

She sliced each of these away to reveal the bone. Then, she continued these cuts, higher and higher into the hand, revealing the bones of the corpse's middle finger.

The carpals.

The metacarpals.

Working her way up the lifeless fingers, she cut into the joints and phalanges of the middle fingertip, wondering what the incisions would feel like if the cadaver were still alive.

She stopped every once in a while to make a note of something she saw. Some anomaly. She drew the hand in her notebook in great detail, labeling everything she found. That was the grim assignment and she had to learn every part.

Every cadaver was different, but she avoided looking at their necrotic faces as much as she could while she worked. She wanted to make sure she was focused on the job. It made the atmosphere of the place more bearable.

It was bad enough they made her study in the old stone morgue alone, but they made her do it at night, too. "It would be improper for you to do this with the rest of the students," the head professor told her. What he really meant was that it wasn't proper at all for a woman to learn to be a doctor and he was trying to scare her from the profession.

But she was determined. More than once she'd thought of turning the scalpel on him when he said something to try to discourage her and send her back to a "proper" life she wanted no part of. It was nearing the start of the twentieth century and she'd be damned if she wasn't part of a change for women for the better, even if she were the only one for now.

The candle flashed with a gust of air and it drew her attention up, away from the exposed hand below her.

What she saw was a field of bodies covered with white sheets, still ghosts in the darkness. The noses and breasts of each silent corpse made peaks and valleys of the white mountains of their temporary graves.

A shiver ran cold across her shoulders.

Once the students were done with their examinations, the cadavers would be buried in the pauper's grave. Until then, they'd be poked and prodded. All in the name of science. And learning. And being better doctors.

A tinkling echo bounced across the stone walls.

Was that a boot-step?

No. It sounded more like…water?

TINK-Tink-tink-tink.

Was there a leak somewhere?

She wiped the blood from her hands on the white laboratory apron she wore over her bustled dress and clutched the scalpel like a dagger. Looking down at her hands, she tightened her grip around the scalpel, knowing she would cut into the living as easily as the dead. She must have looked like quite a sight. Her apron was covered in spatters of blood and formaldehyde like an ink-soaked illustration in a penny dreadful.

From the corner of her eye, she caught a flash of motion and turned toward it. Perhaps it was the breeze, but one of the white sheets that hung over another student's cadavers swayed back and forth.

"Hello?" she asked.

But her voice echoed like the sound that drew her attention.

There it was again.

TINK-Tink-tink-tink.

"Hello?" she called out again. "Professor?"

But she knew her professor was gone. He never stayed for her late-night study sessions in the morgue. He was, no doubt, warm at the gentlemen's club, smoking a pipe near a fire in a hardwood room, and carrying on with any number of the other important men in town.

The sound echoed again.

Louder this time.

TINK-TINK-Tink-tink.

It wasn't water. That much she knew. Or dripping of any sort. It was more like the tapping of stone with a blade.

Her guard was up when she imagined it could be a fellow student. One of those vapid young men, bred with a silver spoon in his mouth, creeping into the necromantic classroom on a cold, dark night.

She tightened her fist around the scalpel and narrowed her eyes, hoping it would help her see more clearly through the greasy smoke of the candles. The edge of the knife wavered not at all, steady in her hand like the surgeon she hoped to become.

"Hello?"

She took a step and her heels clicked against the stone floor. The sound she made was distinctly different than the one that haunted her.

If it were a step, it marked the gait of someone sneaking at speed. Or perhaps it was someone hobbling. Which made her think of that fellow student with the brace on his leg. He had one lazy eye that followed his gaze just a second too late.

TINK-TINK-TINK-Tink-tink.

She took another step before the wind picked up.

A gust came through the hallway, matched to the sound of a door opening. The sheets covering the inert bodies flapped and flew. The candle flames quivered in the wind until they winked out, one by one, and the room was black.

And there she stood, gripping the scalpel tighter.

The only breathing body in the room.

Orange lantern light filled the corridor that led to the outside. It offered spare lines of brightness tracing against the contours of the white sheets, reflected off the stone walls.

The door closed and the cold air stilled.

"Hello?" she wanted to say, but nothing came out.

Backing up a step, she couldn't hear the sound of her heels over the slow but heavy footfalls bearing down from the corridor. As the light grew brighter, the sound of labored breathing filled the space.

The wheezing wasn't hers, though.

She held her breath and wondered if she should make a sound. Or if she should hide.

Some part of her argued that she should crawl up onto one of the empty stone slabs and cover herself with a sheet. She'd hold her breath and pretend to be a cadaver and hope no one noticed that she was the only corpse wearing clothes and shoes beneath the shroud.

But the light and sounds were too close.

She couldn't see for sure, but she knew her knuckles were white against the handle of the scalpel. She would be ready to slice open whomever or whatever intruded on her lesson time. The morgue was in the basement and there were no windows. She had nowhere to run.

All she could do was stay and meet whatever terrifying fate the world had in store for her.

Something caught in her throat when she finally glimpsed flesh. White, pale flesh. Shambling toward her. But she couldn't reconcile the sight with the sound. A lantern was held out in front of the staggering tangle of limbs, its fingers bony and bruised, covered in dirt. The legs were faced backward and a bare backside shone at the level of a head. How was it even walking? Or moving?

How was it wheezing?

Did it even have lungs?

She knew more light would illuminate the problem, but she wasn't sure she wanted to see.

Moving unnaturally, it jerked toward her and she gasped, unable to hold her breath any longer.

The foul creature took another few steps into the room and she found herself backing up in time with it, holding the scalpel far in front of her.

The bright, mirrored light of the lantern shone in her face, practically blinding her. She squinted and held a hand up over her eyes, reaching out toward the light as if she could touch it if she tried hard enough.

The light swung away from her and she blinked.

She could no longer see much outside of the bright light of the lamp and the dancing red blob in her own vision. She wondered if this was how a moth felt as it danced near a flame, blind to everything but the one light.

A heaving moan startled her.

The monster exerted great effort and something big came toward her. She swiped instinctively with the scalpel, but all she found was air.

"There we are, love," a gnarled voice said in a thick cockney accent.

She blinked again and could barely believe her eyes. The one form had become two.

But it wasn't speaking to her.

It seemed as though the owner of the voice was talking to the naked body.

The scene before her came into focus, but it didn't help her make sense of it. And it certainly didn't help her feel any more safe.

There was a naked man draped on one of the stone tables, face up. His eyes were open, but they were as dead as he was.

The corpse had been flopped onto the table by a man in tattered clothes. The shabby man was the one clutching the lantern and wheezing with effort.

He was disheveled and if she had seen him on the street, she'd have run in the other direction. His clothes were frayed. His hands were long and thin, just like a corpse. Bony. He wore fingerless gloves and his spindly fingers were caked in as much dirt as his face.

He spotted her and cocked his head in her direction like a curious bird.

"What's this then?" he said thickly.

This time it was aimed at her.

She didn't know if she could even speak until the words tumbled from her chest like dice from a cup. "Who are you? What are you doing here?"

She waved the scalpel in the man's general direction, lacking the precision with the blade she hoped to learn.

"Who am I? I'm the resurrectionist, love..."

The answer brought her no comfort.

"The what?" she said, breathless.

He wiped some of the dirt and sweat from his brow and reached into his coat to withdraw a cigarette. He put it in his mouth and patted around his coat pockets for a match. "I mean, you think these folks just show up here, dearie? That they just walk in and die on the table?"

She looked down at the fresh cadaver, and then to the resurrectionist, splitting her attention between both of them. "I...I don't..."

She didn't quite know what he was saying. And she definitely didn't know how to reply.

The man laughed. "I didn't know anyone was gonna be here, if you know what I mean, else I'd've come at a different time, but when you snatch a corpse, you bring it back when you've got it, if you know what I mean?" He finally found a match in his front pocket and smiled as he scraped it against the stone wall and lit his cigarette, puffing on it happily.

She tilted her head. "What?"

He let out a whole breath of smoke and waved his hand and the cigarette over the bodies in the morgue. "We pluck 'em out 'a the ground. Or other places—tombs, mausoleums, and the like. I even got one right outta the mortuary, bribed the widow. Surely, a fine woman like yourself don't want to know too much about it, do you?"

And to that, she didn't know what to say.

Because he was right. She didn't.

She'd never thought of where they'd come from before. Stealing them, though...That was unseemly.

"Tell you what," he said. "I can see you're none too pleased about our little encounter here. Help me get him to a table, and I'll light your candle and be on my way."

He pointed to one of the empty tables at the back of the room and the stack of covers on the rack behind them. Then, he twisted his neck back and forth until the bones in his back and shoulders popped. "Diggin' is hard work," he said, as though that explained everything.

Then he leaned over and grasped the dead man by his ankles.

But she stood there, frozen.

He looked up at her and furrowed his brow. "Oh, come on. You can cut 'em up but you can't help a sorry old man move 'em?"

She looked between the corpse and the man.

Then she looked down at the wrists of the dead man. Not unlike the wrists of the woman she was dissecting on the table.

They were all just as dead.

And someone would cut into them sooner than later.

She obliged, putting the cork atop her scalpel and then putting the whole thing in the pocket of her apron. Next, she wrapped her hands around the wrists. She never quite liked touching the dead flesh with her own fingers. The wrists were cold, colder than a normal corpse. He'd been out in the snow with this one and the flakes of it had only just melted in the relative warmth of the morgue.

For just a second, the fingers of the dead grazed the inside of her arm and the cold flesh forced a shiver up her back.

"All right, then," he said. "Let's give it the old heave-ho and I'll be out of here in a split and you'll be able to go back to cuttin' corpses in peace and relative quiet then, love."

She held her breath and braced.

He counted. "All right, a one and a two and a three. That's right."

The only thing she liked less than the cold touch of the corpse was the dead weight and stiffness of it in her arms.

"There we go," he said as they carried the man, inch by inch across the stone floor.

She backed up slowly, careful not to bump into any of the other tables or bodies. The last thing she wanted to do was to make a further mess of the morgue. She had to make sure this was the only corpse she had to lift tonight.

They angled themselves around to the closest empty table and lifted the dead man onto the surface.

"That's it," he said as she went to the rack of covers and lifted it up high. She unfurled it like a flag and let it drift down to cover the new addition to the collection.

She didn't say a word to him.

Her heart raced—it hadn't stopped—and she just wanted him to leave.

"I'll be away then," he said as though he'd read her mind. He clutched the cigarette between his teeth, tipped his cap and tightened his scarf and went back to retrieve his lantern. That's when he stopped and looked down at her book, examining the drawing of the torn open hands. "You draw them well. Most who come here can't draw worth nothing, but yours is elegant."

"Oh," she stuttered. "Uh, thank you."

"I must warn, though, be careful with that one. I wouldn't work on him if you knew what was good for you."

She wanted to know what he meant by that, but before she could ask, he turned to face her and pulled the lantern back. The light flickered on his craggy face from below, giving him all the terrifying charm of a disembodied face telling stories. "Cursed he is. You'll see it in his hands. Best leave him for the rest."

Her eyes flicked over to the corpse she'd helped move and she couldn't see anything out of the ordinary, but she hadn't looked too closely.

"Tell your headmaster I'll be by tomorrow to collect on this one. And if you're not staying much later he might get another one besides."

"I'm, uh..." She didn't know. She didn't know what she was going to do. Some part of her said she would leave and simply never return. Was any of this worth it? Did she want to be a doctor that badly? "I'll be here another short while. But after that, it's all yours."

He pulled another match from his pocket, struck it against the stone, and lit the candle closest to the exit for her on his way out.

"Good night then, doctor," he said, skulking back out the way he'd come.

She didn't have the wherewithal to say anything back to him.

The door opened.

The wind burst through the hallway, almost extinguishing the little bit of light she was grateful he'd left her.

When the door closed behind him, she heard the scrape of a shovel against the stone as it echoed in the morgue.

Perhaps he'd been using it as a walking stick…?

She looked around, over the field of bodies, sure one of them would come alive again. That was just the sort of night she was having.

"There's nothing for it," she said to the corpses.

And without explaining herself further to them, she went back to where she'd been standing and stared at the exposed bones of the hand and wrist she'd been working on.

Looking at the blood and bone and muscle, all exposed in layers, she wondered how different it felt from the cold, uncut wrist of the other dead man.

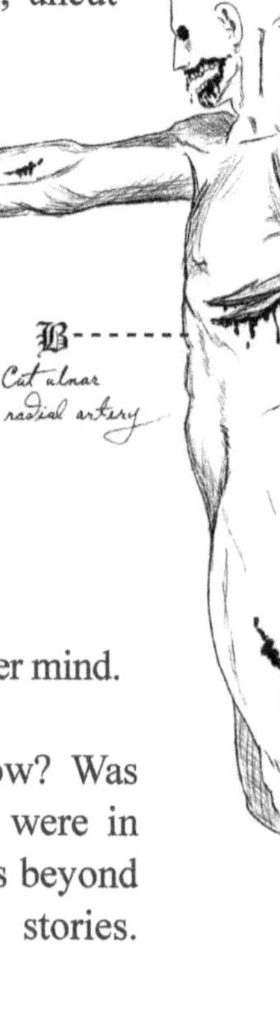

Reaching for the dissected hand, she found her own shaking. Not a good thing for a doctor, and she realized that her heart was pounding. That was it, it was just a fright.

But the word he used echoed in her mind.

Cursed.

That's what he'd said. But how? Was such a thing even possible? They were in the modern world now, and she was beyond superstition, folklore, and ghost stories. Perhaps he meant something else?

Curiosity got the better of her.

Taking in a deep breath, she crept over to the new addition, reaching out for its hands, looking for some mark or blemish that would announce them to be cursed.

The breeze kicked up. The one light left blew out and blackness took the room.

Standing there, holding the dead man's hands, she realized she was in a room full of the dead in the pure black of night and panic rose in her.

It was her own scream she heard when the hand she held gripped back, clutching her wrist tightly.

Pulling away, she felt the body slump to the floor, trying to drag her down with it. She kicked hard, sightless in the dark, trying to extricate herself. Again and again she hit until her hand was freed.

Backing away, hoping whatever curse animated the hand hadn't animated the rest of his naked corpse, she raced to the place she expected to find a candlestick, bumping into other tables on her way.

Reaching into her apron, she withdrew a match and struck it, pausing to see the room before her.

Just as it had been before.

Her heart pounded.

Relighting the candle with a quivering match, she decided firmly to only do her doctoring by day. If the other students had a problem with her, they could come and damn well face the dead alone at night by themselves. Looking down at her hands, trembling from her ordeal, she knew she was through with it.

Bryan Young (he/they) works across many different media. His work as a writer and producer has been called "filmmaking gold" by *The New York Times*. He's also published comic books with Slave Labor Graphics and Image Comics. He's been a regular contributor for the *Huffington Post*, *StarWars.com*, *Star Wars Insider* magazine, *SYFY*, */ Film*, and was the founder and editor in chief of the geek news and review site *Big Shiny Robot!* In 2014, he wrote the critically acclaimed history book, *A Children's Illustrated History of Presidential*

Assassination. He co-authored *Robotech: The Macross Saga RPG* has written five novels in the BattleTech Universe. His latest non-fiction book, *The Big Bang Theory Book of Lists* is a #1 Bestseller on Amazon. His work has won two Diamond Quill awards and in 2023 he was named Writer of the Year by the League of Utah Writers. He teaches writing for *Writer's Digest*, *Script Magazine*, and at the University of Utah. Follow him across social media @swankmotron or visit swankmotron.com.

In Your Image

Kai Delmas

Life becomes death becomes life.

I believe.

Life is unending if we choose to make it so. If we believe and understand.

We discard the old. A waste.

We must ingest the old, become the new. We must seek renewal, be reborn in your image.

Ouroboros watch over me.

My body is not what makes me. My soul is pure and my will is strong. I can change. I will change.

Yesterday I lay in the sun for an hour. Naked, no shade, no clouds.

Samantha would have scolded me for my foolishness. But she left. She didn't understand me before and she wouldn't understand me now.

My skin is pink and it stings when I move. I wish for the itching to begin, for my skin to peel. Oh, Ouroboros, remake me.

Two more nights of aches and itching have passed. The first layer of skin is dead, loose, free. I rub across it, making tiny rolls of skin. I pull at the patches on my arms and legs, my chest and face. They come away in bigger and bigger pieces.

I peel off the old and do what I must to become new.

It tastes of nothing when I place it on my tongue. Some larger pieces have hints of salt. And after I swallow there's an aftertaste of sweetness.

There's much more to eat. I can't let any of it go to waste.

Samantha would have thought me disgusting. Maybe a part of her always did. Is that why she always yelled at me? Is that why she left?

It's her loss. For I will become something better.

In your image.

The first layer is gone but there are many more. The sun burns stronger, my skin reddens more easily. And it peels. It sheds.

I consume it all. I lick my wounds where I begin to blister and bleed. Nothing is wasted.

She thought I would never amount to anything. She thought I didn't have it in me to change.

I'll show her.

Samantha will see me when I am reborn.

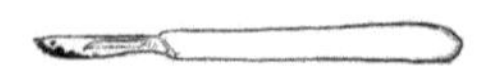

Ouroboros watches over me.

My skin turns hard, scabs become scales. Old becomes new. In your image.

My fingers and toes ache. They thicken, swelling around the nails. The skin splits and bleeds. A nail clatters to the floor. My clumsy fingers can't pick it up, so I lick it off the ground.

It's hard. Can't be chewed. So I swallow it whole. The other nails will fall off soon.

Why wait?

I lift my swollen fingers to my lips and pluck the nails from each with my teeth. Then do the same with my toes.

In with the old. To become the new.

My thighs fused overnight. I can no longer walk. I get used to crawling, to eating my shed skin off the floor. Every day I eat, every day I transform.

If Samantha could see me now. Behold me as I was meant to be.

Would she change her mind? Take me back?

Or would she run away screaming, cursing me? Would she hit me again?

It doesn't matter. Soon I will be something new. I won't need her anymore. I will be better.

In your image.

My teeth wobble and crack. They tumble from my bleeding gums. I don't let them get far.

Some scrape against my throat as I swallow. Others go down easy.

My forked tongue flicks to the roof of my mouth to dislodge the rest. I can feel new fangs growing in.

My arms are one with my torso. My legs, my feet, my toes are gone. Only a tail remains. My old skin has split down the middle. So much dead skin.

I twist and turn. I slither across the floor out of my old self.

My jaw opens wide. Wider. In with the old. What I was, is no more. I am new. Reborn.

In your image.

I no longer need you Samantha. I am better now. I am pure.

My new form slithers through your open window.

My transformation has taught me many things. Most important of all, I was not the problem. I was not bad. Unworthy. Worthless.

Weak, maybe.

But I am strong now.

You're unaware of me as I circle your bed. You only begin to stir when I wrap myself around you. Too late.

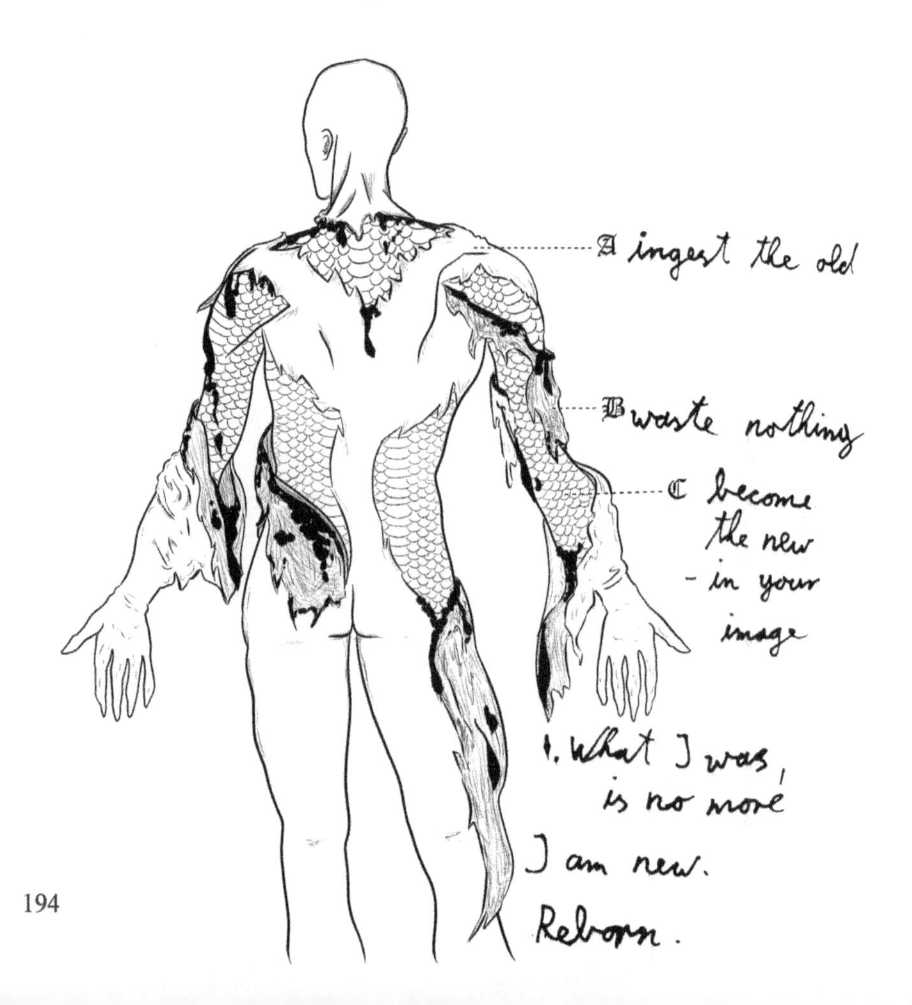

I cut off your scream with the thick scales of my tail coiling around your mouth and neck.

I watch the terror in your eyes.

Oh, Samantha. Ouroboros has granted me not only rebirth but wisdom as well.

You were the problem. You were unhappy and you chose to blame me. I didn't deserve that.

All this time you should have looked upon yourself. That is the only way to better your life. To change.

Well, there is one other way to change.

My fangs flash in the moonlight and my jaw opens wide.

In with the old. Become the new.

In your image.

Kai Delmas loves creating worlds and magic systems. He is a slush reader for *Apex Magazine* and *The Cosmic Background*. His fiction can be found in *Zooscape*, *Martian*, *Crepuscular*, and several Shacklebound anthologies. His debut drabble collection, "Darkness Rises, Hope Remains," was published by Shacklebound Books. If you like his work you can support him at: patreon.com/kaidelmas and find him on Twitter @KaiDelmas or Bluesky @kaidelmas.bsky.social

VINCENT IS A POSEUR ASSHOLE!

DAVID WORN

A parasite. Maybe that's what it was.

I'd read that some parasites stay alive by making themselves useful to the host. Little symbiotic critters that give with one hand and take with the other. If that's what was going on, then the Universe sure had a weird fucking idea about what people would find useful.

But I'm getting ahead of myself.

I'll never forget the first time I saw someone *splash*. It may sound callous, but more than anything, it was the smell. Well, that and the fact that some of it got on my favorite skirt.

It happened as I was on my way to campus for a studio booking. The Art Matters festival was coming up, and as a senior in the art program, I was expected to exhibit a year-end project. So far I had no ideas, no installation, no nothing. It was fucking Vincent! That Instagram poseur asshole had gotten into my head. His little robotic installations draped in animal carcasses were making waves in the circles we ran in. Even our unflappable professors seemed impressed by his work.

But here's the rub: dead animal installations were my thing. When Vincent started in the program, all he did was make shitty little robots with LED lights. Cute, but without any deeper meaning or subtext. After we were paired together on an assignment and he saw my process, he started covering his robots in fur and dead animals. Suddenly, people thought he was edgy. That he had something to say. Bullshit! Vincent only lived for the likes and subscribes.

Anyway, enough about that fucking poseur.

I was headed towards the metro to catch a train downtown. I was late, as usual, and I arrived at the Mont-Royal station just in time to see the ass end of my train disappear down the tunnel.

"Shit."

"Missed it again, hunh?" said a gruff Quebecois voice.

It was Pierre. He sat on a piece of cardboard, his back against the wall, with a can of change and a bilingual sign that read: "Veteran / Vétéran"

"Yep. How's tricks today?" I asked.

"Slow. No love for veteran amputees," he said, rubbing his stump just above the knee. I never knew if this was part of his act or if it really did bother him.

"You're not a veteran," I said.

He gestured to the passengers on the platform. "They don't know that."

There was a pause while I waited for him to ask me the thing.

"So…" he began, "did you bring me breakfast?"

I pulled out an apple from the pocket of my leather jacket and tossed it to him.

He caught it and flashed me a disgusted look. "When you gonna bring me something good? I want a damn smoked meat sandwich."

"Eat your fucking apple, Pierre."

Other passengers trickled off the escalator. A man, dressed in a tan business suit, stumbled into another passenger. He looked like any other office drone taking the morning metro, except for the fact that he was walking around like his legs were made of rubber. He walked past us and stopped by the platform. His torso wobbled back and forth and

I thought he was going to fall on his ass until, like a roly-poly doll, he righted himself.

"What do you make of that guy?" I asked.

Pierre glanced towards the man. "*Trou-de-cul,* never gives me any change."

Then it happened. My first splash.

Later, after the chaos of that first day, when the news reconstructed the timeline of this new global epidemic, I pieced together that this must have been one of the first splashes in the whole world. So yeah, I was at ground zero.

Someone screamed as the man in the suit collapsed in on himself. His entire body turned into a bloody mush that spilled out of his clothing, splashing the pavement like a tub of water dumped out onto a curb. The pressure of all that liquid dropping to the ground caused parts of him to shoot out of his clothing in a torrent of blood, bodily fluids, and…something else.

A single leg, naked but for the man's socks. It sailed out on a sea of blood and liquidized tissues. The growing puddle carried it along until it came to rest inches from Pierre's own stump

The limb lay facing Pierre's amputated leg like some sort of sick cosmic joke.

For a few moments, we both stared at it. The leg was an exact match for Pierre's. Terminating just above the knee and ending in a flat stump of perfect unblemished flesh. Like it was fresh off the factory floor.

I still remember that strange alien feeling. The sudden surreality of it. I couldn't process what I was looking at—my mind throwing error codes like a computer trying to divide by zero.

Then Pierre reached for the limb.

"Pierre, what the fuck?" I cried.

But it was too late. He brought the leg up to his. Stump to stump. Pulling it into his flesh. If I hadn't been right next to him, I might not have noticed the little wisps of skin reaching out from the unblemished leg. Nor would I have heard the faint sucking sound as the limb pulled itself that last half inch until it was completely fused to Pierre.

His face was aglow with a big dumb smile, like a kid on Christmas who'd just been given a fucking Xbox. Pierre slowly got up, using the wall behind him for support. He took a tentative step on his new leg. He wobbled for a second, but the leg held firm.

The next train arrived and the doors opened to a mob of screaming passengers shoving past each other as they spilled out of the train and onto the platform.

My mind was on fucking holiday as I turned from Pierre to the fleeing crowd and back again. I was confused, maybe even in shock. I remember thinking that if everyone else was running, I should probably run too.

So I left Pierre with his new leg and made for the escalator. As I merged with the mass of fleeing passengers, I craned my neck to see towards the now-empty train car.

There, in the middle of the open doors, a puddle of blood and pulped viscera leaked out onto the platform. Inside the puddle was an empty dress, a purse, and a pair of purple pumps.

And a hand.

A pure and perfect hand. The stump covered with taut new flesh, ready to welcome a new owner.

Two weeks later, after the world went to shit, I found myself sitting on a couch in Amy's apartment. We were pre-gaming before heading out to a loft party for festival artists and volunteers. I was on my phone again, doomscrolling through my social media feeds while Amy rolled us a joint.

"Jesus Christ, you won't believe this one." I pointed my phone at her. On the screen was a post from some woman in Los Angeles.

> **Dana Akimbo @dirtybird** *12h* So I was dining at Dresden and Brad Pitt just splashed! No joke. He left behind a finger. Wish it had been his…you know! ;) #celebritysplash #celebritydick

Clive Rooney @splashbroker *12h* @dirtybird
I'll give you 10k in Bitcoin for the finger if you can prove it's Mr. Pitt's. DM ME ASAP!

Amy whistled. "Ten-thousand bucks. Shit, that's not nothing."

"It's sick though, right? Selling pure parts?" I asked.

"Yeah. Besides, fingers aren't that special." Amy sealed the joint and lit it. "My neighbor says she saw someone splash and leave behind a perfect lung! Says an ambulance came and picked it up. She thinks they're going to try and get it to fuse with a lung recipient."

I got an alert on my phone.

"Oh shit, no way!" I exclaimed.

"Who is it this time?" Amy asked.

"Russel fucking Brand."

Amy's eyes went wide. "But isn't he vegan? Fuck…there goes that theory. I saw a YouTube that said it was only killing meat eaters."

We sat in silence for a moment, passing the joint back and forth. Thinking of Russel. Amy broke the silence.

"What are you doing for Art Matters?" she asked.

"Not sure. I have a pig carcass in my freezer. I was thinking of 3D printing human arms and covering them with latex, but with people splashing into blood and guts everywhere, it feels like it's not the right time to make art out of dead animal parts."

Amy took a drag and exhaled a thick plume of smoke. "Why a pig?"

"You've heard how their body parts are compatible with people, right? Like that study from a while back where they washed out the cells in a pig heart and replaced them with human stem cells? So, like, we can transplant their organs into us, to make us live. And yet we still fucking eat bacon. It's practically cannibalism." She passed me the joint. "So the piece is about exploring those similarities between who we are and the things we eat. I was going to call it 'Your children could one day be bacon.'"

"That's fucking great," Amy laughed. "Hey, do you think pure body parts would merge with the pig?"

"What, the carcass?"

"Yeah. What if instead of fake hands, you put pure hands on it?"

"That's wrong!"

"Oh, sweet Charlie. It would be perfect for your message. We're so like the victims of the corporate meat industry that pure hands are willing to merge with a pig! Babe, if it works, it's gonna fucking shake up the *bourgeoisie*!"

"But fuck…" I said, shaking my head, "Human remains? I could get in trouble."

"Everyone's using them. It's all over eBay. Besides, it's not like they're normal body parts that decompose. They're pure! Little gifts."

Amy was on a roll now, a bit tipsy, a bit high, and excited about doing something taboo.

"Like what about your friend with the leg," she said.

"Pierre."

"Exactly. That pure leg showed up, and boom! Life changed. What's Pierre doing now?"

"Still begging for money."

"Really? Shit." Amy sighed. "Okay, sure. But now he can beg and walk."

"That doesn't make it right."

"What's the alternative? Throw out the pure legs and hands and ears? Treat them as medical waste?"

I was getting exasperated. I knew Amy. When she got like this, she wouldn't let go. But it still felt wrong to me. It felt like—

It felt like something Vincent would do.

"Amy, have you fucking looked at YouTube and Instagram lately? It's getting out of hand!"

I was referencing the recent trend among B-list influencers of posting videos and images of themselves with pure body parts attached. Permanently disfiguring themselves for likes and subscribes. The rarer the part, the more popular the post. Something truly rare, like a nose or a woman's breast, and the algorithm shot you right to the top of people's feeds.

For instance, there was a teenager in Ottawa who arranged dozens of pure fingers on her shaved head like a grotesque form of hair. They wiggled whenever she furrowed her brow. And in L.A., a bunch of influencer bros filmed a prank video where they attached a mismatched pair of pure breasts to a kid who had been sleeping off a hangover.

There were also the deaths.

One kid died of asphyxiation as the lung he'd put on his back ripped a new bronchial tube into his trachea. In Vancouver, a teenager filmed herself adding an extra heart to her chest. The pure heart never synchronized with her original one, and the two working together raised her blood pressure so high that she bled to death from aneurysms all over her body. YouTube took that one down instantly, but it was reposted to LiveLeak within minutes.

So far, no one had found a pure brain, but I shuddered to think what some kid on TikTok would do if they ever got their hands on one.

To Amy, this only served to normalize the use of pure body parts. Everyone was doing it. Why, it would be a shame not to!

"You know Vincent is going to jump on that bandwagon if he hasn't already," Amy said. "He's probably already got some stupid pure parts robot lined up for Art Matters."

"Fuck."

Amy was right. Of course, Vincent would stoop to that level. I sank back into the couch, already feeling like I'd lost. Vincent was destined to be the star of the show. That fucking asshole would once again beat me at my own game.

I needed to get smashed.

"Do you have any vodka?" I asked.

The loft party was in full swing when we arrived. The humidity hit us instantly, the air thick with the smell of sweat and weed. At the back of the room, a group of people were dancing to house music. A cloud of cigarette smoke hung above them.

We had just sat down on an empty lounge chair when we were greeted by a familiar nasally voice.

Vincent.

"Well, if it isn't Charlie and Amy Chen!" he said, taking a seat on the sofa facing us. His little art collective minion, Jean-Francois, came and perched himself on the sofa's arm. Next to them, a couple was five seconds away from making out.

Vincent reached into his satchel, pulled out a cigar box, and placed it on the coffee table between us. He looked directly at me—a greasy smirk crept across his face.

"I'm sure you will appreciate the artistic uses of this little beauty." With a dramatic flourish, he opened the lid.

"Behold."

Inside, resting on a bed of bubble wrap, was a pure penis. It lay flaccid, cushioned on its own scrotum. Nestled in a small tuft of black pubic hair. It was like something out of a novelty cake video.

Amy giggled. "It's a bit small. Is it yours?"

Vincent scowled at her. The couple next to him stopped flirting and stared at the contents of the box.

"Is that a pure cock?" the girl asked.

"It is," Vincent responded smugly.

"I heard they're super rare! Where did you get it?"

"Artists never reveal their sources. It's going to be the centerpiece of my installation at the Art Matters showing."

Vincent gave me a shit-eating grin.

What a fucking asshole.

A passerby stopped to gawk at the artifact.

"Holy shit. Is that a pure dick? That's amazing!"

"Can I touch it?" asked the girl on the couch.

"Yeah, go on, *touch it!*" Vincent said, eating up the attention.

The girl reached over and put her index finger on the pure penis. The guy next to her looked on uneasily.

"Oh look at you, little boy. Such a shy little thing." She cooed, caressing the dick with her finger.

Amy and I exchanged eye-rolls.

"Is it gonna get hard?" she asked Vincent.

The guy she was with tried to change the subject: "I saw some chick on Instagram put a pure ear on herself. She says she can hear all these new frequencies and shit. It's like a superpower!"

I blurted out, "That's so fucking stupid."

"No, it's not," replied Vincent. "It's the new transhumanism! Pure part body mod is the future. That's what my piece is about and it's why I'm gonna win. Making installations with animal carcasses is so last year."

Asshole!

I felt Amy tug at my arm. "Come on, let's dance."

We left Vincent and his admirers and joined the sweaty mass of people dancing to the thumping beat. Once inside the crowd, I found it easy to forget about him. Amy and I shared another joint and sang along to the diva vocals.

As always happened when Amy and I went out, some guy or some girl would come sliding in, trying to break up our team. Sometimes Amy entertained them, sometimes she went home with them, but tonight she had my back. Amy gave this particular dude the finger and he slinked back to his friends.

We sat out on the fire escape for a time, cooling off and mingling with acquaintances who came outside for a smoke.

Eventually, we found ourselves back on the same lounge chair. A group of people now stood around the coffee table, admiring Vincent's pure dick. Vincent, however, was nowhere to be found. Instead, his minion J.F. was watching over the cock like a hawk, making sure no one would run off with it. He cradled the box protectively with his hands and answered questions from the onlookers in a slurred voice. He looked fucking plastered.

"Hey J.F., where's your master?" asked Amy.

"He's not my master, okay? We're co-equal partners of FUCK ARTS collective," he replied in an annoyed voice.

Amy couldn't resist teasing him. "FUCK ARTS collective? Ohhhh, *you mean FARTS?*"

Jean-Francois' eyes widened, and he looked about to cry.

"Fuck you, bitches. No one cares about your dead animal installations. Vincent's work is groundbreaking!"

"Chill, dickface," said Amy.

"I'm not a dickface!"

There was a pause, then his face lit up with a fucking eureka.

"But this is a dickface."

He reached into the box and grabbed the pure cock by the shaft and held it in front of his forehead. The stump hovered inches from his skin, and again I saw the hungry wisps of new flesh reach out.

"J.F., don't," I shouted.

"It's okay, I'm not actually dumb enough to let the stump touch me," he said.

He stood up and wagged the flaccid dick around, pursing his lips and posing like a sexy runway model. The crowd around him roared with laughter. Maybe it was the weed, or the liquor, or just the insane incongruity of it all, but Amy and I couldn't help but join in.

I noticed him first.

The drunk guy stumbling around and bumping into people behind J.F. Before I could say anything to warn him, the guy tripped on the edge of an area rug and slammed into J.F.'s back. There was a slapping sound as J.F.'s forehead smacked into the fleshy stump of the pure dick.

Time stood still.

J.F. stared up at the pure cock in his hands. He let go and it stayed aloft. His hands traveled up and felt around, brushing against the thing's balls. He took a gentle exploratory tug but it held firm. The skin of the stump had fused to his forehead.

"No! No, no, no!" J.F.'s voice rose to a hysterical pitch. He pulled on the flaccid shaft of the penis, desperately trying to remove the dick from his head.

"FUUUUUCK."

From across the room, Vincent came running.

"That better not be my dick on your face," he yelled.

Vincent ran up and grabbed at the scrotum behind J.F.'s hands and pulled with all his might.

"It's not coming off. Oh my God!" J.F. wailed.

The drunk guy who had tripped into J.F. stood watching. Slowly, it dawned on him that he had somehow caused this.

"Oh, shit. I'm sorry, eh."

He moved in and got his hands on the glands of the penis and started pulling on the tip. The uncircumcised foreskin of the pure dick stretched out so far it looked like it might tear.

"Give it back! I need it for my show you fucking idiot," Vincent yelled.

Next to me, Amy exclaimed, "Holy shit" amidst fits of giggles.

As news of the accident spread through the party, a crowd gathered around us and watched as the three men, their arms locked together in some insane form of twister, grunted as they pulled and tugged on the pure dick.

And then, from somewhere nearby, we heard a familiar sound.

Splash.

The wet squelch of someone splashing out. Blood shot out across the floor and everyone looked around to see who it was. I felt something wet against my leg. I jumped up, pulling Amy with me as a miniskirt and a pair of pink thongs floated by on a river of blood and liquidized viscera. The smell hadn't hit us yet, but it was coming.

Someone slipped in the people puddle and fell, sending a hand—a perfect pure hand—skidding across the floor towards us. As the crowd broke up and rushed for the exit, Amy grabbed the hand, threw it into her handbag, and gave me a mischievous wink.

Vincent noticed.

He knows exactly what that's for, I thought. Well, fuck it! Let him have a taste of his own medicine. I decided then and there that I *would* use the pure parts. I would make my fucking installation into something shocking and new. I wasn't going to let this copycat poseur asshole upstage me anymore.

I gave Vincent the finger and followed Amy out of the loft and into the night. Still giddy from the excitement and alcohol, we entered a metro station and descended the escalator toward the platform. Amy opened her bag and pulled out the pure hand.

"Be careful with that thing," I squealed.

Amy laughed. "It's perfectly safe, as long as we don't touch the stump."

"Who even was that?"

"Pretty sure it was Catherine."

"Oh shit, I liked her. She did those video installations. I gave her a hand setting up the projectors once."

"Well, now she'll be the one giving you a hand!"

"Amy!" I scolded.

From below, a crowd of people rushed back up the escalator in the wrong direction.

"What's going on?" I asked.

"Someone splashed," said one guy. "I'd take the stairs if I were you."

Looking over the man's shoulder, I saw a few drunk guys at the bottom of the escalator daring themselves to jump over the people puddle. One by one they cleared it, all except for the last of them who missed his jump and landed on his ass in the mush.

"*Calisse, mes Diesels,*" he swore in French, referring to either his designer jeans or designer sneakers.

As we walked past the puddle, Amy spotted another pure hand obscured by the escalator handrail.

She picked it up and waved it at me.

"Two down, two to go!"

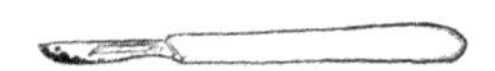

Things were fucking glorious!

The artistic block that had been wearing me down these past months was gone. Working with the pure hands was inspiring. It felt transgressive, like the first time I'd used an animal carcass. Ever since Vincent started copying my style, I felt like I was playing catchup at my own game. His flashy robotic bullshit was like a strobe light sucking up all the attention.

But not this time motherfucker. This time, *I* was going to be the one to shock the *bourgeoisie.*

In the days leading up to the festival, I spent every waking moment at the studio, gobbling up open slots and cancellations, no matter the hour. There was, however, still the problem of the hands. We lucked out in finding two pure hands the night of the party, but since then, nothing. Amy was on the lookout, inspecting people puddles she came across. Most times these were already picked over. She did find a foot once, and we briefly considered whether the pig carcass should have two hands and two feet, but ultimately I felt like four hands worked better visually. At any rate, with only days to go, she managed to find a local pure parts broker who sold us two mismatched hands for $250 in crypto. I'd have to live off Kraft Dinner and bum cigarettes for the next month, but to see the look on Vincent's face when my installation trounced whatever shitty robot he exhibited was going to be worth it.

Meanwhile, the world kept turning. A rash of spontaneous liquifications among online influencers who had done pure parts body mod had spooked the authorities. The University's president had written an email imploring students to stop collecting, selling, or using pure parts. He'd framed it as *out of respect for the deceased*—yeah, that ship has sailed buddy. Things got so bad that Health Canada went so far as to announce a buyback program for anyone hoarding pure parts.

Anyway, whatever. The world is always going to shit in some way or another. *Plus ça change, plus c'est la même chose.*

Meanwhile, my installation was fucking baller! The pure hands had merged seamlessly with the pig carcass, the new flesh sucking itself into the sockets where the pig's legs had once been. I kept the whole thing in my freezer and planned to stuff it full of dry ice before the showing so it didn't stink up the exhibit space.

In the studio, I built a funhouse version of a child's bedroom, with a pig-sized bed and a pig-sized toybox. I'd even photoshopped the pig into those generic family photo inserts you get when you buy cheap photo frames and placed them around the room. The night of the showing, the pig was going to sit in the middle of the installation with a bright red ball in front of its snout as if caught mid-play. The artwork label would read: *"Your child could one day, too, become someone else's bacon."*

When the big day finally came, Amy helped me lug my cooler with the pig carcass in it to the festival space at the Montreal Musée d'Art Contemporain. I was setting it all up when Amy called over to me.

"You'll never fucking guess who your neighbor is."

I looked up at the space across from mine—a sheet was draped over the installation, but I could make out the hard edges of something mechanical.

Vincent.

"His title is a mouthful of shit," she said.

I came over and read the print on the small artwork label.

> **Vincent Paradis**
> *"The Body is an Illusion to be Deconstructed into Fantastically Engineered Artifacts"*
> Robotics, Microcontrollers, Flesh, Pure Parts.

People were going to eat it up. Pretentious title, robots, pure parts. *Fuck.*

"Yours will be great, hon, don't worry." Amy put her arm around me and led me away from Vincent's installation. "Now, come on, let's go get spectacularly drunk and come back after opening."

When we returned a few hours later, the museum was packed. It was ten o'clock on a Friday night in Montreal and, as is custom, everyone was a little sloppy on the cheap beer and glasses of *depanneur* wine being sold in the foyer. The installations were in the museum's Mezzanine area with other mediums (sculpture, intermedia, visual arts, etc.) in the adjoining gallery rooms. This meant that everyone had to pass through our installations to see any of the other works.

We were the center of the universe and in the middle of it all was my piece.

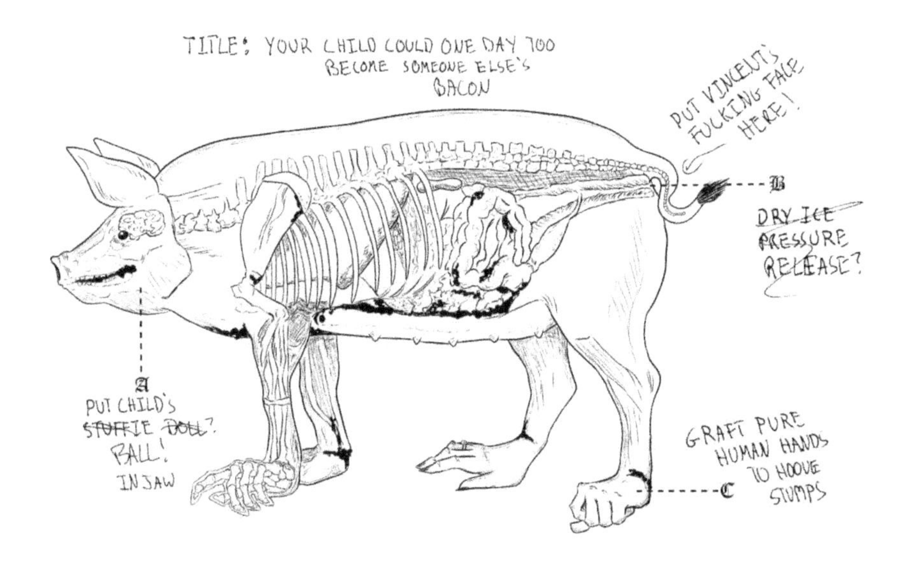

I covered my eyes and told Amy to look.

"Hon, it's packed! You have a ton of people." She pried my hands off my eyes and I saw the wall of people gathered around my piece.

Did they like it? Or were they just collectively trashing it?

One of my classmates walked by and gave me a thumbs-up. "Charlie, your pure parts pig is genius. Nice one!"

As we moved closer to the crowd, I glanced toward Vincent's installation and laughed. There was no one there.

He had done his usual thing, of course. Crappy robots locked in repetitive movements, servo motors, and wiring conspicuously exposed—Vincent never made any effort to hide those. I was pretty sure he did that to make his pieces look *complicated,* as though he alone knew how to solder.

Towering over the smaller robots was a large sheet metal circle covered in faux flesh latex. Around the circumference were dozens of pure fingers and in the middle was a pure foot. It looked sloppy and incongruous, and it dawned on me that *that* was where Vincent's pure dick was supposed to have gone. The entire contraption spun around like a gruesome Carnival wheel. It was eye-catching, sure, but totally meaningless.

Vincent's lap dog, J.F., peeled off from the crowd and intercepted us. He was wearing a winter toque that did little to conceal the bulge of the pure dick still fused to his forehead.

"Vincent is pissed off at you Charlie. Your pig is practically plagiarism," he said.

"The fuck it is! I was using animal parts way before Vincent," I exclaimed.

"Whatever man, I'm just the messenger."

"Hey," said Amy, pointing at his hat. "You know you got some pubes sticking out."

I added, "Yeah, you might want to shave those balls buddy."

J.F. reached up and felt the bottom of the scrotum peeking out from under the lip of his hat and his face fell.

"Why are you such bitches?" He whined and rushed away.

Among the onlookers, I recognized two faculty members from my program nodding approvingly as they eyed my piece. One of the festival organizers spotted me and came over.

"Charlie, your pure parts piece is a hit. A reporter from the *Voir* wants to talk to you."

Then it happened.

There was a gasp from the onlookers followed by a meaty crash. I pushed through the crowd to see.

My pig had fallen off its stand and was lying on the floor, jerking back and forth as the fingers on its pure hands twitched away at high speed.

"Must be a timed circuit. Very clever," said one of the faculty members.

Someone grabbed my arm hard and spun me around.

Vincent.

He looked livid. For a moment I thought he was going to hit me.

"You fucking copycat bitch." He pointed at the pig and then at himself. "I do the robots!"

Vincent shoved past me and crossed over the marked-off space and into my installation. One of the student organizers tried to hold him back, but he shook her off and went over and kicked my pig. His foot embedded into the flesh of the carcass, letting out a whiff of dry ice smoke. As he worked to free his designer sneaker, all four pure hands jerked and twitched with increasing intensity.

"Fucking robot!" shouted Vincent and he kicked the pig carcass again. "Where's the circuitry?"

I didn't understand what was happening. There was no circuitry. No motors. It wasn't supposed to move like that. Something was very wrong with my pig.

Then a voice caught all our attention.

It was Amy. She was in Vincent's installation space, next to his big carnival wheel of fingers.

"Hey Vincent! Oopsies!" Amy sent the enormous wheel crashing over onto the ground, the pure parts scattering across the floor.

Vincent ripped his foot from my pig, nearly tripping over his own leg to get to his installation.

"I'm going to kill you," he shouted at Amy. He reached the broken wheel and ripped one of the pure fingers off its mount.

The smile instantly disappeared from Amy's face as she realized his intention. *He's going to stick it on her!* Vincent jabbed the finger towards Amy, stump first, and was just about to hit her in the face when a student organizer collided with him. He tripped sideways into a middle-aged woman in a dress. As he fell to the ground, the finger brushed the woman's skin and the stump fused to her ankle.

She cried out in horror.

Then she splashed.

The blood and mess hit Vincent in the face, and he gagged on her fluids. The woman's husband stood in shock as he held his wife's empty clothing in his hands.

For a moment the room was quiet, then someone screamed, and the crowd rushed for the exit. But only a part of it. Many still stood around, peering over heads, trying to see what had happened. To see what pure body part this insane cosmic lottery had left behind this time.

It was the woman's arm. From fingertip to shoulder. And Vincent held onto it with both hands, a crazed look in his eyes. He advanced toward Amy, waving the stump at her. She scrambled backwards and fell on her ass into the people puddle.

I was running to her aid when someone grabbed me, locking my arms behind my back. It was J.F. The little FARTS fucker snuck up on me.

"Vincent, forget her. I got Charlie!" he shouted.

Vincent turned and smiled. He left Amy and made his way toward us. The student organizer tried again to intercede, but he waved the stump at her and she backed off. Amy was trying to get back up but kept slipping in the blood and fluids.

She gave me a worried look. Then her eyes lit up.

"Charlie," Amy cried. "Hit him in the nuts!"

I looked down. My arms were pinned. There was no way I could get a hand free.

"Not those nuts. The other ones!"

Unfortunately for J.F., I understood what Amy meant a half second before he did. Using all my strength, I threw my head backward and headbutted him in the pure dick underneath his toque. He let out a high-pitched cry like a squeaky balloon and let go of my arms. As I wiggled free, he collapsed to the ground and clutched his forehead in pain.

Vincent was still coming for me, and I moved to put more distance between us. My ankle brushed against something cold. It was my pig carcass. The pure hands were still twitching violently. They pulled at the flesh of the sockets, causing the entire thing to jerk around like it was being electrocuted.

Then the pig exploded.

The pure hands shot away in every direction. The carcass, quartered by the blast, sprayed Vincent and some of the onlookers with semi-frozen globs of flesh.

The remaining audience took this as their cue to leave and rushed towards the lobby, leaving Amy and me alone with Vincent and J.F.

Vincent watched them leave, then smiled at me. The woman's blood and my pig's flesh clung to his face.

"Call it a hunch," he said, "but I think our pure parts have grown lethal. Maybe merging them with the flesh of dead animals was not the brightest idea, all things considered."

It was about then that I realized that Vincent didn't just intend to disfigure me with pure parts. He intended for them to kill me. As I backed away, I spotted two of the pure hands that had been ejected by the pig explosion. Well, two can play at this game, I thought.

I held up the pure hands, wrist stumps aimed his way. He laughed and jiggled the woman's pure arm towards me.

"Arm beats hand," he said.

I was slowly being led toward a corner of the Mezzanine. I spied J.F. trying to sneak up at me from the other direction. He still clutched at the dick on his forehead, but his face was a mask of rage. He met up with Vincent and they gave each other a fist bump. *Are you fucking kidding me?*

I waved my pure hands back and forth between them, but they were unfazed.

Then, something sailed past Vincent's face and landed on the floor between us. It was a finger. Vincent and J.F. turned to find Amy holding a stack of Vincent's pure fingers from his installation. She threw them like darts. Stump first. Two of them missed, but the third hit J.F. right in the cheek.

His eyes went wide, and his left leg started to twitch. He reached out for his friend, but Vincent pulled away, sensing what was about to happen.

Splash.

J.F.'s liquidized skin and guts spilled to the ground, shooting out his clothes in a torrent of red ichor. The smell was unbearable. Vincent jumped back but wasn't quick enough and his pants got sprayed as a hundred and sixty pounds of liquid crashed to the ground. In the puddle, glistening in a frosting of liquidized brains, was the pure dick. It rode the current afloat on J.F.'s tuque.

Amy threw another finger at Vincent. It missed.

She was out of ammunition.

Vincent grinned at her, drops of congealed blood dripping from his thin mustache, then turned back towards me.

"I think a part of me is going to miss our little rivalry. But frankly, the program just isn't big enough for the two of us. No hard feelings."

He raised the stump of the arm towards me, the pure flesh grew closer and closer. I could see the hungry little wisps reaching out.

I didn't know what to do. I was stuck in the corner with Vincent's fucking arm only three feet away. I had the pure hands, but they were a piss poor weapon against him. A chunk of my exploded pig carcass slid off Vincent's clothes with a wet plop. Then I was struck by an idea. It was a long shot, but maybe it would work…

I jammed the two stumps of the pure hands into each other. They immediately started twitching, just like they had done on the pig carcass.

I threw the conjoined hands at Vincent like a grenade. They sailed through the air, then exploded right in front of his big dumb poseur face. The force of the blast blinded him with bits of ripped flesh and tendon. It sounded like one of those blood cannons they use to shoot splatter in low-budget horror movies.

Vincent staggered back, howling in pain and rubbing at his eyes with his free hand. His other still held onto the arm. He was close to me now, distracted, if only I had something I could—

"Hey babe, need a hand?" Amy threw a pure hand my way. It arced over Vincent's head, and I caught it in a handshake.

I closed the distance between us and, in one smooth motion, brought the stump to Vincent's face.

"You talk too much, asshole."

Then I shoved it into his mouth. The pure flesh was hungry, the wisps grabbing at the skin of his lips. He tried to yell, but what came out was unintelligible.

I left him there, struggling with the hand, and made my way over to Amy.

"You okay?" I asked, looking her over for any pure parts that might have landed on her

"Fine, you?"

"Just perfect."

Covered in blood, bodily fluids, and chunks of God knows what else, we locked arms and made our way toward the museum exit. Behind us, we heard the splash as Vincent's wiry body splattered onto the ground.

He left behind a single part. A knobby little button of flesh.

It was difficult to tell what it was at first, but as we discovered later, a member of the cleanup crew had posted a picture of it on Instagram and a commenter identified what it was.

The world's first pure asshole.

David Worn is a Canadian expat who no longer lives in Montreal but is still very much pining for Le Plateau. His short fiction has recently appeared in *Dark Matter Magazine*, *Shortwave Magazine*, and in the anthologies: *The Darkness Beyond the Stars* and *Howls from the Wreckage: An Anthology of Disaster Horror*. When not writing, he enjoys patching Modular Synths and crushing goombas with his kids. He is available wherever fine cassettes are sold: worncassettes.com and @worncassettes.

ACKNOWLEDGEMENTS

This book was birthed of the horror community. It belongs to the horror community. Without the horror community, despite all its flaws and ups and downs, this book would not exist.

This anthology started as simply an idea. I pitched it to a few writing friends, and the next thing I knew, it became a reality. So thank you to those writers who contributed, who took a leap to work with a first-time editor, who absolutely grossed me out beyond my wildest dreams.

I also want to give major gratitude to Paula, who wrote a better foreword for this book than I ever could have hoped for. Your support and influence for a project like this means the world.

Additionally, I am eternally grateful to every author and editor that responded to my awkward messages asking for blurbs of support. Your backing for this anthology has helped boost its reach, getting these incredible stories in front of more readers.

And last, but certainly not least, I need to thank you, the reader, for taking a chance on this anthology. These projects are not possible without you, and we continue to do them for you. So, thank you for supporting us, and thank you for continuing to support the indie horror community.

If you're an author—new, old, or hopeful—get yourself a writing group. You will be thankful that you did!

—Ryan

About the Foreword Writer

Paula D. Ashe

Paula D. Ashe (she/her) is an author of dark fiction. Her debut collection *We Are Here to Hurt Each Other* (Nictitating Books) was a Shirley Jackson Award winner for Single Author Collection and a Bram Stoker Award Finalist for Superior Achievement in a Fiction Collection. She also served as an associate editor for *Vastarien: A Literary Journal*. She lives in the Midwest USA with her family.

About the Story Illustrator

P.L. McMillan

Besides writing, **P.L. McMillan** creates digital art—like the ones in this anthology! She also has experience as an editor (*Howls from the Dark Ages* and *The Darkness Beyond The Stars: An Anthology of Space Horror*), hosts *PLM Talks* on Youtube (interviewing peers and professionals in the horror industry), and is the co-host of a horror writing craft podcast, *Dead Languages Podcast*.

About the Editor

Ryan Marie Ketterer

Ryan Marie Ketterer is from Malden, Massachusetts. Her writing can be found in *Clarkesworld*, *Cosmic Horror Monthly*, and several other magazines and anthologies. *Welcome to Your Body* is her first foray into the world of editing short fiction. Ryan is a fan of the weird and uncanny, and she finds most of her inspiration from the works of Shirley Jackson and Thomas Ligotti. When she isn't dabbling in the horror scene, Ryan is writing code for a software startup or training for another road race. You can find her on Twitter and Instagram at @RyanMarie47.

Content Warnings

The Hollow March of Decay by Alex Wolfgang: medical procedures, hallucinations, cancer, drug use, body horror, nudity, vomit, bugs, bug bites

A Relationship in Four Haircuts by Ai Jiang: mention of animal death, blood, physical injury, emotional abuse

An Unspeakable Burden by Mary Rajotte: body parts, religious persecution, torture, mutilation, blood, gore

Early Adopter by Julie Sevens: medical procedures, blood, gore

Telling Tales by Christopher O'Halloran: ableism, drug use, vomit, asphyxiation, murder

Braces by Sasha Brown: blood, gore, dental injury, alcohol use, cigarette smoking, emotional abuse, mention of domestic violence

Deeper by Bridget D. Brave: drug use, mention of alcohol use, medical procedures, blood, gore

Run Through the Pain by Taylor Ketterer: bugs, bug bites, mention of alcohol use, hallucinations, medical procedures, blood, gore, vomit, dismemberment

The Rotten Cradle by Demi-Louise Blackburn: body shaming, elder neglect, animal death, hallucinations, body horror, blood, gore, childbirth, death and depictions of grief

Intoxication by Lindsey Ragsdale: alcohol use, vomit, childbirth, body horror, sexual content, cults

Whole Again by Emma E. Murray: death of a child, blood, gore, dismemberment, drug use, vomit, body horror, body parts, hallucinations, suicidal ideation

World of Angel by Johnathan Heart: blood, gore, body horror, child abuse, stalking, infidelity, sexual content, murder, death and depictions of grief

Wandering But Not Lost by P.L. McMillan: body parts, body horror, emotional abuse, pregnancy, mention of infertility, mention of abortion, medical procedures, blood, gore, murder, abduction

Within the Naga's Coils by Rachel Searcey: medical procedures, drug use, illness, body horror, gore, strangulation

The Resurrectionist by Bryan Young: dead bodies, nudity, blood, gore, cigarette smoking

In Your Image by Kai Delmas: nudity, physical injury, blood, gore, cannibalism, body horror, murder

Vincent is a Poseur Asshole! by David Worn: dead animals, blood, gore, dismemberment, murder, body horror, body parts, nudity, drug use, alcohol use, cigarette smoking

SALT HEART PRESS

"Invention, it must be humbly admitted, does not consist in creating out of void but out of chaos."

— Mary Shelley

We at Salt Heart Press seek the best in horror. We live for it, we crave it, we desire it — nothing gives us more pleasure than the thrills and chills found in the perfectly crafted dark tale. As such, it is our mission to seek out fresh voices in the genre, search out the new and unique, the brave and challenging. We want to be scared. We want to be haunted. And we want the same for you.

So take a look at the books we have and keep an eye out for those to come.

CHECK OUT THESE OTHER SPOOKY BOOKS FROM SALT HEART PRESS

Milton Keynes UK
Ingram Content Group UK Ltd.
UKHW010317010624
443378UK00005B/442